SMOKY MOUNTAIN MAGIC

SMOKY MOUNTAIN MAGIC

Horace Kephart

With an introduction by George Ellison and foreword by Libby Kephart Hargrave

Cover and book design by Lisa Horstman
Cover art by Elizabeth Ellison
Editorial assistance by Julie Brown, Valerie Polk, William Ehrenclou, John Hargrave, and Libby Kephart Hargrave
Foreword by Libby Kephart Hargrave
Introduction by George Ellison
Deep Creek map by George Masa courtesy Great Smoky Mountains National Park
Printed in the U.S.A. by Maple-Vail Books

1 2 3 4 5 6 7 8 9 10 11 12 13 14 15 16 17 18 19 20

Text pages are recycled paper containing 30% post-consumer waste.

ISBN 978-0-937207-64-2 (paperback)
ISBN 978-0-937207-65-9

Great Smoky Mountains Association is a private, nonprofit organization which supports the educational, scientific, and historical programs of Great Smoky Mountains National Park. To learn more about our publications, memberships, guided hikes, and other activities, please contact GSMA, 115 Park Headquarters Road, Gatlinburg, TN 37738.
www.SmokiesInformation.org

All purchases benefit Friends of the Smokies, the Horace Kephart Foundation, and Great Smoky Mountains National Park.

GREAT SMOKY MOUNTAINS ASSOCIATION

DEDICATION

To my husband, Dr. John Hargrave, for your hard work and commitment to this project.
To my great-grandparents, thank you for being who you were!

Libby Kephart Hargrave
(Great-granddaughter of the author)

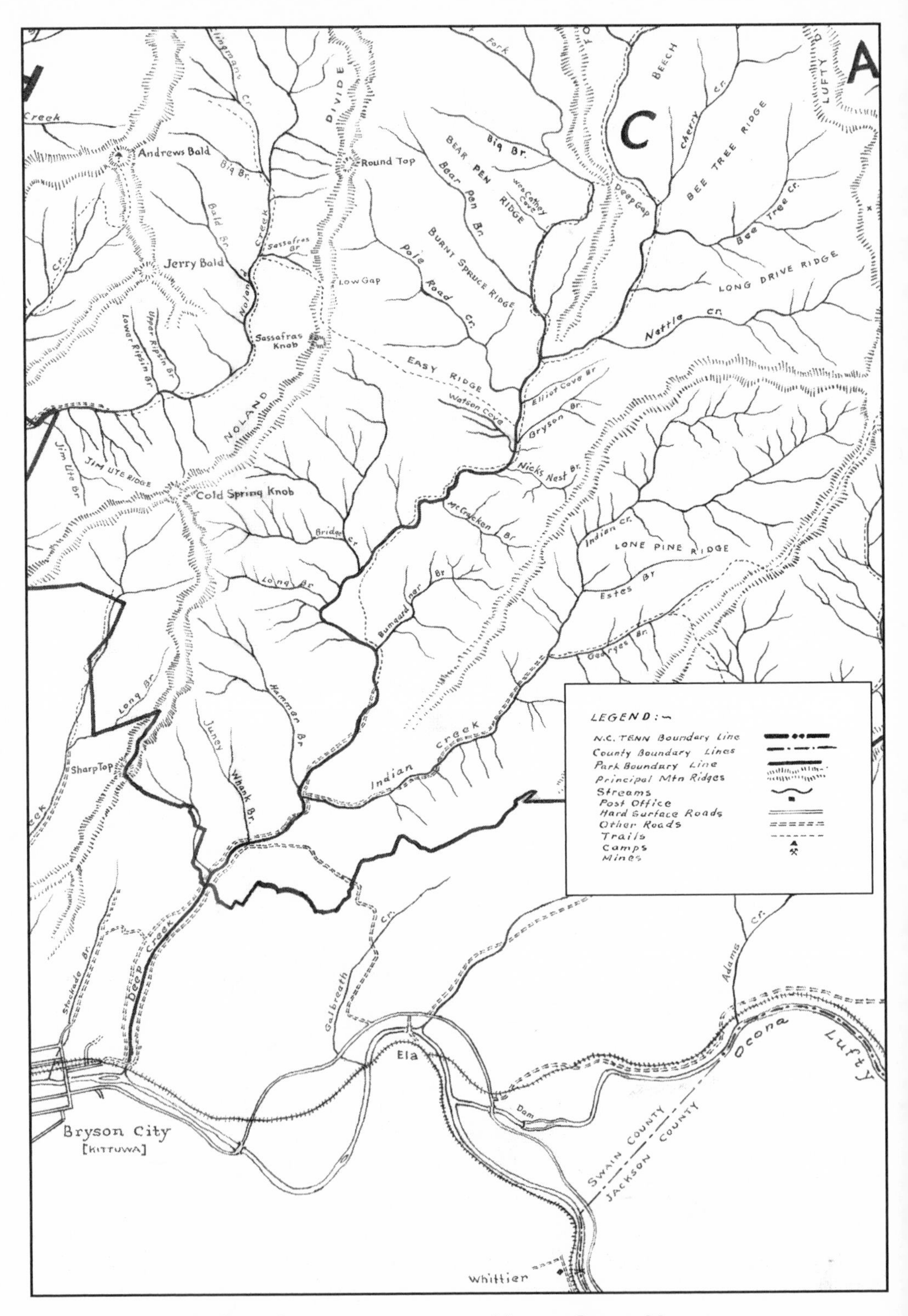

DEEP CREEK AREA CIRCA 1930. MAP BY GEORGE MASA

FOREWORD

Where has *Smoky Mountain Magic* been all these years?

The history of the *Smoky Mountain Magic* manuscript dates back to 1921 when my great-grandfather, Horace S. Kephart, began the research necessary for writing this novel. Multiple preliminary drafts were written during the creative process. In 1929 Horace typed the final manuscript and sent it to a prominent New York publisher, Houghton Mifflin.[1] The manuscript was returned to him. To my knowledge, there is no record of their response.

In 1935, four years after Horace Kephart's untimely death, his personal effects were sold at auction. People bid on Kephart's estate with the understanding that I.K. Stearns, a Bryson City businessman, Kephart admirer, and executor of Kephart's estate, would then repurchase the items and make arrangements to have them saved for future generations. Due to I.K. Stearns' foresight and personal expense—both money and time—a significant amount of Kephart's personal property is preserved. Much of the Kephart legacy, including his writing desk, boots, and outdoor gear is found at Western Carolina University's Mountain Heritage Center. I suggest when you visit the Smoky Mountains, make arrangements to see this extraordinary collection.

Two of Kephart's personal items not sold at the auction were the *Smoky Mountain Magic* manuscript and his Encyclopedia Britannica. These items, along with personal letters and a few books which, I believe, included a Bible that belonged to his sister, Elizabeth Belle Kephart, were the only items Laura Mack Kephart, Horace's wife (my great-grandmother), wished to receive from his estate. When the estate expenses were finally paid and the estate was settled, Laura received a check in the amount of $64.20 along with most of the items she had specifically requested.

It was Laura's hope that her husband's belongings, papers, etc., would be kept in a safe place and not divided up. I.K. Stearns deserves credit for making this wish a reality. Kephart himself recognized Stearns in the dedication of *The Camper's Manual* that was published in 1923. The dedication reads:

TO MY SIDE SWIPE
IRVING STEARNS
who eats my grub at camp
and says he doesn't snore

George Frizzell, head of Special Collections at Hunter Library, George Ellison, who authored the introduction of this book, Ann Wright, Special Collections librarian at Pack Memorial Library, and Peter Koch, education associate at the Mountain Heritage Center, deserve special recognition for their research and scholarship which have likewise preserved Kephart's legacy.

Scholars wonder what happened to many of Kephart's unarchived personal letters and other items. A letter from Laura to I.K. Stearns may explain what happened to some. Stearns wanted Laura to send a particular letter from "Mr. Kephart" back to him.

> January 11, 1940
>
> Dear I.K.
>
> If you want Mr. Kephart's letter back you can't have it because it was burned last night along with the house and every thing material that I own, except the old dress and slippers I had on. It was an old house—about 100 years and went like tinder. I went into speak to Myrtle in the other part of the house. When I went back—or started to—my room was a roaring furnace. Cause unknown, probably a defective flue. The money I had saved for the trip went with the rest—bank book, copyrights, etc.[2]

It is possible that the diary Horace Kephart diligently kept was destroyed in the fire as it has not otherwise been located. Fortunately, the original typed *Smoky Mountain Magic* manuscript was not in the house.

When Laura died in 1954, her children kept the manuscript intact. Eventually it found its way to my grandfather, George Stebbins Kephart, who was Horace and Laura's youngest son. In 1984, two years before his death, George gave the manuscript to his eldest son, Roy Ferris Kephart (my father). In 1997, my father gave the manuscript to me.

In conjunction with the 75th anniversary of the formation of Great Smoky Mountains National Park, Bryson City, North Carolina held a "Horace Kephart Day Celebration" on May 1, 2009 at the historic Calhoun Inn and the Hillside Cemetery where Kephart is buried. Dale Ditmanson, superintendent of Great Smoky Mountains National Park, attended and spoke of Kephart's contributions during the ceremony at the boulder where Kep is buried. I told Superintendent Ditmanson of my intention to contact publishers in hopes of fulfilling my great-grandparents' goal of publishing *Smoky Mountain Magic*. In a later conversation, the superintendent asked if I had considered Great Smoky Mountains Association as publisher of the novel. After meeting with Steve Kemp (interpretive products & services director) and Terry Maddox (executive director), I was confident that turning the manuscript over to the Association was the best way to proceed.

Eighty years after completion of the manuscript, Horace and Laura Kephart's goal to publish *Smoky Mountain Magic* has been achieved.

Horace Kephart's librarian profession integrated seamlessly into his writing profession. Whether writing from a cabin deep in the woods, a remote campsite, or from his office in Bryson City, his librarian's attention to detail is unmistakable. Every word was given careful consideration whether handwritten or typed. In his *Smoky Mountain Magic* journal there are handwritten and typed pages along with newspaper clippings dating back to 1921. With great craftsmanship, he skillfully weaves his knowledge of the mountains, people, and culture of the 1920s Smoky Mountains into his novel of mystery, intrigue, and romance.

Page two of his *Smoky Mountain Magic* journal clearly states his objectives. This practical list, handwritten by Kephart in Journal 18, offers useful guidelines for all writers.[3]

METHOD

Brevity of description. Don't let a love of accuracy of detail produce pages that would be only a weariness to

> the reader. Brilliancy of narrative. The apt word; not the unusual. Ready invention of situations and events. Don't go too far in depicting unpleasant phases of life. Don't preach. Yet be a realist by not deviating from the truth. Touch it up, idealize it, put it in bold relief; but let it be the truth. The diamond is as real as a lump of coal. Uncommon scenes, rare moments, characters transfigured by passion or emotion. Art dreads the commonplace. Most readers live drab lives. Give them color, stir their emotions, let them realize, for the time, their dreams and longings. What they like is the unknown, and what they know can never occur to them. This delight is the oldest and most natural pleasure art can give.

A whole other book could be written just *about* my great-grandfather. He was not an ordinary man. No discussion of his books and articles, his successful efforts to preserve the Smokies as a national park, and other accomplishments seems to be complete without an examination of his marriage and family life. Some of these examinations, past and present, have included untruths. Bearing this in mind, I would like to include the following, not to exonerate him, for he was a complex man, but to present some relevant quotations and history from the Kephart family.

Laura understood and accepted the consequences of Horace's disease. In her 5″ x 7″ bird's eye maple sewing box, she kept a small newspaper article about alcoholism.[4] When Laura opened her sewing box, this carefully kept newspaper article was given a brief, yet empathetic glance. On the rare day when she had a moment to herself, Laura quietly read the article, then carefully placed it back in her sewing box and moved on with the busyness of her days. I can only imagine the sorrow she felt…what was and what could have been. Alcoholism is a cruel disease.

In 1903, Laura and the six children left St. Louis and moved to her hometown of Ithaca, New York. In a letter to my father dated May 31, 1983, my granddad wrote the following:

> It should be noted that Mom, with us kids, moved to Ithaca some time before Dad left St. Louis, eventually

> for the Smokies. We left him. I was 5-6 years old at the time. In Leonard's [Horace and Laura's eldest son] unpublished manuscript he says that Mom brought us together and "with tears running down her cheeks..." said that we were moving to Ithaca, that Dad was not coming with us and that we would be very poor.... From the beginning, and all through the tough years, Mom gave continuing proof of her courage, of her detached understanding of the situation and of her continuing love for Dad. I am convinced that her love was reciprocated....I never heard Mom speak an unkind word against Dad. To the contrary, we learned to love Dad through her, at times with "tears running down our cheeks"....From the beginning, and all through the tough years, Mom gave proof of her courage, her understanding of the situation and her love for Dad.[5]

I believe Laura understood and accepted Horace's need to seek out his "Back of Beyond." She did not leave with acrimony and recrimination in her heart. Her leaving was an act of unconditional love and support. She left to set him free and gave him a chance to heal.

In a letter dated April 9, 1947, three days before the anniversary date of her marriage to Horace, Laura wrote to her son George:

> ...I can only hope you all can say on your 60th anniversary, as I can, that had I known all the years were to bring me, I [still] would have married as I did.
>
> Love, Mama[6]

On July 10, 1947, Great-Granny wrote the following to her granddaughter, Laura Mack Bird, shortly before Laura's marriage to Jim Warren:

> ...If you have to pull through some rough going—well I hope it won't be too rough. If at times you need to share a crust, it won't do you as much harm as getting indigestion, mental and moral, from eating too much plum pudding. If at the end of sixty years you can say,

> "I am content," Life can give you nothing more worth-while....When I met your grandfather he was just another boy that I liked. It rather surprised me when I woke up to the fact that he had ceased to be another and had become the only. He still is.
>
> Love, Granny[7]

Her sense of humor shines through in a letter dated March 25, 1953:

> Dear family,
>
> As letter writers, I think our family would take the Big Prize—if any one could be found to offer one. If any of our children have a gift that way it all comes from their father's side. When it comes to talking I have him beaten to a standstill—unless they happen to hit a subject in which he was very interested.
>
> Love, Mama[8]

Laura Mack Kephart, wife of Horace Kephart, died in 1954 at age 92.

Laura and Horace were enormously proud of their children. All went to college, most to Cornell University. Cornelia married Carlton Moore, a professor in the Agriculture School at Michigan State in East Lansing. Margaret, who never married, was a nurse. Leonard spent 35 years with the Department of Agriculture specializing mainly in seeds. He retired from the World Bank as an agriculture advisor. Lucy married Karl Fernow, a professor in the Agriculture School at Cornell University. George was a forester. From 1934 to1964 he was with the Branch of Forestry of the U.S. Bureau of Indian Affairs retiring as head of the Department of Forestry. In 1977, his book *Campfires Rekindled: A Forester Recalls Life in the Maine Woods of the Twenties* was published. Barbara married Royal Bird, a forester. In 1952, her book, *Calked Shoes: Life in Adirondack Lumber Camps* with photographs by Royal Bird was published.

I have been asked on several occasions, "How does the family feel about Kep's living so far from his wife and children and the rare visits home?" My answer is rather simple: "I, Laura White Mack, take thee Horace to be my lawful wedded husband, to have and to hold from this day forward, for better for worse, for richer for poorer...

I, Horace Sowers Kephart, take thee Laura to be my lawful wedded wife, to have and to hold from this day forward... in sickness and in health, to love and to cherish, til death us do part."

Horace dearly loved his Laura. Horace dearly loved his children and grandchildren. In a letter to his youngest daughter, Barbara, he wrote:

> May 9, 1927
>
> My dear Barbara:
>
> I'm back, once more, in the Smokies, but my heart was left back yonder. I lost it to the brave mother and the kids who made my visit so wonderful after all these years of separation.
>
> I have firm faith that there's a good time coming when we'll see each other often and when Cornelia and George and their families will be with us, too. I'm writing to all of you, just a little note of love and good hope and thankfulness.
>
> Dad[9]

Their marriage was unconventional, yet it survived the years in spite of the occasional severe criticism and disapproval from individuals who did not comprehend the depth of love and commitment to the marriage vows Horace and Laura exchanged on April 12, 1887.

When you visit Bryson City, North Carolina, plan your own "Horace Kephart" day (or two!). Visit Hillside Cemetery where he is buried, and while downtown go to Slope Street and read the Horace Kephart highway marker. A short five mile drive from downtown Bryson City is Deep Creek, the primary Swain County entrance to Great Smoky Mountains National Park. The Deep Creek area is the mountain setting Kephart writes about in *Smoky Mountain Magic*. Today, the area offers day hikes, backpacking, picnic areas, camping, and horseback riding. This is a must!

Other sites related to Horace Kephart in the park include Kephart Prong Trail, Kephart Shelter (at the end of Kephart Prong) and Mt. Kephart (just off the Appalachian Trail).

All of these destinations will give you insight into the magical places Horace Kephart wrote about, treasured, and dedicated many years of his life to. I hope you enjoy the beauty and history as you find your own "Back of Beyond" in the Smokies.

Libby Kephart Hargrave
Pensacola, Florida

NOTES

[1]Kephart, Horace letter to Houghton Mifflin, dated 16 August 1929. Letter in possession of Kevin Beauchesne.

[2]Kephart, Laura letter to I.K. Stearns dated 11 January 1940. Pack Memorial Library.

[3]Kephart, Horace, *Smoky Mountain Magic* Journal 18. Western Carolina University, Hunter Library, Special Collections.

[4]Woomert, Alison, personal communication (Horace Kephart's great-granddaughter).

[5]Kephart, George S. letter to Roy Kephart dated 31 May 1983. In possession of Libby Kephart Hargrave (Horace Kephart's great-granddaughter).

[6]Kephart, Laura letter to George S. Kephart dated 9 April 1947. In possession of Libby Kephart Hargrave (Horace Kephart's great-granddaughter).

[7]Ibid., letter to her granddaughter, Laura Mack Bird, dated 10 July 1947. In possession of Rich and Rick Warren (Horace Kephart's great-grandsons).

[8]Ibid., letter to her family dated 25 March 1953. In possession of Libby Kephart Hargrave (Horace Kephart's great-granddaughter).

[9]Kephart, Horace, letter to his youngest daughter, Barbara Kephart (Bird), dated 9 May 1927. Letter in possession of Sally Woomert Hinder, (Kephart's great-granddaughter).

ACKNOWLEDGMENTS

Horace Kephart spent eight years researching and writing this novel. Eighty years after completion, it is published. Why now? The right "team" of people, all with the same intention, came together with the same goals: 1) publish his book and 2) proceeds must benefit Great Smoky Mountains National Park. This has been achieved with the help of the following people: Dale Ditmanson, superintendent of Great Smoky Mountains National Park; Dr. John Hargrave, my husband; Terry Maddox, executive director, Great Smoky Mountains Association; Steve Kemp, interpretive products and services director, Great Smoky Mountains Association; George Ellison, writer; Elizabeth Ellison, artist; George Frizzell, head of Special Collections, Hunter Library, Western Carolina University; Luke Hyde, member of the board of directors of the Friends of Great Smoky Mountains National Park, and owner of the Historic Calhoun Inn; Karen Wilmot, director, Bryson City—Swain County Chamber of Commerce.

In addition, the following family and professional friends deserve recognition for their invaluable contributions: Martha Kephart Tiernan, my mother; Laura Kephart Pearson, Joanne Kephart Bleichner, Linda Kephart, my sisters; Jennifer Hargrave Geric, my step-daughter; Frances Kephart, widow of Roy Ferris Kephart; George Overton Kephart, cousin; Barbara Kephart Crane, cousin; Alison Woomert, cousin; Sally Woomert Hinder, cousin; Elaine Stewart, office manager, North Carolina office, Friends of the Great Smoky Mountains National Park; Janet McCue, associate university librarian, Cornell University; Dennis Stephens, associate professor emeritus, University of Alaska Fairbanks, and director, Alaska Center for Horace Kephart Studies; Ann Wright, special collections librarian, Pack Memorial Library; Zoe Rhine, special collections librarian, Pack Memorial Library; Jason

Brady, special collections assistant, Hunter Library, Western Carolina University and John White, documentary film maker.

My grandfather, George Stebbins Kephart and my father, Roy Ferris Kephart did not live to see this novel published. Thank you both for trusting that I would, some day, find the right "team."

It has been a pleasure and honor to work with everyone involved with this project.

INTRODUCTION

The railway that would become known as the Murphy Branch was completed in 1891. It extended from Asheville to Waynesville over the Balsam Mountains to Sylva and the adjacent village of Dillsboro. From there, the original tracks continued to Bryson City (where Deep Creek empties into the Tuckasegee River) on down to Bushnell (where Hazel Creek once emptied into the Little Tennessee River, now Lake Fontana) and finally up through the precipitous Nantahala Gorge to Andrews and Murphy.

The Murphy Branch helped transform the region where ever it was extended. The North Carolina flank of the Great Smokies, in particular, became directly accessible for representatives of logging, mining, and land-investment companies. In their wake came homesteaders, missionaries, tourists, sportsmen, convalescents, anthropologists, and wayward travelers seeking a place of refuge.

One day in August 1904, an individual in his early 40s, of below average height and medium build stepped off the westbound train onto the platform of the depot at Dillsboro and looked around. According to Clarence Miller, a former colleague in St. Louis, he was a man with "an aura of loneliness" who maintained an initial "barrier of reserve." He also displayed "quick decisive movements that bespoke muscular strength and coordination. His eyes were dark. . . . His bristling black mustache seemed to contrast violently with his finely modeled features."

Horace Kephart arrived in the Great Smokies having left behind a botched career as a librarian and a wife and six children. All the details that sparked this midlife crisis are not fully known or agreed upon, but it's widely recognized that alcoholism was a contributing factor.

At that point in time, Kephart seemed an unlikely candidate for anything more than an obscure existence. No one who knew him would have forecast literary prominence, a substantial role in establishing the first large national park in the eastern United States, and increased recognition on the regional and national levels into the twenty-first century. Against all odds, however, that's exactly what has transpired.

Kephart is today the writer most closely associated in the national consciousness with Great Smoky Mountains National Park (GSMNP). His *Camping and Woodcraft* is securely established as one of the cornerstones of American outdoor writing, having been continuously in print since 1906. The place of *Our Southern Highlanders*—first published in 1913, with an expanded edition in 1922—as one of the classics of southern Appalachian literature is generally accepted, if still debated in some quarters.

Two months before his death in an automobile accident in 1931, the U.S. Geographic Board designated a 6,217-foot peak traversed by the Appalachian Trail several miles northeast of Newfound Gap in the Smokies as Mount Kephart—an unprecedented honor previously reserved for individuals only after their deaths.

Kephart was chosen in 2000 by the *Raleigh News and Observer* as one of "North Carolina's 100 Most Influential People of the Century," while the *Asheville Citizen-Times* named him one of "Western North Carolina's 50 Most Influential People of the Century," noting that after arriving in the Southern mountains he "became one of the region's greatest advocates."

Throughout 2004, Hunter Library at Western Carolina University celebrated the 100th anniversary of Kephart's arrival in western North Carolina. As an extension of those events, the library's Special Collections department and the on-campus Mountain Heritage Center established a frequently accessed online exhibit titled "Horace Kephart: Revealing an Enigma" that recreates his life and work.

Kephart's depiction in 2009 as a central and captivating figure in the GSMNP segment of "The National Parks: America's Best Idea"—a six-episode, 12-hour PBS series directed by Ken Burns—brings national attention to the story of his life, literary career, and role as park advocate.

Although there has been disagreement in regard to specific incidents, the overall outline and basic ingredients of that story have been general knowledge for some years, dating from the chapter devoted to him in Michael Frome's *Strangers in High Places: The Story of the Great Smoky Mountains* (1966); my biographical introduction to the reissue of *Our Southern Highlanders* (1976); and Jim Casada's biographical introduction to the reissue of *Camping and Woodcraft* (1988). But the publication of this curious and often delightful novel, *Smoky Mountain Magic*, 80 years after Kephart apparently completed the final manuscript, is a surprising development—one that brings a thought provoking addition to the story. Before considering several aspects of *Smoky Mountain Magic*, which is autobiographical in many regards, a review of relevant factors in Kephart's life will be useful.

Horace Kephart was born on September 8, 1862, in East Salem, Pennsylvania. His ancestors had been among the first settlers west of the Susquehanna. The strenuous do-without but colorful pioneering experiences in central Pennsylvania of Isaiah Kephart, his father, became the core of the family's traditional lore. Isaiah, who subsequently recreated those experiences in a series of articles published in 1893 as "Pioneer Life in the Alleghenies," maintained a supportive relationship with his only son throughout his lifetime.

In 1867, the family moved to Iowa, where Isaiah was first a farmer, then a school principal, and finally a teacher of natural sciences at Western College (now Coe College) near Cedar Rapids. The farm had been situated near Jefferson in central Iowa, which was still part of the American frontier. In an autobiographical essay published in 1922 titled "Horace Kephart *By* Himself" (note the italic emphasis), Kephart evoked an image of himself at that time—and maintained it to a certain extent throughout his lifetime—as an earnest and sometimes lonely, yet self-sufficient figure, like "dear old Robinson Crusoe." Looking back, he reminisced about encountering "wild Indians," "building a cave out of sod," and other adventures "before the day of fences."

Kephart attended Western College for a year. After the family returned to Pennsylvania, he entered Lebanon Valley College, graduating in 1879, "not without misgivings on the part of the faculty as to my orthodoxy and sundry other qualifications." While attending Boston University that fall, he discovered what he described as "the blessed privilege of studying whatever I pleased in the Boston Public Library" and enrolled in the graduate school at Cornell University in Ithaca, New York.

That institution's first librarian, Willard Fiske, became Kephart's mentor and, in time, a friend. Upon his resignation in 1885, Fiske invited Kephart to his villa in Florence, Italy, to catalog an enormous collection of materials by and about Francis Petrarch, the fourteenth-century Italian poet. As a by-product of his association with Fiske, Kephart subsequently translated Dante's *Vita nuova* and studied various languages, including French, Spanish, Finnish, and Swedish. In the process, he developed a lifelong interest in and an ear for the nuances of language that were fully realized after his arrival in the Great Smokies.

He had become engaged to Laura Mack of Ithaca before going to Italy. Upon his return in 1886, he accepted a position at Yale College as an assistant librarian, and the following year married Laura. Having developed a passionate interest in American frontier history, he accepted, in 1890, the directorship of the St. Louis Mercantile Association, "the oldest library west of the Mississippi." Here he built one of the most complete collections of Western Americana then in existence and became an authority in that field.

The Kepharts settled into a pattern of respectable family life, a wide range of civic obligations, and various social activities. By 1897, he and Laura had a family of four daughters and two sons. He became an exceptionally competent librarian, with articles published in scholarly journals on classification, cataloging, book binding, and similar topics. Clarence Miller, who succeeded him as director of the Mercantile Library, noted that even though Kephart "lived almost exclusively in a world of his own" he was "always accessible to the staff or the public....The range of his information seemed incredible to us who drew upon it daily. All of his answers revealed a broad basis of understanding as well as a photographic memory. There were occasions when...he would laugh in an almost boyish manner and add a delightful comment." He was seemingly content in St. Louis and on his way to being recognized as one of the foremost librarians in the country.

But something happened. By the late 1890s, his former outlook on life and his aspirations for the future were under revision. His last publication pertaining to professional librarianship appeared in the *Library Journal* in December 1897; thereafter, his articles were published in popular magazines such as *Forest and Stream* about topics like sharp shooting, camping and woodcraft, and cave exploration. He became increasingly disillusioned with the tenets of his home, civic, and social life.

"I love the wilderness because there are no shams in it," he inscribed as an epigram on the title page of "Songs of Barbarism," a 100-page bound notebook dated "St. Louis 1901." Into this notebook, he copied excerpts from various sources, primarily those by authors extolling the virtues of a self-sufficient wilderness or frontier lifestyle as opposed to the decadence of an overly material urban existence.

A serious drinking problem emerged that was, perhaps, more symptomatic of his overall discontent than prime cause. But it did become chronic, debilitating him periodically for the rest of his life. Miller was told that Kephart "could alter his personality by taking a single drink." He drifted away from former friends and began to make frequent extended solitary excursions into the Ozark Mountains and the Arkansas swamps. In retrospect, he seemed intent upon steering a course that would inevitably bring about drastic change.

Miller observed that the wilderness trips "began to alienate the library's directors." Late in 1903, Kephart was forced to resign. Before Christmas, without financial resources, Laura took the children back to her family home in Ithaca. The downward spiral continued into late March 1904, when Kephart was hospitalized, after suffering what Miller described as "a complete nervous collapse." Janet McCue cites reports indicating that prior to being hospitalized, Kephart had written a note saying "that he would end his life." Isaiah Kephart came to St. Louis and accompanied his son to Dayton, Ohio, where he now served as editor of the Methodist newspaper, *The Religious Telescope*.

While trying to sort things out—to see what he might make of a life that was now in such disarray—Kephart returned to Pennsylvania and visited the cemetery where many of his ancestors were buried, recording the inscriptions of each headstone. Back in Dayton at his father's home, he became increasingly preoccupied with the notion of forging a literary career while living in a setting similar to the one experienced by his father and their pioneer ancestors. He anticipated—perhaps with Isaiah's encouragement—that residing in and writing about such a place and its people, if he could find it, might become part of a healing process.

In later years, Kephart was often guarded, sometimes evasive, when giving reasons for choosing western North Carolina. There was no doubt an element of chance in the decision. It's probable, despite his denial of having done so, that he read travel accounts and studied government documents, many of which were available by the early twentieth century. As articulated with verve nine years later in *Our Southern Highlanders*, he was looking for "a strange land and a people that had the charm of originality"—a "Back of Beyond" where he could "begin again." Almost as an aside, he noted that he had wanted "to realize the past in the present, seeing with my own eyes what life must have been to my pioneer ancestors of a century or two before." By the time of his 1922 autobiographical essay, he was placing emphasis on locating remote mountainous terrain as a key objective:

> *My passion for the mountains may be inherited, as my ancestors were Swiss....In the summer of 1904, finding that I must abandon professional work and city life, I came to western North Carolina looking for a big primitive forest....Knowing nobody who had ever been here, I took a topographic map and picked out on it...what seemed to be the wildest part of this region; and there I went. It was in Swain County, amid the Great Smoky Mountains, near the Tennessee line.*

Kephart left Dayton by train and arrived in Asheville in late July or early August 1904. He lingered there a day or so, purchasing gear and consulting with a physician. After arriving in Dillsboro via the Murphy Branch, he walked west for about a mile on the tracks before turning north up Dicks Creek, a tributary of the Tuckasegee River. Here he obtained permission from a local family to establish a camp, situated about where present day U.S. 74 crosses the creek. Somewhat elaborate, it featured a canvas covered lean-to, a free-standing canvas pantry, and a railed fence. He christened it "Camp Toco" or "Dakwah-i"—a Cherokee word, he noted in a photo caption, which means "fish monster place," after a pool in the nearby Tuckasegee River. He lived there from August 7 until October 27, 1904. His notes and photos indicate that, from the moment of arrival, he traveled in the immediate area so as to start observing and recording the region's places and inhabitants, including the Cherokees, whose Annual Association of the Eastern Band was being held.

In October, Kephart traveled westward on the Murphy Branch to

Bryson City, where he perhaps took a first look at the beautiful Deep Creek watershed, which begins as a trickle below the present day Newfound Gap Road. But the population along Deep Creek at that time was sparse—there was no extended community of the sort he was seeking. Farther west, he ventured up Hazel Creek from the now inundated village of Bushnell and discovered the remote settlement—"made up of forty-two households…scattered over an area eight miles long by two wide…a mere slash in the wilderness that encompassed it"—he had been searching for. He felt "as though he had been carried back…on the wings of time and had awakened in the eighteenth century."

Kephart obtained permission from a copper mining company that had gone into litigation to live in one of its vacant cabins. It was located near Medlin, a crossroads settlement consisting of a store and several houses, where the Sugar Fork enters Hazel Creek, ten miles or so above its former confluence with the Little Tennessee River. He refurbished the dwelling, which was situated in the apex formed by the trail and the Little Fork on the west side of the creek, and moved in. That remote site on "the Little Fork of the Sugar Fork of Hazel Creek" became the vantage point from which he studied the land and its people for three years.

Since the early 1970s, I've gone there at intervals, sometimes with others and sometimes by myself. After examining the debris left over from the old-time mining operation, I always climb the wooded slope above the Little Fork and sit for a while, listening to the wind in the tuliptrees and the soft murmur of the creek far below. Even today, except that the cabin is gone, the setting and sounds are not so very different from that day well over a century ago when Kephart moved there and started to explore the "mysterious beckoning hinterland which rose right back of my chimney and spread upward, outward, almost to the three cardinal points of the compass, mile after mile, hour after hour of lusty climbing—an Eden still unpopulated and unspoiled."

An interview conducted in 1926 by F.A. Behymer, who had known Kephart in St. Louis, was published by the *St. Louis Post-Dispatch* as "Horace Kephart, Driven from Library by Broken Health, Reborn in Woods." In it, Kephart recalled that,

> *Seldom during those three years as a forest exile did I feel lonesome in the daytime; but when supper would be over and black night closed in on my hermitage, and the owls began*

> *calling all the blue devils of the woods, one needed some indoor occupation to keep…in good cheer."*
>
> *It was the old life calling, the life of books that he had left [Behymer surmised]. For such a man there could be a beginning again but the old life could not be entirely disowned….Out of the thousands of books that he had intimately known [as a librarian] there were only a few he could carry with him into the solitudes. He selected them with care, twenty of them [including Dante, Shakespeare, Poe, and R.L. Stevenson, as well as field manuals for birds, plants, and minerals]….The old man had become a new man, but the new man was still a man of books…and when the owls began calling, it was in his books that he found comfort. He took up writing, as it was inevitable that he would, setting down by night his experiences of the day.*

Kephart became preoccupied with living efficiently in this remote setting. Despite outdoor experiences dating back to childhood, he discovered that he now "had to make shift in a different way, and fashion many appliances from the materials found on the spot . . . seeking not novelties but practical results." These "results" he published in outdoor magazines. By 1906, he had compiled enough material to put together the first edition of *The Book of Camping and Woodcraft: A Guidebook for Those Who Travel in the Wilderness*, published by the Outing Publishing Company in New York. An expanded two-volume edition appeared in 1917, and in 1921 it came out in a hefty "two volumes in one" format as *Camping and Woodcraft: A Handbook for Vacation Campers and for Travelers in the Wilderness*. (References herein to *Camping and Woodcraft* are to the 1921 edition.) In the process of expansion and revision, it became a compendium of anecdotes, recipes, adventures, and practical advice on tent camping, path finding, route sketching, bark utensils, knot tying, backcountry exploration, bee hunting, and more. It remains remarkably useful and readable. Not a few Kephart aficionados consider it to be his best book.

In time, Kephart also entered into the lives of the two hundred or so residents of Hazel Creek, the largest stream on the North Carolina side of the Great Smokies. Along the watershed with its numerous tributaries, he became a neighbor and, in some instances, a friend. He was accepted as much as any outsider should desire—because he wanted to learn from the mountain people, not tell them what to do. He studied their ways and listened closely to the manner in which they expressed themselves about their lives. He was especially captivated by their humor.

Journal entries Kephart made under countless subject headings recorded details about almost every aspect of their lives as well as his reflections upon those details. He was a fallen librarian, but he inevitably retained a librarian's mindset. His materials were always categorized and often indexed. Relevant items that might be of use were cross-referenced in the outlines and drafts of specific articles and books he was working on at the time. Duplicate copies were commonplace. Very little was ever discarded. Systematically compiled from 1904 into the 1920s in what eventually became 27 canvas-bound, ledger-sized volumes, these journals became depositories of firsthand observation that Kephart drew upon during the composition of both *Our Southern Highlanders* and *Smoky Mountain Magic*.

Continuing to support and—in many ways—identify with his son's endeavors, Isaiah Kephart visited Hazel Creek. As mentioned, they had for years shared an ongoing interest in their pioneer heritage in the Allegheny Mountains of Pennsylvania. They now had the mountain culture Horace Kephart had discovered in the Great Smokies to consider. As they traveled about, the son took photos of his father inspecting a primitive mill and riding horseback at a herder's cabin situated along the high divide between North Carolina and Tennessee.

Bob Barnett was Kephart's closest friend during the Hazel Creek years and on into the early 1920s. Barnett warrants special attention here because of the significant part he played in Kephart's life, which has never been fully appreciated, and because he served as the model for Tom Burbank, a pivotal character throughout *Smoky Mountain Magic*. Although Barnett was the younger man by 18 years, Kephart admired him tremendously. In a "Roving with Kephart" column published in *All Outdoors* magazine in 1921, he described a recent visit from Barnett:

> *He was the big, fat Bob who figures in* Camping and Woodcraft *and* Our Southern Highlanders. *He came years ago, to the old mine site where I'd been living alone with the bobcats and hoot-owls, and became caretaker for the company that had possession. It was an abandoned place—*

> *that is, no one ever lived there—and I welcomed a neighbor. Soon I shifted quarters to his house. We lived together, in various necks of the woods, for several years. Bob is now at Aquone, N.C., on the upper Nantahala, where he keeps open house for all comers.*

In *Camping and Woodcraft*, Kephart credited Barnett as being "one of the best woodsmen in this country, a man so genuinely a scholar in his chosen lore that he could well afford to say, as once he did to me: 'I've studied these woods and mountains all my life, Kep, like you do your books, and I don't know them all yet, no sirree.'"

Many of the dialect witticisms entered in Kephart's journals were originally uttered by Barnett: "Bob whittled Old Pete Laney's store-bought axe-handle for him and remarked: 'Thar! I'll see that Pete'll have a decent axe-handle fer his women-folks to chop wood with, anyhow.'"

In the "Back of Beyond" chapter of *Our Southern Highlanders*, when the two friends were stymied by the marauding tactics of a "slab-sided tusky old boar" (which Kephart has christened "Belial," after one of Dante's devils), Bob remarked in frustration: "That Be-liar would cross hell on a rotten rail to get in my 'tater patch!"

The years after Kephart left the Great Smokies in 1907 until he returned in 1910 have been more or less a mystery. In the 1922 autobiographical essay, he mentioned traveling "in other parts of the Appalachians...comparing what I found there with what I knew in the Smokies." In the *Life of Rev. Isaiah L. Kephart, D.D.*, published in Dayton in 1909, a brief note indicated that his son "served for a number of years as librarian of the Mercantile Library at St. Louis, Missouri, and is now residing at Ithaca, New York, engaged in literary pursuits." Relying upon a letter Laura wrote to a family friend in December 1909, McCue describes an unsuccessful "attempt" Horace made from late 1908 until May 1909 "to reconcile with his wife and rejoin civilization."

A letter recently archived at Western Carolina University from Kephart to Louis Hampton, a friend who still lived on Hazel Creek, provides additional information as to his whereabouts and activities. It is dated Oct. 5, 1909, and addressed from Lindale, Georgia (near Rome), where he was living with the Barnett family. Kephart advised Hampton that he had been "to Dayton to look after my father who was very sick [and] died a year ago. Then I went to New York and Pennsylvania, and back to Dayton, and finally came down here two weeks ago. I will stay with the Barnetts until spring, and then take a long trip through the mountains from Georgia to Virginia and Kentucky, taking photographs for my books." In closing, he observed that, "Bob has a good job and a nice home. I have plenty of writing to do, and am saving money to buy a place in the Smokies. The Barnetts have a girl baby. She is a pretty little thing, but has one bad habit, for she pisses in my lap every day. Bob is fatter than ever, and his wife is quite stout. My own health is good."

While in Lindale, Kephart was no doubt consulting with "Mistress Bob"—as he usually referred to Barnett's wife—who was renowned for her backcountry culinary skills. His little volume *Camp Cookery*, published in 1910, was dedicated: "To Mistress Bob, who taught me some clever expedients of backwoods cookery that are lost arts wherever the old forest has been leveled." She reappeared in the expanded edition of *Camping and Woodcraft*, wherein Kephart described with obvious delight "a mess of greens of her own picking...an *olla podrida*...cooked together in the same pot, with a slice of pork" that resulted in a 'wild salat,' as she called it." And in *Smoky Mountain Magic* she emerged yet again as the model for Tom Burbank's wife, Sylvia ("Sylvy") Burbank.

Kephart returned to the Great Smokies early in 1910. He chose not to settle on Hazel Creek. The W.M. Ritter Company had begun operations there and was in the process of running a railway spur, the Smoky Mountain Railroad, up the watershed. It would not be the same. Instead, he stayed for a while, yet again, with the Barnett family, who had moved from Georgia to "the last house up Deep Creek." This house was situated at the Bryson Place about 10 miles north of Bryson City—precisely where the Burbank family resides in *Smoky Mountain Magic.*

By the early 1920s, Kephart was settled in Bryson City and the Barnetts had moved to Aquone, a remote community about 30 miles west of Bryson City. Barnett passed away in 1934, when he was 54 years old, and was buried near Mars Hill, North Carolina. It's unlikely that Kephart admired or valued any of his friends more than he did Bob Barnett—not even George Masa, the Japanese photographer with whom he also formed a special bond.

Kephart never bought "a place in the Smokies." From late 1910 until his death in 1931, he made his home in Bryson City. He found suitable accommodations at the Cooper House, a rambling 16-room hotel (sometimes described as a boardinghouse) on the north side of Main Street just west of the town square that had been established by "Uncle Billy" Cooper in 1890. It was popular because of "the quality maintained in meals and rooms" and because it "was located closer to the court house in Bryson City than any other hotel of similar size." After becoming the Kephart Tavern in 1939, the structure was "razed" in 1953, as described in an article that appeared shortly thereafter in *The Smoky Mountain Times*. Kephart also rented office space over Bennett's Drug Store, situated around the corner on Everett Street, overlooking the Tuckasegee River.

After his next book, *Sporting Firearms*, was published in 1912, the Outing Publishing Company issued the first edition of *Our Southern Highlanders* in 1913. The Macmillan Company reprinted that text in 1921, then published a true second edition in 1922 that added three new chapters and a sub-title: "*A Narrative of Adventure in the Southern Appalachians and a Study of Life among the Mountaineers.*" It has had enduring and widespread popularity as a lively portrayal of the lives, places, and adventures it described. Kephart was able to produce a book that has become one of the staples of both southern Appalachian and American regional literature by crafting a vigorous and sharply honed style of writing that was often humorous. And his journals were always there, providing the broad range of materials he liked to have at his disposal before selecting what was required for a specific scene or incident. The composition of *Smoky Mountain Magic,* despite being a novel, was executed in a similar fashion.

Kephart continued writing articles and columns for outdoor magazines the rest of his life. He published *The Camper's Manual* in 1923 and served as general editor of "The Outing Library," a series that reprinted famous tales of adventure. In 1927, a controversial and historically significant Paramount Pictures silent film titled *Stark Love* was shot in Graham County, situated to the west of Bryson City on the state line with Tennessee.

In a manuscript titled "The Making of *Stark Love*: From *The Paramount Adventure*," writer-director Karl Brown, a former student of silent film legend D. W. Griffith, provided recollections of "his efforts to find amateur actors in an area where movies were considered sinful by most" and his relationship with Kephart. Brown had chanced upon a copy of *Our Southern Highlanders* and intuited that the author was someone who could provide assistance. So he went to Bryson City in the fall of 1925, at a time when Kephart was struggling with the composition of *Smoky Mountain Magic* and during the exact year in which the novel was set. Although highly colored, Brown's account is one of the more interesting and detailed descriptions of Kephart from that or any period:

> *We stored our gear in baggage rooms [at the Bryson City railway station] while we wandered up the street looking for someone who might give us news of Kephart. Suddenly I saw and recognized him, standing negligently before the town's one hotel....[He] was a small man, something below medium height, but chunky and intrinsically formidable. But the one feature that distinguished him from all other human beings I have ever met was that one of his eyes was a bright blue while the other was a deep brown....We crossed the street and ascended some wonderfully uneven steps to land in an equally wonderful uneven office with a floor that was as wavy as a mild sea.*
>
> *Kephart's desk was of the old rolltop kind, his typewriter, a battered old Underwood 5. The nearby table was piled high with books, papers, magazines and letters, with everything piled on top of everything else. On the floor beside the desk lay a coil of twisted galley-proofs, waiting for some kindly soul to correct them. A few old pipes, thick-crusted and rank, lay on the desk while cloth bags of Havana clippings were handy to fuel these mephitic tobacco burners.*
>
> *Kephart leaned back in his creaky-springed swivel chair and said, as a sort of cue, "Well?"....I decided then and there that this was no man to fool with. There was something so direct and honest in his bearing that he reminded me of others of his kind...so, even though I knew in advance it would be an uphill job, I decided to be as honest as I could manage, considering that I was somewhat out of practice.*

Kephart, who had already heard about Brown's desire to portray mountain people, advised him to "be a gentleman and you'll be treated like one" and that "honesty is not only the best policy: it is the only one." He introduced Brown around and arranged for a mountain guide to assist him in Graham County.

As his fame grew in the 1920s, Kephart often sought refuge from visitors by camping at the Bryson Place, presently a designated horse camp in GSMNP, where there is a marker commemorating his use of the site. Photos of hunting parties at the Bryson Place taken in the 1920s and reproduced in Bob Plott's *A History of Hunting in the Great Smoky Mountains* (2008) show several log structures still standing that Kephart might have used.

He would sometimes go there and stay for weeks on end. This wasn't the "go light" style of camping Kephart often advocated in his books and articles. It was a "permanent camp" or "base camp" operation fortified via one or more wagonloads of supplies from Bryson City, which included a small folding desk and writing materials as well as various firearms and camping gear—equipment on which he was a recognized national authority and often field tested for various companies.

But Kephart also enjoyed camping off the beaten trail, by himself, in hidden sites he called "masked camps." The one that he drew a map for in *Camping and Woodcraft* (vol. 2, page 233, Fig. 68) closely approximates the setting at the unexplored Nick's Nest watershed (adjacent to and just south of the Bryson Place), where the main character in *Smoky Mountain Magic* camps to evade detection.

It would be wrong, however, to suppose that Kephart was always a loner. He liked his privacy, but he also had many friends from all walks of life. He took part in the civic affairs of Swain County and Bryson City as a member of the Chamber of Commerce and a town alderman. During 1929 to 1930, he was president of the North Carolina Literary & Historical Association.

Great Smoky Mountains National Park wasn't officially founded until 1934, but Kephart died knowing that it was going to be a reality. Since the early 1920s, he had devoted much of his time and energy to the national park movement, joining forces with George Masa, whose photographic studio was in Asheville. But Masa spent as much time in Bryson City and the Great Smokies with "Kep" as he could. They were close friends and a formidable duo when it came to promoting the park concept. Kephart wrote magazine and newspaper articles articulating the concept, always emphasizing the potential economic benefits for the region as much as wilderness preservation. These articles were illustrated by Masa's powerful images.

A few months after Kephart's death, when state officials from North Carolina and Tennessee went to Washington, D.C. to transfer titles of lands purchased for the park over to the U.S. government, Secretary of the Interior Ray Lyman Wilbur noted the "persistent and idealistic interest of Mr. Kephart, who not only knew these mountains and loved the people, but saw in them a national treasure."

Rightly, no single individual has been recognized as the father or mother of GSMNP. Many on the local, regional, and national levels contributed significantly. Kephart's name has stood out through the years because he has become something of a legendary figure associated directly with the history and lore of both the pre-park Great Smokies and GSMNP as it exists today. His public explanation for the long years devoted to the park movement was to the point: "I owe my life to these mountains and I want them preserved that others might benefit by them as I have." It was that simple.

The recent appearance of the 1929 typescript of *Smoky Mountain Magic* and Libby Kephart Hargrave's commentary regarding its provenance come as sort of a revelation that Kephart was—during most of the 1920s, when he was well into his 60s and approaching 70—devoting significant amounts of time and energy to an endeavor other than the national park movement. I knew he was working on a novel during those years, but I hadn't realized it was such an ambitious undertaking. Perhaps the negative aspects, for someone like Kephart, of a highly visible enterprise like promoting the concept of a national park were balanced out, to some extent, by the solitary pursuit of writing a novel. Since he realized there would be no direct remuneration from his efforts on behalf of the park movement, he was no doubt hoping for financial success with the novel.

While conducting research in the early 1970s at Pack Memorial Library in Asheville and Western Carolina University for a biographical introduction to the 1976 reissue of *Our Southern Highlanders,* I encountered numerous scattered pages of several incomplete draft versions of the novel. This was before the Kephart materials at both facilities had been properly archived, as they are today. I summarily dismissed *Smoky Mountain Magic* in the introduction, observing with unwarranted confidence that it "had a barely adequate title, but Kephart's talent was for factual delineation, not fiction."

Libby and I first discussed the 1929 typescript, in passing, in the fall of 2008. I was pleased to finally have an opportunity to read a comprehensible text and did so with interest when she mailed a photocopy the following spring. My earlier assessment was wrong. *Smoky Mountain Magic* is a good title that evokes the novel's primary incidents and themes. And Kephart was capable of writing fiction that is not only vigorous and entertaining but, at times, surprisingly innovative.

Kephart labored over this novel. Plot and characters varied from draft to draft more often than not—and sometimes even within the same draft. Given that sort of background, the 1929 text of nearly 73,000 words is surprisingly cohesive; in part, because the story is firmly rooted in a specific setting. All of the action takes place in June 1925 in Swain County, North Carolina, in the Cherokee communities of either Soco or Big Cove; along the Deep Creek watershed in what became GSMNP; or in Bryson City, which is called "Kittuwa" in the novel. (That name is borrowed from the ancient Cherokee ceremonial mound and mother town situated just east of Bryson City on lands presently—but not in Kephart's time—owned by the Eastern Band of the Cherokee Indians.) Almost every river, creek, road, ridge, and peak mentioned in the text can be found on a map of the area.

Smoky Mountain Magic features a primary storyline comprised of a Victorian-style romance and a narrative of exploration and adventure. It includes strange entities like the Uktenas, giant serpents with horns; hidden images of ancient dragons; frequent interplay with the Little People, the Cherokee version of Irish leprechauns; a "witch" named Old Hex; ruminations about telepathy; and magic crystals. For John Cabarrus, the protagonist, Nick's Nest—a nearly impenetrable, boulder-strewn watershed that he explores—is an ethereal cathedral-like setting; for locals, who know it as "Dog-eater Holler," it's named after "a varmint that ain't a rael animal, but a ha'nt, and cracks a dog's bones and eats him alive [and] some says hit will devour a man, too."

The character Tom Burbank (Bob Barnett) is working as the warden for a lumber company, accompanied by his wife, Sylvia or "Sylvy" as he calls her, and their young daughter. Barnett's humor, savvy, woodcraft, and competence are traits clearly reflected in Kephart's depiction of Burbank. Throughout the novel, Burbank and his harmonious family serve as a positive counterbalance for less attractive representatives of mountain culture like the "shiftless" Lumbos.

Not surprisingly, *Smoky Mountain Magic* is also rich in Cherokee lore. Kephart had authored an impressive series of magazine articles about the Cherokees that Laura Kephart collected and published in 1936 as *The Cherokees of the Smoky Mountains*. Still, the range of knowledge he displays in the novel regarding their history and culture is substantial. It is apparent that he studied the work of anthropologist James Mooney, who lived on the reservation for several summers in the late 1880s and published his monumental *Myths of the Cherokee* in 1900. But many of Kephart's characterizations are obviously based on personal experience with the Cherokee, especially those involving demeanor and language.

The descriptions of the natural world encountered along Deep Creek are accurately drawn—and they are sometimes beautifully rendered, particularly during Cabarrus's initial exploration of Nick's Nest. There are scenes throughout in which Kephart is able to transform his skills as a writer of descriptive prose into those of a novelist. One of these occurs as Cabarrus is taking a break to eat lunch and smoke above Nick's Run, a tiny stream that feeds into the Nick's Nest watershed:

> *It was a hot day, even at this altitude. Cabarrus fell into a dreamy reverie. Somehow once more he got to thinking of Indian Myra and the Little People...Somewhere back in the inscrutable thicket were quick, gentle sounds of mice or ground-squirrels overturning leaves. Then abruptly it all stopped, as if in hushed attention to some obtruding scent of fox or shadow of a bird of prey. Profound silence followed, save for the never ceasing clamor of Nick's Run. All creatures in the woods seemed to be listening, some tense with dread, some avid with predaceous greed. Now and again a soft sigh came from the tree-tops, or a gentle sibilant murmur of rivulets flowing underground; but all living things were quiet, until at last their strained ears were soothed by a mourning-dove cooing low.*

Creating a dreamscape and employing descriptions like "inscrutable thicket" are not the sort of stylistic devices a reader familiar with *Camping and Woodcraft* and *Our Southern Highlanders* would have expected from Kephart, not even in a novel.

As a librarian in St. Louis, he had access to numerous journals and diaries that, when subsequently published in book form, became an integral part of Western regional literature. Upon his arrival in the Great Smokies, he created his own journals and a diary (now lost) to draw upon. By the time he started writing his novel, Kephart had already gathered so much relevant material that the portion of Journal 18 set aside for *Smoky Mountain Magic* added but 68 pages of new items. These include plot summaries, drafts of possible scenes, landscape descriptions, and pages of clippings and notes devoted to prospecting, geology, mining, and minerals. Accumulating information in his journals and then sifting through it for what he needed at a given moment was the way he had always worked. He wasn't about to alter this approach because he was working on a novel for the first time.

To a great extent, it is Kephart's utilization of Appalachian language—carefully recorded with full appreciation of its linguistic roots—that brings both *Our Southern Highlanders* and *Smoky Mountain Magic* to life. "I have myself taken down from the lips of Carolina mountaineers some eight hundred dialectical or obsolete words," he estimated. About this topic, he wrote a chapter titled "The Mountain Dialect" for *Our Southern Highlanders,* and an article published in 1917 in *Dialect Notes* titled "A Word-List From the Mountains of Western North Carolina," comprised of about 400 words and expressions.

In *Smoky Mountain Voices: A Lexicon of Southern Appalachian Speech Based on the Research of Horace Kephart* (1993), Harold Farwell and Karl Nicholas noted that on both of those occasions Kephart emphasized "the most novel qualities of the language." After surveying his journal entries, which were recorded from various locales as well as from an array of printed sources, they concluded: "Of all this material…that which seems of incontestable value now is the record of speech he heard among his neighbors in Bryson City and up Hazel Creek, that is, in the immediate vicinity of the Smoky Mountains." The dialect employed in *Smoky Mountain Magic* is pervasive and it is certainly lively and colorful—probably an accurate rendering of the sort of language anyone would have encountered up Deep Creek during the first quarter of the last century.

As might be expected in a first novel, John Cabarrus is modeled in many ways on its author, even though Kephart, in real life, was quite a bit older than his fictional creation. Cabarrus was influenced as a boy by his grandfather, Abelard Dale, to love the natural world "on the old home-place" in the Great Smokies, just as Kephart had been influenced by his father, Isaiah Kephart, to cherish their family's pioneer heritage. In Journal 18, Kephart's notations under the heading "Background," seem to indicate he was using his father, when he was a "Professor of Natural Sciences...at Western [College]," as one of the models for Cabarrus's grandfather.

Cabarrus wants to return to the setting on Deep Creek associated with his youth. Kephart discovered Hazel Creek as a place in the Great Smokies, where he could "begin again" and "realize the past in the present."

Kephart arrived in Swain County by train. Cabarrus arrives not quite 21 years later by automobile. He avoids town and heads for the backcountry, castigating the changes that have taken place in the years he had been away: "Highways," he murmured; "paved streets; electric lights; automobiles....Fourteen years!"

Along the trail he quickly tires and exclaims, "This is what cities and automobiles do to a man"—a sentiment straight out of Kephart's "Songs of Barbarism" notebook.

When he first meets Marian Wentworth, the novel's heroine, she asks, "Is your party near by?" To which he brusquely replies, "I have no party, I am alone."

Kephart, when he arrived on the "Little Fork of the Sugar Fork of Hazel Creek," immediately began to explore the "mysterious beckoning hinterland...an Eden still unpopulated and unspoiled." Upon his arrival on Deep Creek, "Cabarrus rejoiced in the vigor and variety of this unspoiled Eden."

The parallels Kephart establishes in the opening chapters between himself, when he arrived in the Great Smokies in 1904, and his fictional character Cabarrus, when he arrived in 1925, are interesting. There are no indications that he's trying to conceal the literary relationship. In the long run, however, the change Cabarrus undergoes during the course of the novel is where attention will be focused. Readers familiar with Kephart's life and work will wonder, as they near the conclusion of *Smoky Mountain Magic,* to what extent Cabarrus's disposition and aspirations reflect the author's perspectives during the 1920s. At one point toward the end of the novel, for instance, while secluded in Nick's Nest in the "abominable chilly fog and dripping wetness of the woods [and] oppressed with a feeling of futility," Cabarrus realized "that he no longer wanted to live alone."

On April 2, 1931, at the age of 68, Horace Kephart was killed in an automobile accident east of Bryson City. He was buried in the cemetery overlooking the town that had been his home for just over 20 years. Marking his grave is a large boulder moved there by friends. The grave has frequent visitors, often from distant places. They seem to come for many different reasons. His story includes the self-inflicted loss of profession and separation from family as well as intervals of chronic alcoholism. It also includes accomplishments of considerable substance that, until now, could have been summarized as "a significant role in founding Great Smoky Mountains National Park and the authorship of *Camping and Woodcraft* (1906), a cornerstone of American outdoor literature, and *Our Southern Highlanders* (1913), one of the classics of southern Appalachian literature." Any future consideration will have to include: "*Smoky Mountain Magic* (2009), the posthumous novel that evokes the life, lore, and landscapes of the pre-park Great Smoky Mountains."

George Ellison
Bryson City, North Carolina

Works Cited

The on-campus Mountain Heritage Center and the Special Collections department at Hunter Library, Western Carolina University, Cullowhee, NC, maintain a permanent online exhibit titled "Horace Kephart: Revealing an Enigma" that provides biographical information, a timeline, and a bibliography. There are numerous images from Kephart's photograph album (featuring many of the scenes and people discussed in the introduction), pages from his journals, his maps, and personal items: *www.wcu.edu/404.asp*.

Anon. 1934. "'Bob' Barnett Dies at Home Near Aquone." *The Franklin* (NC) *Press* (September 27).

Anon. 1953. "Razing of Kephart Tavern Marks New Era of Progress for Bryson City." *The Smoky Mountain Times* (March 12).

Behymer, F. A. 1926. "Horace Kephart, Driven from Library by Broken Health, Reborn in Woods." *St. Louis Post-Dispatch*, as reprinted in the *Asheville Citizen-Times* (December 12).

Bonesteel, Paul, director. 2003. *The Mystery of George Masa*. Asheville, NC: Bonesteel Films.

Burns, Ken, director. 2009. "Great Smoky Mountains National Park" segment of *The National Parks: America's Best Idea*. Walpol, NH: Florentine Films.

Ellison, George. 1987. "A Quest for Wilderness." In *Wildlife in North Carolina*, ed. Jim Dean. Chapel Hill, NC: University of North Carolina Press.

_____. 1988. "Horace Kephart." In *The Heritage of Swain County, North Carolina*, ed. Hazel C. Jenkins. Winston-Salem, NC: History Division of Hunter Publishing.

_____. 1988. "Horace Sowers Kephart." In *Dictionary of North Carolina Biography*, ed. William S. Powell, Vol. 3. Chapel Hill, NC: University of North Carolina Press.

_____. 2005. "Horace Kephart: Outdoorsman, Writer and Park Advocate." *Mountain Passages: Natural and Cultural History of Western North Carolina and the Great Smoky Mountains*. Charleston, SC: The History Press.

_____. 2005. "*Stark Love*: Karl Brown's 1927 Mountain Movie." *Mountain Passages: Natural and Cultural History of Western North Carolina and the Great Smoky Mountains*. Charleston, SC: The History Press.

Farwell, Harold F., Jr., and J. Karl Nicholas, eds. *Smoky Mountain Voices: A Lexicon of Southern Appalachian Speech Based on the Research of Horace Kephart*. Lexington, KY: University Press of Kentucky.

Frome, Michael. 1994. *Strangers in High Places: The Story of the Great Smoky Mountains*. "Expanded Edition" of 1966 first edition, Knoxville, TN: University of Tennessee Press.

Hart, William A., Jr. 1997. "George Masa: The Best Mountaineer." In *May We All Remember Well, A Journal of the History & Culture of Western North Carolina*. Vol. 1. Asheville, NC: Robert S. Brunk Auction Services Inc.

Kephart, Horace. 1906. *The Book of Camping and Woodcraft: A Guidebook for Those Who Travel in the Wilderness*. NY: Outing Publishing Company; and as a facsimile of the "Two Volumes in One" edition, 1917, with a biographical introduction by Jim Casada, *Camping and Woodcraft: A Handbook for Vacation Campers and for Those Travelers in the Wilderness* (Knoxville, TN: University of Tennessee Press, 1988.)

_______. 1910. *Camp Cookery*. NY: Outing Publishing Company.

______. 1912. *Sporting Firearms*. NY: Outing Publishing Company.

______. 1913. *Our Southern Highlanders*. NY: Outing Publishing Company; and as a facsimile of the 1922 edition, which added three new chapters, with a biographical introduction by George Ellison, *Our Southern Highlanders: A Narrative of Adventure in the Southern Appalachians and a Study of Life among the Mountaineers* (Knoxville, TN: University of Tennessee Press, 1976).

______. 1917. "A Word-List From the Mountains of Western North Carolina." *Dialect Notes* 4.

______. 1922. "Horace Kephart *By* Himself." *North Carolina Library Bulletin* 5.

______. 1923. *The Camper's Manual*. NY: Outing Publishing Company.

______. 1925. *A National Park in the Great Smoky Mountains*. Photographs by George Masa. Bryson City, NC: Swain County Chamber of Commerce.

______. 1936. *The Cherokees of the Smoky Mountains*. Ithaca, NY: Atkinson Press. Reissued with an introduction by John Finger, Gatlinburg, TN: Great Smoky Mountains Natural History Association, 1983.

Kephart, Rev. Cyrus J. and Rev. William R. Funk. 1909. *Life of Rev. Isaiah L. Kephart, D.D.* Dayton, OH: United Brethren Publishing House.

Kephart, Isaiah. 1893. "Pioneer Life in the Alleghenies." *Religious Telescope* (Jan. 4-Feb 8).

McCue, Janet. No date. "Horace Kephart: the Librarian and His Libraries." Draft copy of a 27-page paper. McCue, director of the Albert R. Mann Library at Cornell University, describes Kephart's career as a librarian at Cornell and in St. Louis.

Mooney, James. 1992. *James Mooney's History, Myths, and Sacred Formulas of the Cherokees*. Introduction by George Ellison. Asheville, NC: Historical Images.

Miller, Clarence E. 1959. "Horace Kephart, A Personal Glimpse." *Missouri Historical Society Bulletin 16*.

Pierce, Daniel S. 2000. *The Great Smokies: From Natural Habitat to National Park*. Knoxville: University of Tennessee Press.

Plott, Bob. 2008. *A History of Hunting in the Great Smoky Mountains National Park*. Charleston, SC: The History Press.

(With the sort of meticulous care his fellow librarian, Horace Kephart, would admire, George Frizzell, head of Special Collections at Hunter Library, has helped preserve a significant portion of Kephart's legacy, while at the same time—with patience and humor—providing generous public access to those materials. Aside from his archival skills, George is also the most knowledgeable person regarding the entire range of Kephart's life and work that I know. In addition to his assistance, I'd also like to acknowledge: Anne Bridges, Paul Bonesteel, Quintin Ellison, John Hargrave, Neeley House, Luke Hyde, Steve Kemp, Janet McCue, Frank March, Bob Plott, Susan Shumaker, Aileen Silverstone, Karen Wilmot, and Ken Wise.)

ONE

A giant of a man lay flat on the cabin floor playing solitaire with a scuffed and grimy deck of cards. Up to the waist he was wet from wading trout streams. His sodden shoes were draining, upside down, on the porch. He sprawled on the floor like a schoolboy, one leg bent upward from the knee, his bare toes wriggling. Little pools of water dripped from him as he played.

There was sound of bustling in the kitchen ell. His wife called to him from beyond the open doorway: "Tom, you come and git me some wood."

Tom silently stacked a red jack on a black queen.

"O Tom!"

"Cain't now; I'm busy."

"You come right along!"

"Be still. I'm breakin' the bank."

"Aw, Tom, I got to scour the house today."

"What fer?"

"W'y, you know the preacher-man is visitin' folks all up and down the creek. He's liable to drap in on us any time."

"Well, my dog don't bite."

"Tom, I'd be ashamed! What you reckon he'd think, seein' this house lookin' like a hen-run?"

"Him? He'd think 'Halleluiah! Chicken dinner!'"

"You quit your dev'lin' and git me some wood."

"I put a handle in that axe jist to fit you, Sylvy."

"'Tain't no use keepin' a dog and doin' your own barkin'," retorted Sylvia. "You git busy!"

"Am busy.— Dodrot them black cyards!— Git you a fence-rail."

"I say fence-rail! You've burnt all the nigh ones your own self, on wet mornin's. You're so improvidin'!"

"Now whar'd you git that mouthful? School-marm been here? Im-pro-vidin'!"

"Tom," called the woman plaintively, "the stove'll be plumb out!"

"Be still; I'm makin' money."

"All right, Mister Bank-robber; cold bread and stale coffee 'll be your portion."

Long silence in the front room. Then Tom began talking to himself, or pretending to do so, but loud enough for his words to carry all over the place.—

"My wife casts up laziness to me, sometimes; but I don't mind: for it's so. I'm so improvidin' that I hain't laid up a jug o' liquor for a rainy day.—Ten on nine; red eight; come black seven. Whoop! Thar it is."

Little Margaret had been following her mother about the kitchen, seeking to help her with baby imitativeness. Now she came toddling into the living-room. She frowned upon the prostrate man and shook an admonitory finger at him like an old woman.

"Daddy," she bade, "you det thum wood."

Big Tom dropped the cards, caught up the child in his great brown hands, tossed and tousled her till she pealed with glee, playfully spanked her, kissed the corn-colored curls and set her down. Then he rose ponderously and went into the kitchen.

"Damn these wash-days and scour-days!" he complained. "A woman's allers findin' something to do that a man cain't see no sense in."

He seized his wife by the waist, twirled her around, lifted her level with his six-foot-two, and gave her a loud smack on the lips.

The astonished woman turned red in the face. It was the first time Tom had kissed her in Lord-'a-mercy only knows when.

"What you blushin' for, Sylvy? Lots o' gals, nowadays, has to paint their faces to look thataway."

"Oh, you great big ruffian triflin' thing!" laughed his wife. "If you don't git a soon shave you'll haffter be scalded like a pig to git the bristles off. Now go 'long, you, and see you cut enough wood to last a *time*." Strong emphasis on the last word made it mean a long time, a time worth reckoning.

Tom obediently put on his shoes and went out to the back yard. A heavy double-bitted axe lay across the chopping-block. Its edge was bright from recent grinding.

In a turn of devilment, Tom picked up the dangerous tool by the very tip of its handle, grasping only a couple of inches of the wood between his thumb and two bent fingers. So, holding the helve by the least possible grip, he extended his arm to full length, the axe pointing forward like an outthrust sword. Then slowly, to prove his strength, he bent his wrist toward him and tipped back the axe. Steadily, perilously, the heavy blade moved toward his upturned face in the arc of a circle. The keen bright edge approached his lips; but still his arm was held rigid and only slightly bent.

Sylvia screamed: "Tom! My God! What you doin'? Tom! You'll split your head wide open!"

Tom smilingly let the axe drop nearer, nearer, till he kissed its razor edge. Then deliberately he swung the heavy tool backward in its arc, flourished it in salute, and said: "I allers kiss the bitt after kissin' a woman. 'Tain't so sharp as her tongue is sometimes, and I got to keep my narve up, so's I don't git hacked."

He swung the axe over his shoulder and stepped forth to do his chore.

"Aw, Tom!" Sylvia ran after him, threw her arms around his brawny neck, drew him back, and snuggled her soft cheek against his bristly jowl. Little Margaret laughed and danced about them.

Away, then, went Tom, whistling up his dog.

Down below the house was an old field, worn out, given over to sedge, briers and sassafras bushes. Years ago it had been cleared for corn by the first settler in this wilderness. He, instead of felling and logging the trees, had saved time and toil by simply "deadening" them, girdling the trunks with axe-cuts through the sapwood all around. They died, the bark shed off, and they stood gaunt in the spectral ugliness of skinned and weathered boles. One tenant after another, as time went by, had cut some of them down for firewood. Only three or four remained, of all that skeleton host, and there they stood, white and air-seasoned and bone-hard to the core.

Tom strode along, singing in a hearty treble:

"When fust I married, I lived on Spillcorn
And worked like the devil, the livelong day.
My wife did the cookin' for Wild Bill Rathborn.
They tuk it in head they's goin' to run away."

He cast a contemptuous glance over the stony field.

"Never be wuth a cuss to raise or graze on," he thought. "My mule Jaybo has to take to the linn sprouts and bushes in the woods to pick a livin'."

He scanned the heavily timbered ridge that rose steeply from the water's edge on the far side of the creek.

"Could make a clearin' yander, I reckon; but, shucks, it's too straight-up-and-down to plow. Me and Sylvy 'd haffter hoe it on our knees. Two-three year o' spindly corn, and by then the soil would all be washed down into the creek. All these fur-back Smokies is good for is turkey and pheasant, 'coon and mink, wildcat and bear. I can make more a-huntin' and trappin' than by tryin' to raise a crap whar there's more rocks than dirt."

He skipped a verse of his ballad and sang:

"Another man killed on Sourwood Mountain—
Shot him when the chickens was a-crowin' for day—
And that was the last o' Wild Bill Rathborn.
Tell them boys they'd better stay away."

"Well," he continued soliloquizing, "anyhow, this is shore a joyful place to live and breathe in. God never made purtier woods or cooler waters than we got right here in the Smoky Mountains. And it's five miles to the nighest mean neighbor."

"They found Wild Bill on Sourwood Mountain,
Layin' on his back with his head agin' a tree,
With a forty-four Colt's and a Smith and Wesson—
Ever'body says they belonged to me.

I got a woman on Sourwood Mountain;
She's been the cause of the killin' o' three;
But I'm goin' to stay on Sourwood Mountain,
Though they swear by the devil they're a-goin' to git me."

Tom sang with the care-free abandon of one who celebrates some other fellow's trouble. Had it been his own, he would have kept his mouth shut.

He felled one of the chestnut trees. It crashed to the ground, the slender top snapping into several pieces. The unbroken trunk made a log like a telegraph pole, thirty feet long, a foot thick at the butt and tapering to nine inches at the upper end. Tom lifted the small end, got his shoulder under it, pushed forward, heaving the log higher, and so worked along until the center of gravity was on his shoulder. Then he swung the butt clear from the ground and strode off, carrying his axe in his left hand. Uphill he went, to the house, bearing at one load a quarter of a ton of firewood.

Sylvia greeted him with mild reproof.— "You'll bust your back doin' that, some day, leetle feller."

"Huh!" snorted Tom, "I'm too active to plow and too stout to split rails: so this is the least I'm allowed to trifle with."

Mischievously his wife answered: "Deary me! If you're so gaily as all that, do you 'low it would strain you to he'p me with the scourin' when you've cut some wood?"

Tom made a wry face.— "Doctor said lye soapsuds would crack my leetle tender feet and dirt would git in and pizen me. I've obleege to be plumb keerful not to git damp in ary water dingier than trout-fish swim in."

Tom made the chips fly. Skilled axeman that he was, he piled up enough stovewood in twenty minutes to last a week.

Then, under the great iron wash-pot in the yard, he laid kindling and knots. He filled the pot with water from the spring-branch and quickly had a fire going under it. Nor did he return to his card game, but hung around until the water was steaming hot, then filled a bucket, took off his shoes, seized a stubby old broom, and silently went to work scrubbing the living-room floor.

Sylvia stared as if the world were coming to an end.— "Sights and wonders!" she exclaimed. "Marjy, yore pappy must be under down-right conviction o' sin!"

Margaret, half sensing the miraculous turn of affairs, crossed her hands upon her chubby waist and sighed, like a little old dame in church.

Sylvia scoured pots and pans, tidied up the kitchen, swept the hard bare earth around the house, and was ready for finishing touches in the living-room by the time Tom was through scrubbing.

"Thar," exclaimed Tom, as he lit his pipe, "I aim to rest my bones for a spell or two."

"Pore folks has a pore way," said Sylvia, "but there ain't no excuse for a dirty house. Wish t' we had money to buy a few purties for the fire-board and some colored picters to hang on the wall."

"Sylvy," said Tom, "they's purtier picters framed in our open doorway than ary rich man has on his walls. And our'n keep changin' with sunshine and shadders and storms, so's a body never gits tired lookin' at 'em."

Sylvia stepped to the front doorway, as though to enjoy the scenery, but really to hide a surge of emotion that might betray itself in her face. She looked out over the sparse pasture, the roaring creek on the farther side, the steep wooded mountains that everywhere walled in their little cove. Plaintively she answered: "I ain't a-complainin' none; but, Tom, honey, I do wish t' you'd git somethin' better to do than jist runnin' trespassers offen a company's property and fightin' fires the triflin' scoundrels sets in the woods. You're so big and strong! Hit ain't right, us to drag around thisaway, looked down on as keerless folks—with Marjy—Marjy growin' up—to be a big gal—afore we know it."

Sylvia's under lip quivered and she had to fight back the tears.

Tom looked hard at the fireplace and at the bare log wall of their humble home. He, too, fought something back. His face turned wan under its coat of tan. Long he sat there, humped on a stubby little splint-bottomed chair, puffing his pipe and saying nothing.

At last he answered gently: "I reckon you're lonesome in this 'way-back, fur-off place. But a body's bound to stand up for his home-place, even if 't ain't more 'n a log pen with a roof over. And there's sich a thing as loyalty. W'y, I believe if I was in hell I'd brag about the country."

Sylvia laughed. With quick rebound of spirits she turned and slipped into Tom's lap. She snuggled to him, saying: "Wherever you bide, Tom, I'll be thar, too, a-braggin' with you."

"Don't you git downcast, gal," said he bravely: "I've got plans. The day's comin' when there'll be developments here. Then there'll be plenty for me to do. I stand well with the company and they've as good as promised to make me a foreman. That'll be long before Marjy's growed up. You jist wait and see."

TWO

Tom Burbank's home was only ten miles from Kittuwa, the county seat, but the road was so rough that a wagon never took less than three hours to make the trip. There was a mountain to cross. The last five miles from town were through virgin forest. The creek had to be forded seventeen times in those five miles. The bottom of every ford was thickly strewn with slick round boulders. After a heavy rain the creek would be impassable until the flood ran down.

The road ended at Tom's place. Beyond and on either side loomed the wilderness: mountain after mountain, mile-high, or more, above sea-level, each marked by climatic zones of vegetation, one group above another, so that magnolias of the South bloomed within sight of spruces like those of sub-arctic Canada.

Sometime after the Civil War a wandering hunter had found here the Eden of his heart's desire. He, like Daniel Boone when leaving Kentucky for the far West, was sick of "what men call their laws and their justice." He sought wild free woods where he might live by himself, unhampered and unbeholden, lord of himself and his surroundings.

Ten miles up Deep Creek, after struggling through wild waters and along steep mountain walls, he found a place where the defile spread apart to a width of a hundred and fifty yards. Here was level bottom land sufficient for his needs. Projecting into it, and commanding a view up and down the creek to the nearest bends, was a low promontory, the flat-topped point of a ridge, that was large enough for a house site and a garden. A clear cold brook came from the mountain's heart and ran past this vantage point.

Here the hunter built a log cabin of two rooms, with rough stone chimneys and a clapboard roof. And here he abode many a year. But the evil day came when an intruder built a hut within five miles of him, half-way up the creek from Kittuwa. That was too close for the old-timer's comfort: so he moved and followed his daemon toward the setting sun.

Then came tenants of a baser sort, one succeeding the other; woods-loafers, shiftless folk, a sly and secretive breed, suspicious, fierce in the vanity of their own low caste. None of them stayed long on the place; but by turns they wore out the narrow strips of corn-land, cut all firewood that stood handy, ravaged the cabin of shelves and loft floors to use as kindling, and left it a ramshackle, filthy pen.

At last Burbank came on the scene, induced to serve as warden for a timber company that now owned most of the surrounding wilderness. Tom and his thrifty wife cleaned up the old place, repaired it, added a kitchen wing, and fixed up the back room for "company," if so be that visitors should ever come to such a far-off, lonesome place.

Two years, now, had they dwelt in this solitude; and in that time all the visitors they had entertained overnight were a few bear hunters, some timber cruisers, an itinerant missionary and a fugitive from across the Smokies in Tennessee.

Today, as Tom and Sylvia rested after their spell of house-cleaning, little Margaret played in the front yard under a gnarled old apple tree where she kept her "play-purties," the bits of bright tin and broken crockery that furnished her very own kitchenette. She swept the ground with a cedar spray and built a tottery bed of sticks for her rag doll Josephine. The red hound drowsily watched her as he lay sunning with nose between his paws.

Soft airs wafted from the woodland bearing honey scent of basswood and spicy fragrance of tree azalea. Wild bees buzzed softly around the child, harmlessly minding their own affairs. Out of the deep forest back of the house came a low, dove-like twitter from a "quillaree," as the mountain folk call the wood thrush. High overhead the intense blue was mottled here and there with tufts of languorous white cloud. The world all round about was dreamy.

But suddenly the hound sprang to his feet and bayed loud warning, his nose pointing down the creek where ran the road to town.

Margaret jumped as if stung. One glance showed her a horseman coming. With the instinctive fear of intruders that she shared with the wild creatures of the woods, she spilled her playthings, snatched Josephine from her bed, and fled for the house as fast as her stumpy little legs could carry her.

Sylvia, always alert, hurried to the porch. Tom, phlegmatic, relit his pipe before allowing curiosity to draw him to the doorway.

"Lookee yander, comin'!" cried Sylvia, staring at a slim khaki-clad figure approaching on a bay horse.

"Some young sprout from town," conjectured Tom. "One o' them furriners, likely, that gads about in soldier clothes and never shot a rabbit in his life."

"Soldier nothin'," disputed Sylvia. "W'y, Tom, as I live and breathe, *it's a woman*—and her with breeches on!"

"Good Lord!" sighed Tom, with mock concern. "Jist when I left all my varmint traps in the woods, here comes a rare new specimen!"

"Tom, now have some manners. She may be some*body*," cautioned Sylvia, meaning someone of consequence.

"Yeah," agreed Tom, "her body does look right slightly, from here, anyhow."

Sylvia ignored him. She went down the porch steps and into the yard to greet the stranger. Outwardly calm, she felt her heart surging with excitement; for here came the first woman to venture so far up Deep Creek since the Burbanks settled in the backwoods; and she was coming alone!

"Must be a brave gal, or a fool—one," thought Sylvia, eager to determine which.

Girl and horse disappeared for a moment under the bank where the front yard abruptly dropped off and the pasture bottom began. The horse took the steep grade at a hand-gallop. The girl came flying into view with hair waving and a merry whoop ringing from her pretty throat. Expertly she checked her horse and sprang from the saddle, a bewitching creature, all grace and friendliness and radiant good cheer.

"Good morning," she saluted. "Is this where the Burbanks live?"

"Yes: I'm Mrs. Burbank," answered Sylvia. "This is my husband."

She yearned to throw her arms around the happy, wholesome-looking girl, but native dignity was holding her in leash.

Tom, however, was in no wise backward. He shook hands with the girl, took the bridle reins from her without asking leave, and hitched her horse to the apple tree, as a mere matter of course. Folks who came to his place must stop and chat.

"I'm Marian Wentworth," said the girl to Sylvia. "I'm in Kittuwa for the summer and am collecting plants for our herbarium in college.

This is a glorious collecting ground! I made some finds this morning on my way up here. Let me show you!"

She opened one of the saddlebags on her horse and brought out a light plant-press, such as collectors use in the field. Unstrapping it, she laid out several specimens.

"This is *pyrularia*. Here's a twig of some strange *crataegus* that isn't in my botany. This is *Morongia uncinata*."

"It's wha-a-at?" interrupted Tom.

She repeated the latin name and added "sensitive brier."

"Huh!" grunted Tom. We call it toe-eetch. You walk into it in your bare feet and you'll git a lot o' leetle prickles atween your toes that'll eetch like flea-bites."

Marian laughed.— "I don't suppose there have been many collectors up here. So much the better: I'm on virgin ground."

"There was one, last summer," said Tom. "He was a professor and was studyin' bugism. I went with him, now and then, to watch his capers and see he didn't come to no harm. He tuk right kindly to me and tried to give me an education in what spiders and t'rantulas and daddy-long-legs was good for. Well, one day, he like to had a fit: he'd captured a new specie of gran'daddy. You never seed a man take on so over a new baby or a prize calf. But, now, what d' you think that fool went and done?"

"What did he do?" asked Marian.

"Well, sir—ma'am—he went home and named that blasted gran'daddy after *me*! Gave a long-legged stinky bug my name! And he printed it in a book!"

Marian struggled to keep her face straight.— "But he meant to honor you," she explained.

Tom looked daggers.— "Honor me? Honor the bug, you mean. Just think! And I'll be John Henry if he didn't write me a letter sayin' that, owin' to me having showed sich an intrust in science, he was namin' a new specie of hellakapoop after me!"

Tom stuttered and choked. Under his breath he said something the women were not to hear; but they did hear it and they burst into inextinguishable laughter. Tom stalked off, muttering something about "a passel o' folls."

Left to themselves, the women chatted freely. Marian said "The woods are charming. I've never enjoyed a day more. But there are some evil-looking people in the last two cabins I passed on my way up here, just before one enters the big forest. Who are they?"

"The Lumbos; a triflin' set."

"Two of the women made mean remarks as I passed, and they knew I overheard them. Do you think my breeches are unbecoming?"

"Law-*zee*! I only wisht I dar'd wear the like. Look at me, now, and think how on rainy days I have to trapes out in the wet and go draggin' around in this long skirt like a drabble-tailed chicken. And that bobbed hair o' yourn—I declar I envy you. Hit's sich a task for a workin' woman to do her hair when it's as long as mine; and if I slight it— w'y, my head looks like a stump full o' gran-daddies."

Tom had lingered within earshot. Now he snorted: "Thar it goes, agin—gran' daddies!" He moved farther off.

"Don't you get lonesome here?" asked Marian.

Sylvia sighed.— "Winters it's lonesome—seems like, sometimes, I'd die! But when spring comes, and all through the summer and fall, there's ginerally men passin' every three-four days."

"But no women?"

"Nary from the settle*ments*. Oncet a month, or so, old Granny Vine comes acrost yan mountain, or I go to her place. The Vines live only a couple o' miles from here; but it's a fearful steep climb, goin' and comin'. Whar trees has fell acrost the trail you have to work around them through thickets and briers that nigh tear a body's clothes off. The Vines is wuss off than us; for there ain't no wagon road within a mile o' their place. They've jist a narrer leetle sled-track down to the big road, and a steer to drag the sled over the ground."

"What do you do for pastime when the day's work is done?"

"Winters, I quilt. Pretty evenin' s when it ain't cold weather I often take Marjy and we go a-fishin' up or down the creek. I don't ginerally ketch so very much; but I do love the smell o' the woods, and the clar cool water, and the sunshine dancin' on the riffles, and the foam surgin' below the leetle falls."

"Aren't you afraid of snakes?"

"Not so much. The water snakes is harmless, and Tom claims the blacksnakes is, too; but I know better: I've seed 'em around here six foot long and they're powerful spry and strong. I found one in a quile beside the trail, sound asleep. Ought to had sense enough to let it alone; but I thought o' Marjy playin' around, and I got mad and heaved a rock as big as I could handily lift, and I drapped it right on that snake's quile. God A'mighty! The rock bounced off, like the snake was rubber hose, and he kem at me with head two foot from the ground and mouth wide open. He was so quick I couldn't move, nor hardly bat an eye. But he seed I was too big to swaller; so he run off in the brush."

"Ugh, what a fright it must have given you! Are there any poisonous snakes around here?"

"Tom kills a rattler, now and then, out in the woods. I ain't seed none, myself; but a copperhead bit Tom's bird-dog he had last summer. His head swelled till he didn't look like a dog no more, and he was powerful sick for days. He gradually got better, but he never was much account after that."

"The big wild beasts don't come down here to your place, I suppose."

"They're around, sometimes; but I ain't never yit met up with a wildcat nor much of a big bear. One evenin', though, up nigh the old splash-dam, me and Marjy was gradin' along the bank through a thicket, to git by a deep hole in the creek. Right thar—hope I may die if we didn't walk right up on a leetle cub bear! It was the cutest thing! But I knowed in reason the old mammy bear wasn't fur away and she might wind us and come a-rarin'. People! I grabbed my young-un and I lit out o' thar with my feet poundin' the ground to beat a hen a-peckin'. You could a-played marbles on the tail o' my skirt, I betcha."

So they chatted on; Marian asking eager questions about a mode of life that to her was as strange as if it were on the planet Mars; Sylvia answering with matter-of-fact directness, in the quaint idiom of the mountaineer.

The girl was thrilled by the amazing novelty of the situation. Here, only ten miles back from a national highway, in the very center of eastern America, she was discovering a world that did not even faintly resemble the one in which she had been born and bred. It was as though she had carelessly, unwittingly stepped across some shadowed boundary of sense into a fourth dimension where even the simplest things she had learned in childhood were no longer true. She had been carried back upon the wings of time into a world primeval, and here she sat talking face to face with a daughter of Daniel Boone.

Meantime Tom, in the background and out of hearing, was growing restless. That was a confounding pretty girl. Too pretty to be gadding about in man's clothes, weed-hunting. Weed-hunting indeed! That didn't stand to reason. No such girl would be in such a fool business, unless it was a blind. Now what was she really up to?

Who knew but that she might be one of those dodgasted writers who nose into folks's private affairs, and then go and print them? Or advance agent for a movie concern that would come and film the place and make him and Sylvy ridiculous?

Tom was just obliged to find out more about her. He had a nice smooth line of talk to draw her out. He would entrap her into telling the truth. Yes, it was time he was getting back to see what was going on.

But as Tom rounded the house—what the devil was this? He rubbed his eyes. It was so! Sylvia had her arm around that girl and she, Sylvia Burbank, was sniveling!

He caught some disconnected phrases. Then this:

"Honey, I been dyin' to talk to a woman-person! Let's go in the house. The front room's damp yit, for I been scourin'—leastways Tom has—so let's go back to the company room. It ain't been used in a long time; but every day or so I open it wide to the sunshine, and air the quilts, and dust the pore leetle furniture. Yes, and I keep a jar o' posies thar, fresh from the woods, waitin' for the company that never comes."

"But I've come," soothed Marian.

"Yes, deary; and I wish t' you'd stay. You must stay to dinner, anyhow: I'd be right hurt if you didn't."

"You bet I'll stay for dinner," answered Marian heartily. "Come and we'll have a good long talk!"

The two women went up the steps and into the house together.

Tom stood outside and glared.

"Good God A'mighty!" he gasped. "Ain't Sylvy got no sense at all? She right up and told that gal I'd been a-scourin'! Now it'll be all over the settlement faster than the devil can set out fire. Me scourin' floors! Me pushin' a broom! Me with my pants rolled up, sloppin' soap suds over the place! Of all the damned gossip, now that'll be the candy! Jist becayse I hated to see Sylvy break her back—and there wa'n't nobody around to spy and tattle—I done it to pleasure her. But will anybody believe that? Naw! Every fool on Deep Creek will hot-foot the news around that Tom Burbank—Big Tom—the feller that can lift a hoss—has been henpecked, begod, into scourin' floors! By the jumpin' Jericho, I'll have ten men to lick for this!"

Tom blew up in a blue streak of profanity.

THREE

The state line between North Carolina and Tennessee runs along the crest of the Great Smoky Mountains from the Pigeon River to the Little Tennessee. On the Carolina side the Okonaluftee River, called Lufty for short, comes down out of the Smokies, paralleling Deep Creek and separated from it by a wooded ridge that rises a mile or more above sea-level.

On the same June morning that Marian Wentworth visited the Burbanks on Deep Creek, a young man stopped his dusty sedan at a filling station where the highway from Asheville to Atlanta crosses the Lufty. He called for gas.

"Fill her up," said he.

The gas man was quick-eyed and inquisitive. He glanced inside the car and observed that the tonneau was filled with a big pack-sack and boxes of what might be foodstuffs but certainly were not sample cases.

"Camping?" he asked, by way of being chatty.

"Camping," echoed the driver.

"New York," said the man, reading the license plate.

"New York," repeated the stranger.

"Alone?"

"Alone."

"Long trip for a feller by himself. Don't you get lonesome?"

"Never lonesome. And no: I'm not bootlegging."

The gas man laughed.— "Mind-reader, eh? Well, I'll bet the price of this gas that you've been stopped and searched."

"You win. Now suppose you tell me something: does the highway follow this side of the river all the way to Kittuwa?"

"No: it crosses on a concrete bridge at Governor's Island."

"Can't one take a car down this side from the bridge to Deep Creek?"

"Yes: there's a sort of by-road—the old detour when they were building the highway last year."

"How far up Deep Creek can a car go?"

"Five miles, to Jim Terhune's place; but the road's rough."

"Thanks. Now what is there about me that looks like a bootlegger?"

"It ain't you, yourself; but you being alone with all that camping rig. It looks like a blind. Folks don't go camping alone."

"I do," said the stranger, shortly, and away he went.

Beyond the Lufty bridge he observed a sign at a junction where another road came down from the north. An arrow pointed up the Lufty, from the highway, and the sign read:

Cherokee Indian Reservation. 5 miles.

The young man stopped his car and looked wistfully in that direction.

"I wonder if Myra is still living," he murmured to himself. "She was a good soul, that Indian." He sighed and uttered faintly, "Fourteen years!"

The man back at the filling station halloed and signalled him to keep to the left. He drove on down the highway.

When he came to the concrete bridge where the highway crosses the Tuckaseegee River, he turned sharply to the right, down a bank, and bumped along over the old detour between the river and a railway embankment. So presently he came to the mouth of a glassy-clear stream from the north that debouched here into the Tuckaseegee. There was a sign at the bridge, *Deep Creek*, and another on the farther side marking town limits.

Again the traveller stopped. Again he looked pensively at the surroundings. On the opposite river bank and its hilly background there was a small new suburb. From the bridge he had no view of the main town, owing to a bend of the road and a bluff ahead.

He drove up a grade to the beginning of a street. Before him spread Kittuwa, a village in size but a city in function, with the white dome of a court-house showing above the treetops.

Ten minutes he lingered here, not entering the town, but scanning from afar as if searching for old landmarks and noting changes.

"Highways," he murmured; "paved streets; electric lights; automobiles...Fourteen years!"

Then, slowly, with head bent over the steering-wheel, he backed around and returned to the creek. Here he turned northward, toward the Great Smoky Mountains, following the Deep Creek road.

His watch showed half past ten. He had left Asheville at eight o'clock.

He drove up an open valley covered with pleasant farms and bounded on either side by wooded spurs that sloped down from high ridges in the distance. Farmers that he passed gave him only a cursory glance. They were getting used to tourists, here in the neighborhood of town.

But a couple of miles north from the river there was a marked change. The valley suddenly contracted to a gorge, the road became rough and rocky, the ridges rose like walls almost from the water's edge. There was no outlook on either side, save here and there a narrow field where a brook came down from the mountain and had formed a little cove. He saw sparse cornfields on the sides of ravines as steep as forty or forty-five degrees.

As the character of the country thus abruptly changed, so did that of the inhabitants. These hill dwellers were a different folk from the valley people, less comfortable in appearance, less pleasant in expression, not so preoccupied with their affairs, more curious about the passer-by. They stood and stared after him till he went out of view.

It was hard going. Twice the car stuck in ruts between rocks and he had to jack it up and pile stones in the track before his differential would clear.

All the way he followed the winds of Deep Creek, along ravine walls and up and down steep grades, always bumping over rocks, making five to ten miles an hour.

The creek hurried over rocky shoals, shot over ledges, plunged into long pools where trout lay plainly visible through six to ten feet of cold blue water. It crowded and surged, here and there, through narrow chasms, tossing in waves and setting up a roaring that ascended to the hilltops.

Presently the traveler espied a boy walking on ahead, a quaint figure in overalls that came to his armpits and still had to be rolled up at the bottom to keep from dragging. The boy turned and gazed back at the approaching car. He seemed undersized for his age and had an old-fashioned air. His beady black eyes took shrewd inventory as the car drew nigh.

"Have a ride?" proffered the driver.

The boy hopped in.

"Going far?"

"Next house," answered the boy. "I live thar."

An envelope worked out of the driver's pocket as he twisted in steering the car among the rocks. The boy stooped over and picked it up. Deliberately he spelled the address aloud.

"Mr. John Cab-arrus," he made it out.

"Ca-bar-rus," corrected the stranger, stressing the second syllable and sounding it as in barrel. He pocketed the letter.

"That your name?" asked the boy, meaning only to be sociable.

"Yes."

"Mine's Kittredge McPherson Printer-John Vine Terhune," said the boy with an air of importance.

The stranger emitted a low whistle.

"You seem to have had plenty of godfathers," he observed.

"Kittredge was a senator our folks allers voted for," explained the boy gravely. "Him and George Washington was the greatest men ever lived. Then McPherson, he was the preacher married Pa and Ma. Printer-John—well, they was three John Vines: Long-John, Sick-John and Printer-John who run the paper, oncet, in Kittuwa. Vine was Ma's name afore she married."

"I see. And now, Mr. K. M. P. J. V. Terhune, what might one call you when he is short of breath?"

"Kit."

"All right, Kit; is this the place where we get out?"

They had come to a broad ford that looked impassable for cars. Across the creek was an old frame house set amid apple trees in a wide yard. The house was two stories high, a notable structure for the backwoods, ambitiously begun but never finished. Its unpainted weather-boarding was stained and blackened by the elements. The upper story had neither doors nor windows in the openings left for them by the carpenters when they quit work those many years ago. It was a house to make sensitive people shudder if they passed at night or in stormy weather.

"The creek's down, now," said Kit, "and you can ford it in this cyar."

Cabarrus was dubious; but as he glanced about he could see no parking place on the hither side, amid the big rocks, nor anywhere to turn.

"Lots o' room in our-unses yard," the boy assured him.

"But if the creek should suddenly rise?"

"Then jist wait till it runs down."

"You're sure I won't flood my car or go too deep for the engine?"

"Well, we-uns has a team o' mules to pull you out, if you do."

"I see," remarked Cabarrus sagely. "Now, then, Mary Jane," said he, addressing the car, "let's have no coughing or choking when you get your baptism."

They plunged into the water and went chugging and twisting and bumping over boulders, till they met the main current, and there they jammed a wheel hard fast between rocks.

"Hell!" exploded the stranger.

"Set still," said the boy philosophically; "Dad's comin'."

A very tall and attenuated man appeared from somewhere as if summoned by magic. He, too, was in overalls, like the boy, but they were six inches too short for him. He walked with a peculiar bobbing gait, up and down, up and down, and his long legs spanned a full yard at every step. Nonchalantly he came right into the creek, waded to the car, stooped over, seized one of the wedging rocks, gave a mighty heave and rolled it aside.

"Git ep!" said he, as if to a team of mules.

The car went forward. It plunged into a hole but came gallantly up out of it and bumped along, splashing, to the creek's rim and triumphantly out into the farmyard.

"Travelin'?" asked the tall man. He was wet all over but did not mind it a bit.

"Yes," answered the stranger. "My name's Cabarrus; from New York. I'm on vacation and want to see the Smokies. This seems to be as far as I can get with the car. May I leave it here in your yard while I go hiking in the mountains? I'll pay for the accommodation, of course."

"You're welcome to leave it hyur, and there'll be no charge. There ain't nobody 'll tetch ary thing you have in the cyar, onless it's Bupply, that youngest o' mine, who's a plumb nuisance about nosin' into things that ain't none o' his business. That's him comin'."

The farmer pointed accusingly at a fat boy of seven or eight who was galloping absurdly toward them with a grin on his round moonlike face.

"Hello, son," said Cabarrus to Bupply. "Do you reckon anything would bother my car if I leave it here?"

"There's a hooty big owl out thar in the woods," warned Bupply.

"Well, you can scare it away; can't you?"

"Uh-huh. I shot a great old cockyolly-bird with my bow 'n' arrer."

"Oh, what a lie!" said Kit.

"Did, too," asseverated Bupply.

"Well," said the stranger to the fat boy, "I'll hire you to guard my car, while I'm away, and see that nothing is touched. Here's a new silver dime for you, and I'll give you another when I get back, if everything is O.K. about the car."

Bupply grinned and seized the coin in his chubby paw. Cabarrus patted the boy's head and assured him, "You'll grow up to be a great man, some day, and have a cigar named for you."

Bupply ran off behind the house, reappeared with a bow and arrow, and gravely mounted guard over the stranger's car.

"Come in and rest," invited Terhune the elder.

Cabarrus looked at his watch. "Past eleven," said he. "I want to get far enough up the creek to pick a good camp site for the night: so I'd better be starting. Just follow this wagon road, I suppose."

"Yes: it goes as far as Big Tom Burbank's, and you could stop thar for the night, 'stead o' camping. He'll put you on a trail for the high Smokies, if so be that's whar you're gwine. Better stay to dinner with us," he added cordially.

"No: thank you. Time now to hit the grit. I'll be back in three or four days."

Cabarrus lifted his big pack-sack out of the car, heaved it up on his shoulders and ran his arms through the straps. It was a capacious affair, a Northwest cruiser's pack, and stuffed with sixty pounds of equipment.

Kit gazed at the pack and took in every detail of its design and material.

"I've lived here twelve, goin' on thirteen year," he declared, "and I ain't never seed the like o' that in my time!"

"It's a good thing, grandpop," laughed Cabarrus.

"Bewar' you don't git lost in the mountains," warned Terhune.

"I have a map and compass," said Cabarrus, "and I'm used to the woods."

"I wouldn't confidence them government maps too much," advised the farmer. "They're right enough in the settled parts of this country; but up in the wild mountains, whar you raelly need guidance, they're mainly guesswork. Trust your own eyes and sense. If there comes a thick fog, make camp and wait. Cloud often settles on the mountains and if you go blunderin' around in it you'll git in a bad fix. There's laurel and clifts and blow-downs whar you cain't make a mile in two hours, even in broad day to say nothin' about when the fog's so thick you cain't see a tree till you butt into it."

"I'm fixed for three or four days, come what may," said Cabarrus.

"All right. Now don't cross the next ford above hyur: it's waist-deep, even now. Keep the trail on this side and you'll save several fords. You'll soon come to the Lumbos. They's three cousins of 'em: Youlus; 'Poleon and Alexander. If they're at home they'll want to go along and guide you. Suit yourself. If 'twas me, I'd say 'Good day, gentlemen, and far'well.' They'd eat up all your rations in two meals and tell you a thousand lies. Bear sharp to the right at the last house and take up a steep high bank. Good luck! We'll look for you back about Friday."

"Don't be uneasy if I fail to show up till a day or so later," said the young man. "And I thank you for your kindness to a stranger. Good bye."

Cabarrus took to the trail, his pack bulking large like an old-time pedler's. Soon he disappeared in the woodland. Terhune and Kit went into the house.

Bupply made a horrid face at Kit's back. He stuck his thumbs in the corners of his mouth, pulled it wide toward his ears, drew down his lower eyelids with his finger-tips, turned both eyes inward toward his nose and darted his tongue in and out like a snake. Having relieved his feelings by this performance, he sat himself down under an apple tree, facing the stranger's car, with bow and arrow in his lap.

He was about to drop off to sleep when something roused him to renewed joy of life. A flock of guinea-fowl had been pecking and chasing grasshoppers about the yard. An inquisitive guinea hopped up on the running-board of the car and made as if to fly to the radiator. Bupply rose on one knee, adjusted his arrow, drew it to the head and let drive.

By rare luck the shaft flew true to the mark. It struck the guinea a sound whack directly under its uplifted wing. The bird tumbled to the ground with its breath knocked out. Instantly all the other fowl set up a tremendous clatter.

Kit came dashing from the house with a shotgun, expecting to see a hawk. But there stood the proud Bupply, puffing out his cheeks and chest, the image of Victory in triumphal pose.

"Thar's your cockyolly-bird," said he. "Now, durn you, who's a liar?"

FOUR

The trail ran for a quarter of a mile or so along the side of a wooded hill; then it came to a clearing and skirted the lower edge of a corn-field.

A board shack stood in the very midst of weedy corn that grew to within five feet of the door-sill. It was a mere weatherbeaten box, made of culls, with front and rear doors but no porch nor window. Heat shimmered visibly from the rough planks of the siding and blistered the black roof. Of all the noble trees that once had shaded this spot there was not one left. All had been felled and burnt to clear a space for corn. There was not a shrub nor a vine nor so much as a spear of grass about the house to mask the stark indecency of vandalism that here seemed to vaunt itself and sneer at the clean nobility of the forest beyond the field.

Pigs made free of the narrow runway around the hovel, slept in its hot dust, wallowed in the muck beside the door where dishwater was thrown. Dogs and chickens ran in and out of the common room. Flies swarmed over the all-pervading dirt and stickiness. A sour smell came from the premises.

A slattern of a woman, gaunt, clay-colored, with lascivious eyes, stood in the doorway rubbing snuff on her gums with the chewed end of a twig. Some ragged children hovered about her, feral and furtive-eyed.

Cabarrus said "Good morning," but there was no response until he had passed by: then one of the small boys cried "Good mor-r-ning" to his back in a tone of derision.

"These are some of the Lumbos," judged Cabarrus. "Trash stranded here in a hurrah's-nest."

He soon came to the next house. It was larger than the other, but quite as filthy, and stood unfinished after the lapse of years.

Here the residents were warned of his approach by the baying of a hound, the shrill yapping of a fice, and surly growls from a big black cur.

A woman slowly closed the front door, as he approached, till only a hand-breadth of space was left between it and the jamb. She stood in the darkened interior and peered out at him through the crack.

Cabarrus had to go directly past this door; for so the trail ran. As he walked briskly by, the big cur erected its bristles and came slowly toward him, head down, muttering growls, with hate of humanity stewing in its rheumy eyes. It did not meet him face to face but slipped up behind and followed. Then suddenly it made a rush.

The traveler, encumbered by his bulky pack, barely managed to whirl in time to meet the treacherous assault. There was but one thing he could do, and he did it quickly. Snatching off his hat, he held it out to the dog. The beast seized it. Then Cabarrus kicked. The length of his arm, plus hat, was exactly the length of his leg; so the toe of his boot took the dog just under the jaw, making it bite its own tongue. With a yelp of pain and dismay the cur ran off, bleeding at the mouth.

Then the door of the house flew open. The woman appeared in full view, raging. She was a red-headed, red-faced person, voluble when roused. She let fly a stream of vile abuse, at which Cabarrus merely raised his eyebrows. She redoubled her maledictions, but still the exasperating fellow was airily unperturbed. Her wordy missiles bounced from his serenity like hail from a helmet.

"When my man comes," she shrieked, "he'll beat the hound out o' you for this!"

"Give him my compliments," said Cabarrus sweetly, "and tell him that vicious brutes are likely to get what's coming to them."

He bowed, with a flourish of his hat, as to a grand lady. It struck the woman speechless with rage. Then he turned and went on his way.

Just above the house the trail forked. To the left a path led to a footlog that gave passage over the creek to another Lumbo cabin on the far side. Cabarrus kept to the right, as Terhune had directed, and he mounted the hillside by a trail as steep as a stairway. He bent nearly double under the burden of his equipment and had to halt once for breath, being not inured to such climbing.

The virago rushed to her back yard and let out a long piercing cry, the alarm signal of the mountaineers. Then she began calling "Youlus—Youlus!"

"That's their way of pronouncing Ulysses," chuckled Cabarrus. "She's calling her man from the field. How such people ever pick up classical names, heaven only knows. I suppose she is Penelope, and that would be Circe back yonder in the corn-field chewing snuff."

Resuming his zigzag climb, he soon came to a fairly level pathway that ran along the front of a mountain. Here the forest canopy was dense and its shade delicious. Cabarrus cast off his pack and wiped his streaming brow.

He knew that this short climb was nothing to what he had to surmount before the day was done: so he looked about for a staff, the mountaineer's third leg.

Near by was a sourwood shoot that seemed grown by nature for this special purpose. It was about the thickness of a broom-handle, quite straight and tall and smooth of bark. He cut it to a length that would reach from his heel to his armpit, trimmed the ends, sighted along its straight and perfect taper, balanced the stick in his hand.

Then a sudden impishness seized him. He sprang into the fencing attitude of a crusader wielding a two-handed sword. He lunged, parried, slashed, danced about, executing one maneuver after another, as against an imaginary foe. It would have seemed a ridiculous performance to an onlooker, had there been any but a few startled chipmunks and chickadees. In this lightsome manner the young man limbered his muscles that had been stiffened by three days of driving a motor car.

He stepped to an opening in the foliage whence he could look down, as from a high window, upon the sordid contrast that he had lately hurried by. A ragged man was hastening from the field to meet a gesticulating woman.

"Aha," breathed the cudgel-player, "Ulysses is coming to see what all the row is about. I warrant Penelope's story will lose nothing in the telling."

Cabarrus put on his pack and stepped forth with recovered jauntiness, whistling a soft trilling air. High above the roaring creek his path led through a tall forest of oak and hickory, chestnut and maple, sourwood and service-berry, black gum, dogwood and blooming laurel. A wild brook came cascading down a cleft in the mountain, and here were hemlocks, witch-hazel and great rhododendron glorious in its wax-white bloom. Thick moss covered the wet rocks and the trunks of old fallen trees. Ferns and flowering umbrella-leaf grew lush in the spray of waterfalls.

He drank deep of the pure cold water, then pressed eagerly forward as if in pursuit of some quest or adventure that had been much upon his mind.

Ere long he came to a green jungle where the trail went down into a ravine. Here a small tributary emptied into Deep Creek. The beaten path swerved to the right and went up this branch. But Cabarrus went straight ahead, crossed the stream, and came out in a small old clearing where a pile of rocks marked the chimney site of a cabin that had fallen in ruin and disappeared years ago. At this point the wagon road came from across the creek by a rocky ford and started up a mountain to avoid a long winding gorge. Cabarrus now took to the road.

On, on he climbed, bearing hard upon his staff. Muscles seldom taxed in lowland life were soon overstrained and remonstrant. Sweat trickled from his brow. His breath came heavily. Every ounce in his pack was growing to be a pound.

On level ground he could have carried that pack a long time without giving it much thought; but ascending the mountain was like climbing stairs up a Woolworth Building, with sixty pounds on one's back, only to find, on reaching the uppermost landing, that a Washington Monument was set on top of it and had still to be surmounted in the same way. He had to stop for breath every few minutes and let his pounding heart slow down.

"This is what cities and automobiles do to a man," he panted. Wistfully he recalled a time—barefoot boyhood-time—when he could have taken this mountain at a run and crossed it like any rabbit.

Had he, perchance, once done so? This very mountain? He closed his eyes. Was he today among long lost but dearly beloved scenes? Was he rejoicing to find them familiar and unchanged?

> "They bring me tokens of myself, they evince them plainly in their possession.
> I wonder where they got those tokens;
> Did I pass this way huge times ago and negligently drop them?"

The forest and undergrowth were so dense that there was no outlook until he had won to the top of the divide. Then abruptly he was brought face to face with the reality of his situation. Beyond this mountain was another, and then a mountain, and then more:

an infinity of mountains, all clad from base to summit in living green. Not an opening, not a bare rock, not even a sign of trailway could be discerned in all that wilderness. He had passed from the presence and dominion of man into a vast solitude where Nature for a million years had reigned unchallenged and undespoiled.

Cabarrus did not tarry long on the mountain-top, for the wind had free sweep and he was perspiring from the climb. Going downhill it was a relief to find muscles coming into play that had not been taxed in climbing. He flexed his knees like springs, to take up the jar of the rough descent, and so with resilient stride and steady rhythm of pace he rapidly covered ground.

Since leaving the Lumbo settlement he had been on the property of the Unaka Pulp and Paper Company. Posters bearing that name were tacked to trees, warning against setting the woods afire and forbidding trespass, particularly hunting, fishing, camping, and grazing cattle on the company's land. On one of these posters he saw a ribald defiance scrawled with pencil:

> the man that Put this up had Better
> Be god Dam careful Ore he will Be left
> in the Woods.

Evidently some of the native mountaineers were rebellious against curtailment of their ancient privilege of doing as they pleased in the wilderness.

The over-mountain road apparently never was worked but was simply left a sport for the elements. On steep slopes it was gullied almost axle-deep. Along the faces of cliffs it was dug out just wide enough for wagon-hubs to clear by an inch or two. In more than one place it slanted perilously toward the edge of a precipice and the outer wheel-track missed the brink by a foot or less. Nowhere could a wheel turn without hitting a rock. Cabarrus was happy to be afoot.

Ere long he came to an icy-cold spring that gushed directly from the rock and was too enticing to pass by untasted. Here he ate lunch. At the next turn of the road he heard the creek, hundreds of feet below, go roaring through its gorges. In ten minutes he had reached it and was wading a ford.

Thence for several miles the road meandered through forest of strikingly different aspect from that of the hillsides. Here in more generous soil the trees grew taller, thicker, and many of them branched out so high from the ground that it would have taken an expert rifleman to drop a squirrel from the lowest limb of one of the big hickories or chestnut trees.

Most remarkable was the variety of species shouldering each other like people of all sorts and lineages crowded together in a metropolis. Pines and hemlocks grew close to tulip and cucumber trees, beech and birch near ash and sugar maple, buckeye and basswood and butternut not far from sycamore and holly. A collector, seeking specimens of different woods, could have procured those of forty or more species within a radius of two hundred yards.

Beneath the forest giants were laurel and rhododendron, dogwood and service-berry, moosewood and silver-bell, azalea and leucothoe. There were scores of species of shrubs, berry bushes and vines, twined and interlocked in mazes hard for a man to push through. Yet there were little glades around brooks and rivulets where Nature had set more orderly gardens and where herbs, orchids, mosses, ferns and fungi were undisturbed by the coarser growths.

Cabarrus rejoiced in the vigor and variety of this unspoiled Eden; but he had no time to linger in it now. Something urged him onward, spurring him to accelerated pace as he neared his objective.

FIVE

For days and weeks his mind's eye had been dwelling on a scene drawn from a time long past but vivid as if thrown upon a screen before him.—

Half a mile or so downstream from where Tom Burbank now was living there was a tract of three hundred acres that the Unaka Pulp Company had failed to acquire. Fifteen years ago this property had been sold to an old man, from somewhere in the East, who came to occupy it, bringing with him a boy of twelve and an Indian woman as housekeeper.

To the country folk the old man was a mystery. They respected him for his scholarship and gentle bearing, but he seemed an eccentric and a dreamer. It was even whispered that he was a pagan who worshipped flowers and birds and trees and objects of stone and crystal.

To the log cabin that stood on the place the old man added a room of better sort, built of hewn pine logs that fitted neatly together, with matched flooring and screened doors and windows.

He brought workmen to clean up the place and he planted flowers and ornamental shrubs and vines selected from the surrounding forest. The Indian servant set out a vegetable garden and took care of a cow that grazed on a meadow below the house.

The old man divided his time between teaching the boy his lessons and roaming the woods for specimens of rare or beautiful things that won his interest or affection.

Within a year of his coming into the wilderness, the old man died. The boy and the Indian woman moved away.

It was this sylvan studio, with its wild gardens and grassy meadow and tiny cultivated spots, set apart from the encompassing wooded mountains but nestling under their shelter, that the young man visioned as he hurried forward.

At two o'clock he came to the eighth ford beyond the mountain he had crossed. He splashed through the stream, indifferent to the chill of its spring-fed water, and climbed the bank on the farther side.

Then suddenly he halted, gave a startled exclamation, and stood rooted to the spot. He was staring at what had once been a close-cropped meadow, open and smooth enough for a golf course, but now abominably grown up in thicket. Sumacs and small pines were crowding each other everywhere, all entangled in meshes of greenbrier and blackberry vines. He could not see fifty feet.

"Abandoned!" he cried aloud.

His eyes, still incredulous, searched for some open vista. Surely this rank intruding growth must be only a fringe around the untended boundary of the field. He moved on up the roadway, which here was all overgrown with bush-clover and wild indigo and trefoil. There was no opening. The whole field had reverted into jungle.

Cabarrus wiped his brow and bit his under lip. His face went white with the instantaneous ruin of his dream. He had expected to find someone in tenancy of the place and keeping up its cultivation: someone of whom he could make inquiries and learn certain things that would help him to plan his future course. But the place was deserted, dead as a neglected graveyard.

Slowly he went on in a daze of perplexity. Then his eyes fell upon a stained poster tacked to a scrub oak beside the road. He stepped up and read it.—

NOTICE:
All persons are hereby notified that any and all trespassing
will be prosecuted to the full extent of the law.
W. G. Matlock.

At sight of the signature a hard look came into the young man's eyes. His mouth contracted to a thin line. The sad expression he had worn was now displaced by the stern rigidity of a fighting face.

"Matlock!" he muttered. "So that scoundrel still holds possession."

He stood for a time with head bowed in thought; then, gripping his staff tightly with the strain of sudden resolution, he started forward.

He had not gone ten yards when something went z-z-z-z, right in front of him, on the ground. Quick as an electric shock his subconsciousness released a spring that checked him and threw him backward in a leap for safety.

In the middle of the road, partly hidden by clumps of weeds, a five-foot rattlesnake had been dozing in the sun. At the thud of a man's footfall it came instantly wide awake and threw itself into a striking coil.

It was a black rattler that had recently shed its skin. Every scale on its refurbished body glittered like a faceted jewel in the sun. The tip of its tail was erect and vibrating so fast that Cabarrus saw only a blur where the rattles whirred.

Then the reptile stopped sounding its alarm and lay silent, tense, with head drawn back in its coil, waiting for the man to advance within striking range. Its horrid eyes met him with a fixed stare.

Cabarrus promptly recovered from the shock and anger blazed within him. The vengeance aroused at sight of Matlock's name passed on to wreck this other deadly thing that lay in his way. He grasped his staff in both hands and measured the distance with his eye, knowing that the snake could not leap more than two-thirds its own length. Then he took a step forward.

The rattlesnake raised its head slightly and poised to meet the expected blow with a counter-stroke. Cabarrus lifted his stick. Both man and serpent struck at the same instant. Cabarrus missed its head but he landed a heavy blow on the thick muscular body.

The rattler struck viciously again at the stick, as a second blow descended, but a few more strokes put it out of action. Cabarrus crushed its head, cut off its rattles for a souvenir, and cast the mutilated body at the foot of the tree that bore Matlock's poster. It was a childish way of showing resentment; but his mind and heart, for the moment, were those of an outraged child—he was a boy of thirteen, again, on the old home-place.

Then he went on up the road, keenly glancing from side to side and at every rock or bush in the way, as one always does for a little while after close encounter with a deadly snake.

Soon he came to the next ford.

"The footbridge is gone," he observed.

He strode into the swift water, which took him to the hips and might have swept him off his feet if he had not used his staff as a brace. Then he came up into another small field of bottom land. It, too, was now naught but a scraggly thicket. At the farther end, alongside the road, a few old logs lay rotting. Beside them were the charred remnants of camp-fires where wandering woodsmen had cooked their meals and slept beneath the stars.

"Here stood the barn," mused Cabarrus sadly.

He turned and looked to the left, toward a steep bank that rose from the thickety flat, forming the edge of an upper field.

Back a little way from its brow stood the blackened ruin of an old log hut, sagging, gaping to wind and weather, desolate. Its porch was gone. The top of the big stone chimney had fallen outward. The doors had been carried away or used for kindling. Clapboards that once covered the chinking between the logs were missing. There was no sign of the "new house" that the old naturalist had added to the original cabin.

"Vandals!" cried Cabarrus aloud. "Too lazy to gather firewood in the forest, they tore down the new house because it was of white pine logs, easy to chop and split and burn!"

The pathway up the bank to the old house was choked with weeds. Bushes and briers grew rank to the door-sill. Amid them, in solitary beauty, bloomed one single shrub of downy hydrangea, its conspicuous white flowers courted by butterflies, its leaves gently waving in the breeze, displaying the silvery sheen of the under side. Cabarrus remembered the very day that the old man had lovingly transplanted it here.

He went up to the deserted cabin. The front steps were gone; so he pushed his way through tall weeds and briers to the back of the house. Here he surveyed the upland where formerly a young orchard and a small corn-field had been.

"Poor Myra!" murmured he. "There isn't a post or a paling to show where her precious garden grew. Thicket and desolation all round about! Even the spring-branch is gullied and choked with trash."

He turned to the gaping doorway. Directly in front of it stood an unpleasant weed, the black nightshade, like a sentinel of the underworld guarding some gruesome den. He struck it down with his staff and stepped inside the ruined hut.

It was a shocking transformation that here met his eye. The rotting floor was littered with animal refuse. Gray little lizards scuttled away and ran up the walls, where they hung and blinked at the intruder. Grime and cobwebs everywhere. Dirt and the mouldy odor of decay.

Yet, ah! The memories that haunted this old place. How often at that stone fireplace....There at the window....Yonder where the table stood....

Cabarrus took off his hat and clasped his brow.

Thus was he standing, meditating upon the wreck, oblivious of everything but the dissolution of his dream, when a bay horse came down the road, bearing a young woman who kept glancing from side to side for anything unusual to add to her plant-press. She spied the hydrangea at the cabin doorway.

"That is what Sylvia calls 'nine-bark,'" she observed. "Good, so she says, for 'most anything that ails you.' Well, it's rare outside the mountains and I must have a specimen."

She hitched her horse to a sapling and climbed the old path to the cabin, her light footfall making no sound. The shrub grew in a snaky-looking place amid rocks and weeds. She glanced circumspectly at the ground, decided to risk it, and pulled the top of the bush toward her to clip off a twig. The shrub was about six feet high and masked the doorway; but as she bent the top downward the interior of the cabin was revealed and she beheld a startling sight.

There stood a man, a young and handsome man, with an expression of profound sadness on his face. He was in profile, with head bent, but he must have seen the bush bend, and may have heard her, for he turned full-face and, as he saw her, astonishment shot into his misty eyes.

"Oh!" exclaimed the girl, "I beg—"

The apology never was finished; for something suddenly happened down by the roadside that diverted both her and the man into instant action.

Her mettlesome horse was impatient at being tied to a tree when there was a rare bit of smooth road ahead and he was in fettle for a race. He had stamped and pawed and backed around the sapling and stuck a hind foot into a hole in the ground. As quick as that foot came out of the hole an infernally hot thing followed and hit him on the belly. He jumped and kicked, and immediately a whole swarm of hot things assailed him. Frantic from the stings, he tore loose from his tether and went madly racing through the thicket.

"My horse!" cried Marian.

Cabarrus leaped out through the doorway and ran headlong after the fugitive animal, with the girl skipping nimbly by his side.

The horse had plunged at random through the brush. In a breath he found himself up to the shoulders in a trout pool. A sheer cliff rising from the farther bank cut him off. He had rid himself of the yellow-jackets and his belly was cool once more; so he gave Cabarrus little trouble in securing him.

The girl petted the horse and then examined the contents of the saddlebags. Her plant-press was a mess. Every sheet of its absorbent, paper was a soggy pulp.

Cabarrus said, "I'm sorry your specimens have suffered."

"Oh, it's nothing," said Marian. "The Burbanks above here, have invited me to visit them and I'm coming back for a week or two: so I can soon duplicate all of these and add hundreds more. This is a wonderfully rich forest."

"It is, indeed. Do you live in Kittuwa?"

"No: in Raleigh. This is my first trip to the mountains."

"I am just setting out to explore them," said he. "I am John Cabarrus, of New York. We may meet again in these woods, I hope."

"We may. I am Marian Wentworth. Are you to stop with the Burbanks?" she asked, wondering, if so, where they could put him.

"No: I camp out, wherever night may find me."

"Do you enjoy that?"

"Intensely: It's a hobby of mine."

"One could envy you. Camping is so independent! You can go where no horse could travel; see country that none but the bear hunters know."

"Yes, and be free at all times to follow the whim of the moment."

"Is your party near by?"

Cabarrus smiled, but his eyes had a wistful look, as though the question recalled to him something not altogether pleasant. He answered: "I have no party; I am alone."

Marian stared. "Oh!" she exclaimed. "But surely you must have a dog for company."

"Not even a dog; but I'm used to going alone."

"But how do you manage, about carrying food and shelter and so on?"

"I have a light kit especially designed for such work. It all stows in my pack-sack."

Marian considered, in silence. This must be a queer fellow: to brave the wild woods all by himself, sleeping in the open without even a dog to sound an alarm. Why would anyone do so?

There was an awkward pause. Cabarrus, to his great disgust, was growing conscious of what he must have looked like when the girl first saw him through the cabin doorway. He was not sure but there were tears in his eyes. Sentimental noodle! What must she think of him?

"This is a charming country to camp in," said Marian, preparing to leave.

"Delightful, save that the gnats are rather bad. I got one in my eye, a bit ago, and it burned like red pepper."

"Oh, did you get it out?"

"Yes—oh, yes," answered he, helping her into the saddle.

"Good bye, Mr. Cabarrus. Thank you so much for catching my horse."

"Good bye, Miss Wentworth. If I come on any rare plants in the woods I'll save them for you."

She cantered off on the bay horse. Cabarrus stood gazing down the road for some time after the last hoof-beat sounded.

"Stunning girl!" thought he. "Rather awkwardly met. But if there were tears in my eyes they've been neatly explained. I didn't know I could be such a ready liar."

But Marian, jogging homeward, was not fooled.

"A gnat in his eye—fiddlesticks! That man was grieving. I've seldom seen a sadder face. What brought him here? What can there be about that old ruined hut to touch him so? Why is he camping alone, far back in the wild woods?....Marian Wentworth, you've met a man of mystery—and he's darned good-looking!"

SIX

Youlus Lumbo was a dour and moody fellow, taciturn, given to brooding. His disposition was septic: grievances festered in him. His own cousins watched him out of the corners of their eyes. Neighbors said of Youlus "He has a gredge agin all humanity and glories in human misery."

When injured, as Youlus often felt himself to be, he was not apt to fly up at once and redress his wrong on the spot. Rather he would take it home and to bed with him, studying it over and over, calculating chances, and biding his time till he might catch his enemy at a disadvantage, then do him the utmost harm with the least risk to himself.

So, when his peppery wife told him that a passing stranger had kicked his dog, Youlus stroked the side of his nose, squinted his pale gray eyes, and quietly asked, "What sort o' lookin' feller?"

"A dude with a suggin on his back as big as all outdoors."

"Rations," observed Youlus, licking his lips. "Aims to stay a spell in the woods. Have a gun?"

"I didn't see none."

"Under his shirt, prob'ly. Right or left-handed?"

"Right-legged; leastways he kicked thataway."

"That ain't what I axed ye. Man don't draw his gun with his leg."

"Didn't use his hands, savin' to fan his hat at me, the fool!"

"How old?"

"Twenty-five, or tharabouts."

"Eyes?"

"Black and dev'lish."

"Ha'r?"

"Short and brown."

"Whiskers?"

"Clus shaved. Didn't I tell ye he was a dude? Shiny-lookin' skin, like he washed all over, ev'ry day."

"Ar-r-rh! Which way d' he go?"

"The upperest trail."

Youlus speculated.— "Mought take the Vine trail and out over Pullback, or mought foller the big road acrost the mountain, ary one."

He stepped outside and ran his eye over the path. At a wet place where wash-water was thrown he saw the clear imprint of a man's foot.

"New boots," he affirmed. "Nails not worn hardly none."

The pattern left by the hobnails he registered indelibly in his memory.

"What you goin' to do about that dog?" demanded his wife.

Youlus was not bothering about the dog, just now. Of course nobody had a right to kick it but himself; but that matter could wait. The first thing in order was to find out who this stranger was and what he was up to.

"Reckon I'll take a turn up the creek," said he to his wife. "Go git me a bite."

The woman asked no further questions. She took down his "suggin" from its peg on the wall. It was a crude but serviceable haversack, home-made from bed-ticking, with a cloth strap to go over the shoulder. She took it to the kitchen and stowed in it a big tin cup, a pone of corn bread, a small chunk of raw salt pork, a few ounces of alleged coffee, a tablespoonful of salt— just that and no more. Her man's rationing for two or three days was accomplished in a minute. He would catch fish, of course, and perhaps shoot something.

Youlus took his Winchester rifle from its rack. It was a .44-40, full magazine. A touch of his thumb through the magazine gate satisfied him, from the spring tension, that plenty of cartridges were in place.

He filled his tobacco-pouch with home-made twist, stuck some matches in his pocket, put on his haversack, and was ready to march. Jack-knife, fish-line and trout flies he always had about him. He never burdened himself with a blanket till dead of winter, if then. Often he had slept out in the open without a blanket when the ground was "all spewed up with frost." If it rained, he soon built a lean-to shelter of bark or boughs and took the drip with stoical philosophy.

His wife wasted no breath asking when he would return. There were no schedules in that house. Nor was there any civility of leave-taking. He just went. He would come back when he got ready.

Youlus took the "upperest" trail. Fresh nail-scrapings on the rocks up the steep ascent confirmed his wife's report of the stranger's course. Thenceforth he traveled rapidly and unconcerned until he came to where the trail turned up toward the Vine place. There he studied the ground until convinced that the man had crossed to the big road. He picked up the tracks at the ford and went on up the mountain, traveling twice as fast uphill as Cabarrus had done, and with no conscious effort.

Soon he caught sight of the stranger plodding on ahead, bowed under his heavy pack-sack. Youlus slowed down and discreetly followed at a distance.

He came down off the mountain and crossed the creek by leaping from one rock to another, never wetting his feet. It was but a short way up the road to Bridge Creek, which came in on the left from the Noland divide.

Here, without warning, he was confronted by a burly man who stepped out from a screen of bushes and stood squarely in the way. The man had a revolver under his arm, in a shoulder-holster, and a badge pinned to his shirt front. It was Big Tom Burbank, who had left home immediately after the noon meal and was patrolling the company's property.

"Howdy, Youlus," said Tom.

"Howdy," returned the Lumbo sourly, stopping perforce.

"Goin' fur?"

"What business is that o' your'n?"

"You're on company property, though warned off, time and agin."

"Yeah, and I'm on a public road, I've as much right to travel hit as you have."

"Sartin; but not to step off o' it, one side or t'other."

"Not to git a drink o' water?" asked Youlus, seeking argument.

"Oh, yes: the company 'd be pleased to know you'd got fond o' water."

Youlus flushed at the gibe.— "'Pears like the public ain't got no rights, no more. We-uns made this road, in the fust place. Hit and the trail beyant is all the way we have of crossin' to Tennessee."

"You aimin' to cross now?"

"I'm aimin' to mind my own business."

"Is firin' the woods your business?"

"Who says I fired the woods?"

"Every leetle bird from hyur to Round Top."

"To hell with your leetle birds, and your gossips, too! 'Way back, sence time begun, the Indians themselves had sense enough to fire the woods every springtime to keep the braysh down so's people could travel. Look at the woods now, sence you've kep' fire out! The ridges is kivvered with huckleberry, buckberry, gooseberry, blackberry and greenbrier till a body cain't hardly push through. The creeks and branches is a mommick o' laurel and dog-hobble that you have to cut through."

"Yeah," agreed Tom, his eyes twinkling, "that does make it aggravatin' for poachers."

"Poachers!" exploded Youlus. "That's the name you give us native-born citizens who've made this country! Our foreparents for ginerations used the wild woods as common property whar anybody could hunt and fish and trap and graze his cattle and fatten his hogs on the mast."

"Yes," said Tom, "and chop down any kind of big tree on the chance of gittin' a pailful o' wild honey or a single 'coon."

"Of course. Well, that was the custom till these companies kem hyur and posted the land. Now us citizens is slapped in the face by a passel o' damned furriners and told to git the hell out o' hyur and starve!"

"I was talkin' about you firin' the woods," said Tom.

"Let's see you prove it! Anyhow, it does the woods good to burn' out the trash every spring, like we-uns allers did to make grass."

"No," declared Tom. "It mars the butts of many big trees. Then decay sets in, like a holler tooth, and the tree's damaged for lumber."

"Lumber!" sneered Youlus. "In fifteen years there won't be a tree of any size left in all this country, and you damn well know it. Then the companies 'll move their machinery and pull up their rails and kerry off their money-profits to some other state, leavin' us nothin' but a barren o' stumps and slashin's. Thousands o' tree-laps layin' sprangled over the ground, dryin' thar, among chips and splinters and everything that burns easy. Comes a spell o' dry weather, a spark gits into that mess o' tinder, and then you *will* have a fire! Hit'll go hell-roarin' over mountain after mountain, burnin' up the very ground itself, and you cain't stop it with all the men in Swain County. But what'll the companies care *then*? Huh! We can burn up and be damned. Talk about your fire protection makes me sick!"

"Some companies does thataway," admitted Tom; "but not our'n. The Unaka Pulp aims to presarve this land and let it reforest itself. That's why it's particular about not lettin' the seedlin's git destroyed by your firin'."

"Tell that to your granny," retorted Lumbo. "When did you see a timber company wait to reforest anything?"

"Well, there's no use argufyin'," said Tom. "If I find you on company property, fishin', huntin', diggin' sang, or the like, I'll take you with a warrant. That's the last word."

"Ketch me!" defied Youlus.

Tom stepped aside. He watched the departing Lumbo with mingled pity and contempt.— "These Lumbos, what are they?" he asked an imaginary audience; then answered: "A shiftless, rovin' set, rangin' the woods three-fourths o' the time, beggarin' their fam'lies at home, filthy as hogs and jist as stubborn. They ain't what's called typical mountaineers, no more than the people in the slums o' New York is typical city folks. But there's enough of 'em, and they do enough dirt, to give us a bad name. Trouble is, there's jist enough sense in what he says to make a difficult case to handle. Some o' his grievances is shared by lots o' industrious, well-meanin', old-fashioned folks who rebel agin anything they're not used to.— Well, I ain't settin' on the seat o' jestice. I've jist got a law to enforce; and, ay gonnies, I'll do it!"

Youlus Lumbo went on up the road. He came within spying distance of the deserted cabin just in time to see Cabarrus catch Marian Wentworth's horse.

SEVEN

When the girl had gone, Cabarrus realized that it was time for him to be looking for a camp site. The roadside was no place for a solitary camper who would be away from his tent most of the time and had not even a dog to guard it. So he went back to the ruined cabin, took up his pack and staff, and started off into the forest where no one would be likely to find his outfit.

Westward from the cabin, between high ridges that came down from the mountain divide that separated Deep Creek from Noland Creek, there was a long cove known to native woodsmen as Turkey-Fly-Up. The Indians gave it that name, in their own tongue, because, so they said, whenever anyone went there, in the old days, wild turkeys would fly up from this favorite haunt of theirs.

A charming brook flowed through the cove and emptied into Deep Creek below the cabin. There had once been a well-beaten trail up this hollow, but Cabarrus found only traces of it here and there. It was astonishing, to one revisiting these woods after the lapse of years, to find so much undergrowth where there had once been open and park-like woods.

On the ridges huckleberry and buckberry and thornless gooseberry bushes grew thick as hair on a dog's back, all meshed together by the exasperating greenbrier that checked a man at every third or fourth step and tore any clothing less armor-like than leather or hunter's duck. Along water-courses, and often halfway up the ridges, the beautiful but baffling leucothoe grew thick as marsh-grass, five to ten feet high, its tough stems interwoven and sometimes impenetrable except by cutting one's way, foot by foot. And wherever trails were not kept open the traveler was often balked by fallen trees, many of them a hundred feet long and five or six feet thick, which forced him to detour.

But up in the cove there were several openings. Cabarrus passed by some pretty camp sites that would have satisfied a less experienced woodsman. One of them was overhung by a leaning tree that might topple without warning, as trees do, in the ancient forest, when their roots have decayed. Another inviting place was endangered by big brittle limbs overhead. He went on till he found a fairly level place, with good natural drainage, that had none but sound trees surrounding it.

There he stopped and cast off his pack, never dreaming of the sinister figure lurking near in the bushes and watching every move he made.

Cabarrus opened the pack and took out a hunter's axe. He cleared off a space about eight feet square on which to set up his little tent and build a fire. He cut three slender poles, about twelve feet long, and a dozen small pointed sticks for tent-pegs.

Then he got out of the pack-sack a five-pound tent of thin, closely woven, waterproofed green cloth. It had a sewed-in floor and a bobbinet front to exclude insects and other pests of the woods.

He stretched the floor and pegged it down. Then he lashed the tops of the poles together with what sailors call a necklace tie, which allows the butts to spread as required. He set up the three poles as a tripod outside the tent.

Over the pole lashing he threw a light rope attached to the tent peak. He hauled on the rope till the tent was drawn up quite taut and true, then he hitched the rope to a stake near one of the front corners. Set up in this fashion, the tent stood as a half-pyramid with vertical front, its doorway unobstructed by any pole or guy-rope.

"Never seed sich a-lookin' tent," muttered the spying Lumbo to himself. Inferentially, that was enough to condemn it as a silly contraption.

The stranger's next move was downright heretical; a profanation and a scandal, according to all traditions of "roughing it."

He got out of his pack a sort of corrugated rubber bag, about four feet long and a bit over two feet wide. He sat down on the ground and went to blowing into it through a tube. The bag swelled up. Cabarrus tested its tension by poking it with his thumb. When it was blown up to just the right resilience, he closed the valve. It was an air-mattress, weighing less than four pounds, but long enough to support a man down to his thighs and very comfortable to rest his bones and keep him off the damp ground.

The camper blew into a small rubber bag and it became an air-pillow. Then he spread the mattress and the pillow on his tent floor and folded over them the best blanket that had ever come into the Smoky Mountains.

"My Lord!" sighed Youlus, "what a dude! All he needs now is a rattle and a sugar-tit. And still the son-of-a-gun's got narve. He knows good and well he's trespassin'; for his tracks went right by that notice o' Matlock's and he cast a dead snake in front of it as a sign o' contempt. I *say* he's got narve, if he knows the kind o' man Matlock is! There's liable to be a killin' over this."

Cabarrus gathered a lot of sound dead wood and stacked it near the tent. Then he went once more to his pack and took out a big pan of peculiar shape. It was somewhat like a wash-basin, but with straight sides flaring broadly outward. He started away from camp with it, and Youlus stole after him.

The stranger followed the brook downstream till he came to a bend with a shallow pool at its lower end. Here he stopped and busied himself in a way that made the spying Lumbo squint and wrinkle his brow.

Cabarrus half filled his pan with sand and gravel from the bottom of the pool. He sank it below the level of the water, held it there a moment, then laid the pan out on the ground and worked up its contents with his hands. Having mixed the mass to his satisfaction, he again sank the pan under water, holding it level, and gave it a number of rapid half-turns. Then he took it out and picked off the coarse gravel that had come to the surface.

Youlus edged as near as he dared, to get a better view.

Once more the stranger put his pan under water. He spun it with half-turns, sloped it away from him, leveled it again, and then went to rocking it forward and backward, but keeping it level and well below the surface of the pool. These maneuvers he repeated many times, until most of the material was washed away, leaving only a couple of spoonfuls of heavy residue in the bottom of the pan, along with a cupful of water.

He now came out of the stream, gave the water a slow whirling motion, then tilted it out and sat down to examine what he had left in the pan. He sorted out some of it and saved the particles in a little cloth bag.

Shadows were now darkening the woodland. The sun had sunk

below the western ridge-top. Cabarrus returned to his camp, made a fire, and began to prepare his evening meal.

Youlus remained crouching in the bushes. His face was pale and the sweat of feverish excitement had broken out on his brow.

"Gold!" he whispered to himself. "Ay, God! he's huntin' gold!"

Years and years of baffled treasure-hunting, greed that no rebuff could conquer, were concentrated in that tense expression.

"Gold!" he repeated. "Gold!"

How often had the three Lumbos, singly or together, scoured these mountains in the hope of finding precious metal! Sometimes they had indeed found it; but only in minute traces, scarcely visible specks amid the sand. Once his cousin 'Poleon had picked up a nugget of gold as big as a bean. Once the three of them discovered a ledge that seemed to contain a fortune. They were millionaires for a week, planning vast schemes and pleasure voyages, already quarreling among themselves over their shares. But the deposit proved to be nothing but copper pyrites and too poor in copper to have any value.

Yes, yes: bitter disappointment, year after poverty-stricken year! And yet there really was gold in these mountains. The Parker mine in Cherokee County was worked before the Revolution. In the first quarter of the 19th century North Carolina furnished all the gold produced in the United States. The southern mountains and piedmont were the nation's chief source of the precious metal until they were eclipsed by the California discoveries in '49. Coming close home, Youlus knew that some of his own neighbors had made at least day's wages by panning gold in nearby streams.

Back of this positive knowledge there were golden legends in which Youlus had firm faith. Stories of rich mines known only to the Indians, who were too superstitious to reveal them. Stories of gold and silver mines secretly worked by whites who were too avaricious or suspicious to tell even their own children where the treasure lay.

But Youlus himself had always been handicapped by his ignorance of how or where to prospect in an intelligent way. He had no book-learning whatever. He had never seen a well-informed prospector at work.

Yet at last luck had turned! Right here in Turkey-Fly-Up, before his own eyes, an expert was on the job, not knowing that he was being watched.

Youlus thanked his stars that he had a dog for this stranger to kick.

That incident had led him straight into possession of a priceless secret. And if there be anything, next to wealth itself, that a mountaineer prizes, it is a secret all his own that he can gloat over and share with no human soul.

What luck, too, that this precious deposit should be on Matlock's land, instead of the Unaka Company's! Tom Burbank could not molest Youlus here. Matlock let the Lumbos hunt and camp on this place as much as they pleased. He hated the Unaka Company as much as they did. More than once he had found use for Youlus in shady transactions and there was a good understanding between them.

Lumbo had no fear that this stranger was in cahoots with Matlook. If such had been the case, Bill Matlock, who trusted no man out of his sight, would have come along; he would be here now, watching every move that the prospector made. No: the fellow was working in secret, consciously trespassing, with the purpose of gathering all the treasure he could slip away with.

So much the better. Youlus could well afford to watch and wait. Let the fool furnish the brains, let him do all the work, and then—Youlus would reap.

The spy leaned back and clasped his knee in a pose of ease and self-satisfaction. Not for a moment did he doubt that this high-strung, daring and efficient stranger would succeed. The man knew his business. He must have known in advance just where to look, for he had come straight to Turkey-Fly-Up, had gone forthright to work, and within an hour he had found something valuable enough to save. He would strike it rich! He would clean up!

Then Youlus would see—. He half closed his eyes in a knowing leer. His mouth grew thin and wide in a sly grin. Ah, yes: he would see—.

Below him the brook gurgled over golden sands. Above him the wind whispered the secret to the leaves and they passed it along, one to the other; but no mortal heard it save the lone spy crouching there.—

"Gold! Gold! Gold!"

EIGHT

Marian was to spend the summer in Kittuwa with her aunt, Mrs. Fielding. The old lady did not at all approve of her niece galloping off into the backwoods and ranging the mountains alone in pursuit of her hobby; but the girl had a partisan in her uncle, Colonel Fielding, who was a sportsman to the core and rather enjoyed her ardor and daring.

When Marian returned all aglow with her project of roughing it for a week or so with the Burbanks in the very heart of the great forest, the Colonel did not offer any serious objection.

"I know Tom Burbank," said he. "A great, big-hearted, honest fellow and a first-class woodsman. But his wife is—"

"Is what?" demanded Marian, noting his hesitation, and quick to defend Sylvia against any aspersion.

"The better one of the two," finished the colonel mischievously. "If that woman had half a chance, she'd be the best cook in the Smoky Mountains."

"Oh! So that's your ideal of womankind. Well, you might be surprised to see how they make shift with what they raise on that stony place and how they get along with so little from the stores. You see, they have no wagon: so it's hard for Tom to pack things out from Kittuwa over that awful road. He has only a little mule called Jaybo and a rag of a saddle with a rope girth. It's the funniest sight when that giant of a Tom gets on Jaybo and goes riding down the road with his feet nearly dragging the ground, like a great fat friar on a donkey. It looks as if Tom ought to get off and carry the mule. But it's not so funny to think of him carrying a can of oil in one hand, and a lamp chimney in the other, ten miles over the mountain, and across seventeen rocky fords, so they may have something better than a pine knot to light their cabin."

"If I had to do it," observed the colonel, "oil would be worth five dollars a gallon, on Deep Creek, and lamp chimneys would not exist."

"Well," planned Marian, "I must have a wagon to carry my trunk; so it may as well take them a lot of canned fruits and vegetables and oil, such as can't very well be packed on Jaybo-back."

"All right; I'll get you a wagon and man who's safe to drive it over that infernal road. Tom, by the way, has nothing to do in mid-summer but patrol the forest, and he can go with you when you're hunting plants."

"Oh, I can look out for myself, uncle."

"I don't know about that," answered the colonel. "Some hard characters follow that trail into the Smokies, at times."

"I have this," said Marian confidently, producing a wee .25 caliber automatic pistol.

"Good Lord!" exclaimed the colonel. "If you draw that trinket on a hill-billy he'll take it for an atomizer and think you're going to spray him with scent."

"Oh, I won't need it for anything but snakes."

"Snakes—yes, of course there are snakes; but in thirty years I've heard of but two people bitten by snakes in this county. More folks have been struck by lightning."

"Well, I'd prefer lightning."

"You'll be in more danger from hornets and wasps and yellow-jackets than from snakes."

"That reminds me," said Marian. "My horse was stung by yellow-jackets this afternoon, near a queer old abandoned hut about a mile this side of the Burbanks' place. It's a romantic ruin, that cabin. Do you know its history?"

Colonel Fielding did not answer for a moment. He sank back in his chair, half closed his eyes, and twirled the tips of his long white mustache between his fingers. Then he said: "It's a tragic story, Marian. I hardly think you'd like it."

"Yes, tell me, please."

"Country folks say the place is haunted."

"Delightful! Now I must have the story."

"Well, let me see," mused the colonel. "This is 1925. It would be seventeen years ago that Abelard Dale came here from the Piedmont with his invalid wife and his little grandson. Dale was an old man, well up in the sixties, but active, wiry, fond of taking long tramps over the hills and prowling about in the woods.

"I can see him now: a tall, thin, stooping, sharp-eyed man, in a rusty black suit and generally bare-headed. He had a shock of stubborn gray hair that stood up like a kingfisher's crest and gave him a militant mien, but he had the most benevolent face I ever saw.

"His pockets always bulged with mineral specimens or boxes of moths and butterflies. He was forever chasing after some wonderful rare thingumadoo to add to his collection or give to a museum. I think he had a little income from selling such things at times when he was hard up, but I fancy it grieved him to do so."

The colonel paused, and Marian asked, "Was he a scientist, uncle, or only a hobby-rider?"

"How shall I say?" wavered the colonel. "He had been a professor of natural history, as they used to call it, in some small college—I forget its name. He was not at all what you nowadays would call a scientist: he didn't dissect or analyze things to find how their innards work or what atoms they're composed of. No: he was a dreamer, more artist than scientist, enjoying the beauties of nature and not caring a rap what wavelengths were in a color or in a wild bird's song. He didn't specialize, but skipped about, from one subject to another, choosing the novelties, the rarities, the exceptions rather than the rules, in the whole realm of nature."

"Frittering," sighed Marian.

"Maybe so; but people loved him for it. I've heard hard-fisted old farmers say, as they smiled at his vagaries, 'Let him be: he's like a leetle child a-playin'."

"One of his hobbies was Indian lore, the myths and customs of the aborigines. Some of our straight-laced friends looked askance at that and whispered that old Professor Dale believed in the Indians' religion. Anyway, the old-fashioned Cherokees on Lufty thought the world and all of him: he was so loyally, pathetically their friend. He even got an Indian woman to come and serve as his wife's nurse and maid-of-all-work—she'd been well trained in such things at the Government school. The strange thing is that the squaw stayed on the job, through thick and thin, to the bitter end."

"Is that Indian woman still living?" asked Marian.

"I think so. She's a half-sister of the ex-chief Degataga, who was here to see me just the other day. Her name is Myra Swimming-Deer."

"Will you ask Degataga about her?"

"Yes; but why?"

"Oh, I want the whole story. She might tell more. It promises well and might be worth writing up."

"I see: you would weave a good yarn out of it and sell it to a magazine. Very well: go to it."

"Professor Dale, as you were saying—"

"Professor Dale was a gentle visionary, trusting everyone, taking a child's roseate view of life. But of plain, hard business sense he had not an atom in his composition. In fact, he despised business; and no business despised him. He got into financial difficulties."

"Congenial soul!" laughed Marian. "I would have liked him."

"You wouldn't have liked what he came to."

"Go on, please."

"On one of Dale's long rambles he found a three-hundred-acre tract of virgin timber, away up Deep Creek, that was advertised for sale to satisfy a mortgage. He cared nothing for property, as such, but he was fascinated by the wild beauty of the place. He felt obliged to buy it and preserve it intact as a rare gem of the wilderness. So he put into it all of his savings.

"Mrs. Dale died in the winter of 1909. The expenses of her long illness and hospital fees had run the old professor deeply in debt. He had borrowed at the bank till it would lend him no more, and then from a skinflint named Matlock who still curses this town with his presence. Matlock runs a store and a real estate business here.

"When Dale was hard pressed and did not know which way to turn, Matlock went to him in the guise of a friend, encouraged Dale to borrow money from him, and took his notes at a ruinous rate of interest. He knew the old professor would consider it a debt of honor and would never go to court with any charge of usury.

"Matlock's scheme was simply this.— He had looked over the Deep Creek property and he saw that it was a strategic point. The day would certainly come when a lumber company would have to buy it; for there was no way of getting a railroad up the creek without running it through this particular tract.

"Soon after Mrs. Dale's death, the old professor moved to the cabin on his Deep Creek land, taking with him his little grandson and the Indian housekeeper, Myra. Then, in 1910, Matlock seized the property.

"Dale pled for time; but he might as well have begged mercy from a tiger. When he saw that he was left without a penny to his name, or a roof overhead, he staggered to the cabin door and fell dead on the threshold."

The old colonel sighed and dropped his head. Marian waited, but he did not continue. So she asked, "What became of the little grandson?"

"Jack Dale? He was only thirteen when the old man died. Little Jack came back to Kittuwa. It seemed he had no living relatives. He went about shining shoes, selling papers, and the like. A shy, big-eyed, sensitive boy, pathetic to look upon. I was about to take care of him myself when the end came without warning."

"The end?"

"Yes. That brute of a Matlock was on a street corner haranguing a group of loafers about prudence and worldly wisdom. He argued that shiftlessness was worse than dishonesty, and, by way of illustration, he made a vile reference to old Professor Dale.

"Little Jack happened to be standing by. To everybody's amazement, the shy little chap seized the first thing handy, which chanced to be an iron axle-nut lying near the curb, and he threw it with such force and aim that Matlock was bowled over. It flattened his nose into his face and he bled like a stuck pig."

"Then what happened to the boy?" asked Marian.

"He ran away and has never been heard of to this day."

"A boy of thirteen, alone in the world and without a penny in his pocket!"

"Alone and with, maybe, fifteen cents."

Marian clenched her hands.— "Then that was the end of it?"

"The end, so far as I know."

Marian said nothing about the sad-faced man whom she had discovered brooding in the ruined cabin. But she made a swift calculation. If he were thirteen in 1911, it would make him twenty-seven now; and that was about the man's real age.

But he had told her that his name was John Cabarrus. Colonel Fielding called him Jack Dale.

Cabarrus. It was a peculiar name: not English nor Scotch nor Irish. Somehow it had a Latin sound.

Where had she heard that name? Never as applied to a man. And yet—why, certainly, it was a county in North Carolina, which probably took its title from some public man of the olden time.

Perhaps the Dales came from Cabarrus County. What more natural, then, than that the boy, fearful of being traced and apprehended, should take an assumed name, and that he should choose one familiar to his childhood but borne by no living person and unlikely, on that account, to entangle him in complications?

She recalled how, when she rode away from the cabin, she had lightly thought of Cabarrus as "A man of mystery," though not really meaning much by the phrase. She now perceived that it might, in very truth, be apt and of more serious import than she had dreamed.

What had he come back to do?

What was he seeking amid the ruins of that abandoned place?

What would happen when he and Matlock met again?

She went to bed that night with puzzles simmering in her head.

The next morning, which was Wednesday, the girl set forth to do her shopping. The wagon was to call for her at one o'clock.

First she went straight to Matlock's store, on the chance of seeing the man of evil repute and making her own offhand estimate of his qualities.

Matlock seldom waited on customers himself, being more interested in deals that he negotiated in a small office in the rear of the building. But at this hour he was in the store, doing some figuring at the desk. When he saw an attractive young woman enter, a stranger, he shouldered the clerks aside and went to her asking what she would like to see.

Matlock was a large, dominant man, big-boned and muscular, with a bluff manner and booming voice. Marian thought she had never seen a face so arresting and yet so repulsive. He had a fine head, if the features had been in keeping with the high intellectual brow, but his lips were thick, his nose as flat as that of a skull, and his eyes were set widely askew.

He regarded her with his right eye, which had a frank and friendly expression, twinkling with good humor. The other eye squinted aside and its lid drooped so that one could not catch its look.

Presently Matlock whifted the axis of his vision and there was a startling change of his expression. The left eye, turning under its lowered lid, suddenly pierced her with a stare as rigid and cold and stony as a snake's.

This instantaneous change of aspect sent a shiver up Marian's spine. It was as if the man had two personalities, one amiable and ingratiating, but the other sinister and lurking, venomous.

Marian made but a single purchase in Matlock's store and she hurried away.

"Ugh!" she shuddered. "What a reptile! Eye of a basilisk! I'd rather meet an honest lion face to face."

NINE

Youlus Lumbo slipped away from his spying post when savory odors from the stranger's cooking aroused his own appetite. He wormed his way through the thicket to a secluded place near the mouth of the brook and proceeded to make camp after the Lumbo fashion.

First he built a fire against a fallen tree trunk. While the sticks were burning down to coals fit to cook over, he arranged his quarters for the night. As the sky was clear, he did not bother to set up a brush shelter. He simply scraped together a bed of leaves, as a wild animal might do.

However, he took the human precaution of piling them under a shade that moonlight would not strike through. If one sleeps in the moonlight he will go crazy. Also he broke off a willow fork and drew a circle with it around his bed. That was to keep witches away. Then he took a piece of rubber band from his pocket, where he always carried it, snipped off a bit and burned it in the fire, so no ghost would bother him that night.

These solemn rites having been performed, Youlus put some ground coffee in his big tin cup, filled it with water, and set it to boil on a pair of bed-sticks over the fire. Then he cut a branch of dogwood that forked into three tines, leaving the stem for a handle. On the fork he laid a chunk of his hard corn bread and fastened it in place with limber twigs woven crosswise. He impaled a slice of fat salt pork, on a sharpened stick, broiled it over the coals, and held his bread under it to catch the dripping grease and get warmed through.

Youlus ate as voraciously as a hound, meantime drinking his black coffee without sugar and getting supreme enjoyment from it. The Lumbo ideal of camp cookery was attained. If some well-meaning but misguided genii had carried him off on a magic carpet and set him to feast at a king's table, Youlus would have sniffed and growled at every dish placed before him and would have bragged about his "old corn bread and sow-belly."

Having dined with gusto, he tossed his broiling-sticks into the fire, stowed the unrinsed cup in his haversack, licked his fingers, and had nothing to do till bedtime. So he chewed tobacco and happily meditated before the fire.

Everything was going fine. He had dreamed, the night before, of a bay horse wading through clear water. A bay horse meant good luck, as everybody knew. Clear water, also, was lucky. But to dream of both together was the surest sign of good fortune that he had ever heard of.

The stranger had found gold within an hour in Turkey-Fly-Up. Of course it was gold. People didn't hunt lead or copper or iron with a washpan in the bottom of a creek branch. There must be oodles of gold around here.

Let the fool work till he got all he could carry, all he could hide away. Then—a body burned to ashes in a log-heap leaves no evidence. Youlus knew of such a case. A man was shot from ambush; the officers knew who did it; but the corpse had been utterly consumed in a log fire, out in the woods, and nobody could be convicted.

When finally the warmth and the firelight made Youlus drowsy, he burrowed into his bed of leaves, without removing any of his clothing, reversed his rifle between his knees and pillowed his head on its butt, pulled his cowl-like hat down over his eyes, and was off for dreamland. He was immune from snakes, for he had a piece of rattlesnake-skin sewed up in his coat, and that was a charm that never was known to fail. As for the heavy dew of a Smoky Mountain night, he cared no more for it than a bear.

Lumbo was up at first peep of day. His breakfast was just what supper had been. He broiled enough pork to have some left over that he would eat cold for lunch. Then, slipping on his haversack and shouldering his rifle, he returned to the neighborhood of the prospector's camp and resumed surveillance.

Cabarrus panned along the brook all morning, to determine the character of the "float" washed down from surrounding rock formations. He worked on until one o'clock and by that time had finished with the stream itself. After a hot lunch at camp, he picked up his staff and started out to look for terraces and exposed ledges of rock along the sides of the ravine, leaving his pan in the tent and his specimens in the little wooden case of his blowpipe kit, which he tucked under his bed.

Lumbo trailed after him until convinced that the prospector would be away from camp for some time. Then he slipped back and made an investigation.

The tent door was tied shut, but he opened it and went in. Between the blanket and the air-mattress he found the little box. Packed neatly in compartments were a blowpipe, a small alcohol lamp, a magnet, a magnifying lens, an agate mortar, crucibles, test tubes, chemicals, and, among other things, the little cloth bag in which Cabarrus had stored the particles and nuggets selected from the residue of his panning.

When Youlus lifted the bag his heart gave a great throb of excitement. The diminutive thing was heavy!

His fingers trembled as he opened the little bag. Then, as he peered into it, confident of seeing the gleam of yellow metal, he choked with disappointment. The stuff was not yellow: it was greenish-black, granular, with a dull sub-metallic luster. Most of the particles were small, but a few were as large as buckshot. They bore not the least resemblance to gold or silver. They did not even look like lead.

Youlus cursed bitterly under his breath. Was it possible that he had been wasting time chasing after a fool?

But the stuff was heavy for its bulk. It was certainly heavier than so much iron or copper ore. And that strapping, bright-eyed, masterful young stranger surely was nobody's fool. He hadn't come here for nothing. He hadn't picked this stuff out of a panful of dirt for nothing.

Youlus recalled what Doc. Terry, the collector of mineral specimens, had told him, one day, in Kittuwa: that some ores rich in gold or silver do not at all resemble the pure metals in appearance—some of them are black. And Lumbo knew only four metals heavier than iron or copper. If this were not an ore of gold or silver, it must be one of lead or quicksilver. A moderate heating would show. So he stole two of the larger nuggets to test for himself.

Replacing everything else that he had touched, Lumbo went outside and refastened the tent door-flaps. With solemn precaution he spat over his left shoulder to break any charm that the prospector might have laid on his mineral specimens. Then he carefully obliterated his own footprints with a bushy twig and retired once more into the thicket.

Waiting for the prospector's return now became very irksome. Youlus was eager to try his stolen metal by fire. Cabarrus seemed to have gone far away. Since he had left his pan behind and had carried no tool for digging, nothing would be gained by watching him any longer that day. So Lumbo went back to his own camp, made a hot fire, heated a rock almost to redness, laid one of the nuggets on it, and watched the stuff to see if it would melt.

It did not show the least sign of melting, even along the edges. Indisputably there was neither lead nor mercury in it. Gold or silver it assuredly must be!

Youlus could have shouted for joy if he had been free to vent his feelings. As it was, he walked round and round, with head thrust forward, eyes glittering, fingers twitching, smiling to himself, chuckling betimes, repeating in whispers "It's gold—it's gold—ay, God, it's gold!"

Meantime Cabarrus was exploring the ridges of Turkey-Fly-Up, but finding little of interest. Nearly everywhere the bed-rock was overlaid with clay and humus in which shrubs, herbs and vines grew thickly, baffling a prospector not equipped with pick or shovel. Even the cliffs were sheathed in living green.

Late in the afternoon he came out on top of a mountain spur overlooking Deep Creek. From the ground there was no outlook through the foliage: so he climbed a tree to get a view of the surrounding country.

Back of him, to the west, the mountain walls rose sharply and cut off all prospect. Northward, however, he could see out over billows of wooded ranges for many miles, even to the crest of the Great Smoky divide.

Below, in the foreground, he saw the Burbank place as though it were a tiny glade peeping from an immensity of forest. It was nearly a mile away to the northeast, yet, by contrast with the vastness of the surrounding wilderness, it seemed that he could almost throw a stone to it.

Turning his gaze now to the eastward, with Deep Creek directly before him, the sky-line was much nearer. It was the undulating crest of a mile-high ridge that separated the waters of Deep Creek from those of the Indian country.

From the top of this eastern divide a series of abutting ridges came steeply down, like ribs from a backbone, and were shorn off at the creek below him, ending there in cliffs or promontories that were thickly overgrown with laurel and rhododendron and stubbornly clinging trees.

Men always shunned that east bank, on account of its almost impassable barriers, and because the Kittuwa road came up along the western side.

On one of the eastern ravines in particular the man in the tree-top fixed his attention. Its mouth was across the creek from the ruined cabin and diagonally upstream. From his high perch Cabarrus could see nearly its whole length, from where it started as a runlet near the summit of the divide, on down a widening and deepening gulch, with gullies joining it here and there, to a chasm choked with jungle where its waters joined in a brawling torrent. The upper slopes were lighted by the westering sun to an emerald glow, but the depths of the ravine lay somber and mysterious in the shadows of the cliffs.

Cabarrus mused,— "Over there, so Myra used to say, the Little People dwell in caves on the mountainsides and under the waterfalls. They are a tiny folk, hardly reaching to a man's knee, but well formed and featured, with long hair reaching nearly to the ground.

"They are fond of music and of dancing. Sometimes, on a summer day, when all else was silent about the cabin, we would hear a far-off mysterious throbbing somewhere in that glen, and Myra would say to me 'Listen: it is the Little People beating their drums!'

"She said they were kind to mortals who think kindly of them; but they play tricks on busybodies and other folk that they do not like. If a man gets too curious and spies on the Little People when they are at their games, or tries to enter their caves without being invited, or pokes behind the small waterfalls with a stick, they will cast a spell upon him so that he loses his way in the woods and goes wandering about in a daze.

"When one finds anything pretty in the woods or among the rocks he must say 'Little People, I want to take this;' for it may belong to them, and if he does not ask permission they will stone him away from the place.

"Myra used to hint to me that old Grandpa Dale brought most of his bright crystals and colored stones from over there; and so, she said, he must be a great friend of the Little People, or they would not let him find such things, or would make them dissolve and fade away before he could take them out of the glen.

"I remember how the old man used to chuckle over her stories, never denying or making sport of them, but enjoying her odd ways of explaining things.

"But he himself gave the place a bad name. He called it Nick's Nest, after the Old Nick, and told me it was a terribly rough and devious gorge, hard to find a way into and worse to get out of. He solemnly forbade me ever to set foot in Nick's Nest, lest I should get lost or snake-bitten or break my neck among the crag-pits.

"Yet for him, somehow, the place had a fascination. There was something eery and uncommon and challenging about it that piqued his fancy and excited his zeal to explore. He said there were recesses in that wild glen that no man had ever entered, and there was no telling what might be found there. Often he would spend a whole day in Nick's Nest, returning at night quite fagged out with his exertions.

"Once I grew overbold and disobeyed him and tried to get into Nick's Nest. But at the very mouth of the ravine I got into a swamp—which in itself was very strange; for there is no other swamp in all this country round about. Every other branch of Deep Creek, so the hunters told me, comes tumbling down out of the mountains and rushes right out into the main stream.

"I got mired and lost under an overhanging jungle of great vines and amid matted dog-hobble and giant laurel. Many old fallen trees blocked the way in every direction, some of them too thick for me to climb over. They seemed to have been thrown pell-mell by a hurricane, at some remote time, and that is probably what caused a swamp to form at the mouth of Nick's Nest; for the trees checked the run-off of the waters, and silt dammed up against them.

"It took me all of two hours to wriggle out of that predicament. I was so frightened by the gloom and horror of the place, by the fear of sinking into its cold and slimy depths, that I never ventured there again, nor told anyone of the experience. Once I asked an old hunter if he had ever been over there. He tried to stare me down; then, when I repeated the question, he answered: 'Nobody ever goes there—nobody with a grain of sense—it's ha'nted!'"

"I asked if the place had a name. He said: 'We-uns calls hit Dog-eater Holler—don't you know what a dog-eater is?' When I shook my head he explained: 'Hit's a varmint that ain't a rael animal, but a ha'nt, and it cracks a dog's bones and eats him alive. Some says hit will devour a man, too.'"

Thus was Cabarrus letting his memory and his fancy play when he was brought up sharply to a sense of present realities by a strange jarring sound that came from the creek gorge, rising above the clamor of the waters with an alien and dissonant quality of its own.

It must be, thought he, a wagon, jolting over the boulders of a ford. He looked southward, where the road came from Kittuwa and the creek ran tortuously among sprangling ridges.

At a point half a mile distant, and five hundred feet below the altitude of his perch, a bit of the road glinted in the sun. The sound came from just beyond it and was carried upward through the void with such clearness that it seemed the wagon must be only a couple of hundred yards away.

Presently he saw a team of powerful old logging horses drawing a high, broad-tired lumber-wagon over the rough road. He lifted his field-glass and made out a man driving, humped forward on his plank seat, and behind him a young woman bouncing on a bed of straw in the wagon-box. There were grocery boxes behind her and a small trunk, roped fast so they could not cannon about and smash things.

"That must be Miss Wentworth," speculated Cabarrus, "on her way to visit the Burbanks. Plucky girl, to be out collecting in so wild a country! Chic and capable girl—devilish pretty, too! It isn't right for her to be running such risks alone. Likely to get lost in the woods. Might sprain an ankle when far from help. Ought to have a brother along, or somebody.

"Ho, hum! Something about her eyes: honest eyes, frank and friendly—eyes that somehow have something—"

Something, it would seem, hard to define; for he got no farther in describing them.

"Let's see: didn't I promise her a rare plant, if I found one in the woods? There's a wonderful orchid of some sort blooming near my camp: the flower a pure white above and its broad under lip all pink and crimpy. I never saw another like it. Maybe it's rare. Anyway, she'd know I thought it was.

"But hell's bells! What am I thinking of? Idiot! come off the perch: get back on the job and let that flower alone."

So the idiot climbed down from the tree; and he came down off the mountain; and he went straightway to where the orchid grew; and he stood gazing at it a long, long time. Then he came away without having seen it, save as one in a dream.

TEN

Every old camper develops a technic of his own. He has certain ways of doing certain things, because system saves time and trouble. Cabarrus in his lone camp was as methodical as if he had been in an army barrack.

Naturally, then, when he went to open his tent and found the tapes tied with granny bows instead of true bow-knots, he knew in a flash that someone had been prying into his affairs.

Inside the tent, at first sight, nothing was amiss. Perhaps some simple-minded mountaineer, meaning no harm, had just peeped in. Such folk are notoriously curious about strangers in their midst, and, having been brought up in small cabins, they have never learned to respect the privacy of others; but there are very few thieves among them.

It was not until Cabarrus opened the case of his blowpipe kit that he saw something wrong. The little cloth bag had not been retied with his own deft neatness. Then he detected that some of the larger specimens were gone.

"So," he muttered. "Spied on from the very beginning. That's rather odd."

It was more than odd: it was mystifying. No soul on earth had been warned of his coming. He had met no one on the way whom he had ever known.

Perchance some old resident had seen him driving up Deep Creek; but who could now recognize in the mature and stalwart figure of John Cabarrus the little Jack Dale of long ago? Even though someone had made him out, why should the man quit his work and steal after Cabarrus, far up into the wild mountains, and spy upon his actions?

Terhune was not that sort; anyway, he was comparatively a newcomer in the settlement.

Ah! the Lumbo whose dog he had kicked. That was plausible. The woman had called; her man had come down from the field. Quarrels over dogs have led to many a homicide in the mountains. The Lumbos were half-wild creatures who lived more in the woods than they did at home. It would be quite in character for Youlus to seize his gun and take after the stranger who had kicked his dog. Then, trailing Cabarrus and finding him panning a stream, the fellow would bottle his wrath and go to spying, as a matter of course.

In any case, the fact stared Cabarrus in the face that an enemy, or at least a busybody, was on his track within twenty-four hours after his return to Deep Creek.

The young man went outside and scanned the ground for telltale marks. There were no footprints other than his own; but he did espy some faint parallel streaks of dust that told, as plain as print to an experienced eye, where tracks had been brushed out with a wisp of hemlock.

Cabarrus scouted around in the neighborhood. Finally, some distance from camp, he found a few imprints of broad shoes thickly studded with small round-headed nails. The heels were worn off at the outer edges.

These tracks led directly into the thicket where it was impossible to follow a man's course. A story-book Indian might have read the "sign," but not so a flesh-and-blood white man. The berry bushes grew shoulder-high and so close together that one could not see where he planted his own feet, much less descry tracks left on the ground by others. The elastic tops closed after a passing man like water. In story-book fashion there should have been some broken twigs or torn leaves or disrupted cobwebs to catch the eye of a follower; but in this instance everything was normal. Had it been morning, the dislodging of dew would have left a noticeable surface mark on the bushes; but it was now near sunset and all the leaves were dry.

Balked in his effort to trail the knave, Cabarrus went back to camp, studying a course of action.

Since a spy might still be on the lookout to see if he took alarm, Cabarrus assumed a careless air, going about with a "Yo-ho-hum" as if nothing had happened. He cooked and ate supper, washed his few dishes, took a leisurely smoke, and then went about in the woods collecting fuel. He was not content with an armful for getting breakfast, but stacked up enough dry wood to last two or three days, as if providing against a spell of rainy weather.

It was now twilight. Cabarrus took off his high boots to ease his feet and he put on a pair of light moccasins with thin pliable soles, which he had brought along for camp slippers and to wear when drying his boots.

He sat around yawning and softly whistling little trifling airs. A horned owl set up a *who-who-who* on the mountainside. The lone camper answered with perfect imitation. The owl promptly gave another *who-who-ah*. And so they went on, exchanging the compliments of the woods.

Some furtive beast moved in the thicket, not far from the tent, slowly pushing bushes aside but making no sound with its padded feet; a wildcat, doubtless, coming to stalk that owl down here in the hollow. Cabarrus smiled at the success of his own mimicry. There was no use trying to shoot the prowler, for the campfire had died down to the merest glow and the cat's eyes gave no reflection.

Cabarrus turned in. He closed the screen at his tent door but left the flaps wide open for ventilation, as was his custom. He could see out through the bobbinet, but no one could see in. He lay there wide awake developing his plan.

To shake off the skulker in his rear, he must move out of Turkey-Fly-Up before morning.

The spy would not linger around here after Cabarrus had so obviously turned in for the night. The fellow would need rest, himself, and he would go far enough away for security while he slept. If he had seen the prospector store up all that wood for future use, he would not dream of finding him decamped in the morning.

Cabarrus was angry at having his routine upset and his hand forced; yet it really made little difference so far as this one locality was concerned. He had already learned all that he cared to know, for the present, about the mineral resources of Turkey-Fly-Up. His real objective was Nick's Nest. He had begun work across the creek from it because here there was a good camp site and because he wanted to study from afar the general contour of Nick's Nest, with its relation to the surrounding country, before choosing a course into it.

It was somewhat of a bore to move camp in the middle of the night; yet even this had its sporting aspect. Cabarrus laughed to himself at the sneak's discomfiture in the morning when he should find that he had no tenderfoot to deal with. It would be fun to outwit him and set him guessing.

It was a clear and starry night. The moon was in the first quarter and it would not set until near three in the morning. Cabarrus lay quiet until ten o'clock. Then he arose, dressed for the march, collected his equipment, took down his little tent, stowed everything in his pack-sack, shouldered it, and moved on down the faint trail to the old cabin and out to the Kittuwa road.

He remembered that in the old days there was a trail from here up the next ravine south of Nick's Nest to the top of the mountain. It connected with the main trail that ran across the mountain from Burbank's place to Vine's and thence on down to the Lumbo settlement. It might now be overgrown from disuse, but he decided to chance it.

He forded the creek, getting wet to the hips. The water was deucedly cold. He blundered around a good deal in the thicket and semi-darkness before he found the beginning of the old trail. It was, as he expected, overgrown in places. Here and there he lost it and had to prowl before he could pick it up again. But after it crossed the bottom land and began the steep ascent of the mountain there was no longer any doubt, for the rains had gullied it ankle-deep, in some places shoulder-deep.

No light from the heavens pierced the depths of the ancient forest he had now entered. Cabarrus had to use his electric torch. He was thirty minutes making the ascent, though the distance was less than a mile and the climb was not over six hundred feet.

He topped out in what was known as Lick-log Gap, from a notched log lying there that was used in salting cattle. Here he came to the well-beaten Pullback trail that ran north to Burbank's.

From his tree-top outlook, that afternoon, Cabarrus had figured that the Pullback trail must cross the upper course of a brook that plunged on down into Nick's Nest. The crossing might be the best point from which to start exploring the ravine.

And now he practiced a bit of Indian strategy, to baffle the skulker in his rear. Instead of turning north along the mountain, toward Burbank's, he proceeded straight ahead toward Kittuwa and went down the far side of the mountain. Purposely he made plain tracks with his hobnailed boots as he jogged heavily down the bare trail.

By and by he came to a clearing. It was the upper field of the Vine place. Here the trail led into a rocky sled-road that was much used. Beyond that point there was slight chance of tracing any individual's footprints.

Cabarrus went aside and changed his clothes, getting out of his wet things and into dry ones from his pack. He put on his moccasins. They had no nails, of course, and made faint tracks very different from those of his big boots. He tied his wet clothing to the outside of the pack. Then he turned back on his course and climbed once more to Lick-log Gap, avoiding the trail as much as he could and leaving no "sign" that would attract notice.

Having returned to the crossing, he now went north toward Nick's Nest, dodging wet or dusty places in the trail by going round them in the thicket. Nothing but a beast trailing by scent could have followed him. He was confident that by having made false tracks down the trail toward Kittuwa he had rid himself of the spy and sent him on a fool's errand.

Cabarrus bivouacked for the rest of the night in a thicket near the upper end of Nick's Nest. At break of day he hurried through breakfast and eagerly started to explore the mysterious gulf that his grandfather had found so interesting but the native mountaineers shunned as something gruesome.

The brook that ran down into Nick's Nest had no local name. Cabarrus called it Nick's Run. He started to follow it from where the trail crossed; but in two minutes he was in trouble. The banks of the brook were a maze of big laurel and shrubby rhododendron so interlocked that he could scarcely wriggle his body through, much less carry his pack.

Hearing a waterfall ahead, he dropped his pack and crawled forward to reconnoiter. The foliage was so dense that he could not see ten feet in any direction. Worming his way along, he came to the top of a chasm where the water plunged down over a series of ledges, some of them twenty feet deep, that were slippery as grease. On either side rose vertical walls of rock. A man by himself and without a rope could neither descend into the gulf at this point nor climb up out of it.

So much, then, he had learned: that Nick's Nest, or Dog-eater Hollow, whichever one chose to call it, was barred from entry at its mouth by a well-nigh impassable swamp and at its upper end by precipices.

Yet the old man, his grandfather, had found some way in and out of it.

There remained the two sides of the ravine to examine. When scanning the country from the tree-top he had noted that the south ridge was considerably higher than the other one. He had not been able to make out details of configuration, even through his field-glass, because every acre of the country was clad in forest and the foliage gave it all a deceptively smooth appearance, with no hint of cliffs and chasms and matted undergrowth.

He crawled back to the trail, shouldered his pack once more, and started along the backbone of the north ridge.

Even here the going was bad. The trees were not so thickly set as in the richer soil of the coves, but there was much kalmia and rhododendron. Berry bushes grew as rank here as anywhere. He had never seen greenbrier thicker or more exasperating.

Cabarrus did not use his hunting knife or his axe to clear a way, for that would have pointed out his course to the first passerby. He just pushed and dodged and floundered ahead, struggling with the briery vines, "fighting his pack." The heavy dew on the bushes was rubbed by friction right through the rainproof fabric of his breeches and soon his feet were sloshing with water that worked down inside his high-topped boots. He got cobwebs in his eyes and had his hat brushed off so many times that he angrily tied it on with his neckerchief and looked like an old country-woman in a bonnet.

The top of the ridge undulated in saddles, one after the other, so that after each descent he had to climb up another hill. There was no outlook through the foliage. Sometimes it was hard to tell whether he was still on the crest of the ridge or had strayed off on some abutting spur.

After half an hour of sweating and toiling through the brush, he came to what seemed a jumping-off-place. There was a steep descent in front and on both sides. He could not see what lay beyond, in any direction. He knew that if this were the end of the promontory over Deep Creek he would be hearing the water roar down below. So it must be that he had come to a deep gap between two pinnacles of the ridge, but which way the ridge ran from here was a matter of guesswork.

He went down a little way on the left, toward Nick's Nest, but came to a cliff that would be dangerous to descend. Then he graded around to the right, seeking the gap, and soon he found it. There was a steep climb ahead. He staggered on, picking his way around fallen trees and clumps of laurel, and finally came out on top of a high knob where three tall pines rose like spires above the forest roof.

Here was an opening, at last. He could see far out over the mountains to the Smoky divide. Burbank's place was on the edge of the woods to the northward. Turkey-Fly-Up was across the creek to the west. At last he was getting true bearings.

ELEVEN

Cabarrus cast off his pack and sat down to rest a bit. The sweep of the prospect was vast, out over a sea of peaks, domes and ridges, sharply outlined in the foreground by bright sunlight and deeply contrasted shade, but gradually growing dimmer in the distance through the haze that nearly always envelopes the Smoky Mountains and has given them their name.

He had scarcely found a seat on a mossy log before he was treated as an intruder. A tufted titmouse flew at him with shrill angry cries. Immediately it was joined by a flock of others, fluttering around his head and chiding: "*Cha—cha—cha—cluck!* Who are you? What are you doing here? Get out! Get out!"

An eagle sailed high overhead, then spiraled down out of the blue, circled low over the Burbank place, suddenly folded its wings and shot headlong to the back yard. Checking itself with an outspread of pinions that cast a broad shadow on the ground, it seized a chicken and made off with it. The other fowl raised a terrible clamor.

Cabarrus, through his field-glass, saw a woman rush out from the house with a gun. She fired at the flying marauder, but it was already out of shotgun range and triumphantly headed for the mountain woods.

It was too cool and breezy on the peak for him to linger there. He took up his pack and started down the southern face of the ridge toward the sound of hurrying water that he knew must be Nick's Run.

The brow of the ridge here was overgrown with small pines. Under their deep evergreen canopy there was no impediment of bushes. But the slope was so steep, and the carpet of pine needles so slippery, that he descended warily, using his staff as an alpenstock to test the footing and maintain his balance. There was no telling when he might come of a sudden to the verge of a precipice.

As it turned out, good fortune now attended him. He came down out of the pines into a thick forest of deciduous trees interspersed with mighty hemlocks. Nearing the bottom of the ravine, he had to push through ferns shoulder-high. Then he came out in a wild garden of shade-loving herbs, such as are never seen in perfection elsewhere than in primeval forest that has suffered no interference by man.

There was lush growth of cohosh, snakeroot, Solomon's seal, trilliums, orchids, Clintonia, angelico or nondo, wild spikenard, Indian cucumber, and scores of other interesting plants. He saw old and thrifty specimens of ginseng—proof positive that no mountaineer had been in this glen for several years; because the dried "sang" root, as the natives call it, brought fourteen dollars a pound in any of the country stores.

There were mushrooms of many varieties, some edible, some poisonous, and a surprising ghostly multitude of that weird parasitic plant—the Indian pipe. Cabarrus had seldom seen such mosses as covered the decaying tree trunks that littered the ground, nor such galax as carpeted the banks.

Nick's Nest was literally choked with vegetation. There were dark arbors of wild grapes, bowers of moonseed and other vines, spreading over the smaller trees. The rope-like stems of the wild sarsaparilla, or Dutchman's pipe, twined round the greater trunks and festooned the high limbs like tropical lianas. Along the banks of the brook the superb leucothoe grew so thickly that he could hardly force his way through it.

When he came to the stream, Cabarrus set down his pack, taking good heed where he was leaving it, so he could infallibly find it again. He drank deep of the sparkling water and then set forth to explore the bottom of the ravine. He had hardly gone twenty paces before he flushed a ruffed grouse that rose with a boom as startling as if a cannon had been fired in the solitude.

Cabarrus knew he must be near the upper edge of the swamp; so he moved off in the other direction, toward the head of the glen. His first concern was to discover a good camping site.

Nick's Nest was a V-shaped trough, three to four hundred feet deep and about half a mile long, from the swamp at its mouth to the cliffs below the Pullback trail. Throughout its course the wild waters of Nick's Run dashed and flashed, chattered and roared, over one cascade after another, between steep rocky banks covered with mosses and ferns and vines dripping in the spray.

Nowhere along the bottom of the gorge did Cabarrus find a spot level enough for a man to lie down on the ground and spend a night. As high as he could see on his right, as he climbed eastward, the mountain rose in a sheer wall, bristling with laurel and rhododendron. On the other side the slope was forty to fifty degrees, densely timbered with tall trees of many species, and the surface was broken with ledges and protruding rocks.

After a long, gradual climb, pushing his way through the undergrowth, he came to shaggy cliffs rising high above the waterside, stately and grim. Here was the cataract that he had discovered when first peering through the laurel at the head of the glen. It came thundering down over ledges that were like steps of a giant's stairway, and then to a steep incline of smooth rock over which it shot with hissing velocity and plunged into a deep pool that boiled and surged and carried a race of froth out into the channel.

There was no exit here, even if Cabarrus had wished to go farther in this direction.

The flanks of the ravine remained to be explored. It was possible that there might be a bench or terrace of level ground somewhere high above the brook. It would be unhandy to carry water to such a place, but the terrace would get more sunlight and be a more wholesome camping place than the gloomy bottom of the ravine.

The northerly frontage was a maze of laurel and it was in perpetual shadow. That would not do at all. So Cabarrus climbed up the other flank, where the sun warmed the mountain, and he began looking there for a biding place.

For an hour he zigzagged up and down along the face of the ridge, finding everywhere under the continuous canopy of trees a variety of floral beauty that entranced him; but nowhere was there a ten-foot square of level ground.

It began to look as if he would have to build a scaffolding against the trees to support his bed. That would be a sorry makeshift for one who was bent on spending at least a week, perhaps a month or more, in this locality.

At last, as he was about to resign himself to the necessity of occupying a very comfortless roost, he came out on the top of a cliff that jutted from the side of the ravine. Here he stepped to the edge to get a view of what lay beyond.

A cry of surprise escaped him at the abrupt change of aspect. Before and below him, as far as he could see through the foliage, great rocks were tumbled and scattered in confusion. Under sheer walls or overhanging ledges of the mountainside were hundreds of detached rocks, split and upheaved and thrown at all angles.

Their edges were mostly sharp, as if recently quarried by Cyclopes. They were colored by lichens to a mottle of gray and brown, though many were cushioned over with thick moss. On some of the greater ones birch trees stood, apparently growing out of the bare stone, their roots penetrating the crevices or twining around the rock like tentacles of octopi.

Between the boulders and under their uptilted ends were innumerable crannies and dens, some of them very gruesome black holes, fit for multitudes of foxes and wildcats, likely breeding-places for rattlesnakes.

All over and among the shattered and strewn masses were rank ferns and vines, masking the cracks in which a man might wedge fast his foot or turn an ankle, concealing pitfalls into which he might slip and break his bones.

But above this formidable barrier, along the mountain front, was the very location that Cabarrus had struggled so hard to find.—

Overhead was an outthrust ledge of very solid and trusty granite covering a semi-circular alcove of bare rock, thus forming a roofed and dry and clean recess like a half dome, with a nearly level rock floor some twenty feet in extent either way.

On the far side of this vaulted room was a cleft in the ledge from which poured a bold spring of water from the living rock. It fell into a tiny pool embowered in ferns and delicate mountain flowers. The water in the stone basin was transparent as a glass lens. Its run-off disappeared down the slope under the riven rocks and passed underground to its outlet in Nick's Run.

The whole front of the ledge was masked by the evergreen tops of huge hemlock trees that provided perpetual concealment. But overhead there was no barrier to the sunlight that streamed down into the alcove as through a skylight in a high roof, keeping the place dry and wholesome to occupy.

If ever there was an ideal spot for a hermitage, safe from intrusion, or a secure hiding-place for a refugee, it was this unknown natural fortress high up on the scarped side of Nick's Nest.

The place was safe from detection, even in winter when the leaves of all but the evergreens had fallen. No one scouting along the bottom of the ravine would suspect its existence. It was unapproachable from above; indeed it could not even be seen from the brink of that frowning precipice. There was but one way over which a trail could be made to it, and Cabarrus, by skilful scouting, aided by sheer good luck, had discovered where the entrance lay.

Aglow with eagerness, the prospector started forward to take possession of his new-found wilderness home. Instinctively he named it The Alcove. He was already figuring how he would make a secret pathway to it from the outer world, over which he would bring supplies with which to live in snug comfort while pursuing his labors of discovery.

Picking his way cautiously over a barrier of fallen rocks he arrived on the smooth floor of the niche and began to scan the features of the strange retreat that Nature had provided as if in prevision of his needs.

The floor sloped slightly toward the outer edge, where there was a straight drop of ten feet to the nearest of the great stone blocks that littered the declivity toward Nick's Run.

The granite ceiling swept upward and outward in an arch. The back and side walls of the Alcove were of soft rock that had weather out in a great pocket. The winds and waters and frosts of many centuries had attacked this soft stratum and eroded it, while the hard upper end lower strata remained firm and whole.

The place was remarkably dry and clean. There was no sign of its being occupied at any time by wild beasts. Probably it was too large and open for them, save as an occasional sunning-place. They preferred to den in the dark and narrow holes, all round about, that could be more easily defended.

Cabarrus was pleased at finding there were no crevices in the rear wall, such as most caves or rock-shelters have, where snakes might harbor. He saw that mud-dauber wasps had plastered their gray nests on the ceiling and walls; but they were welcome, for they would keep his place free from spiders.

While scanning the wall of his cliff-dwelling his eyes were arrested by a peculiar marking that was not conspicuous and yet showed plainly enough when he fixed attention on it. On the west side, near the spring, was something that did not look like a natural feature. He stepped close to examine it.

At the height of his shoulder was a symbol carved in the rock and evidently the work of man. It was a fantastic thing, crudely resembling a Chinese picture of a dragon, with arched back, three-toed feet, whip-like tail and snaky neck. But where the head would be there was only a broad line from which protruded four claw-like things that evidently were meant for fangs shot from an open mouth.

The carving seemed very old. Its surface bore the patina of centuries. At some time in the remote past an Indian hunter must have discovered this secret recess in the mountain and left his sign manual here.

With what tool had he accomplished the engraving?

Cabarrus was thrilled by finding the answer lying at his very feet. There on the Alcove floor, half hidden in fine sand that the winds of ages had ground from the encompassing rock, lay a flint implement about seven inches long, slender and shaped to fit the hand. He picked it up. One end was sharpened to a chisel edge and the other was battered as if often hit with a stone hammer.

Somehow the hammer marks on that primitive tool gave it a very near and intimate significance. Cabarrus felt akin to that Man of the Stone Age who had carved the glyph upon the rock. He had a weird feeling that he was himself a fellow cliff-dweller, meeting life on its simplest terms. He seemed not only miles but eons removed from the complex of civilization. He was not just close to Nature but was actually one with her.

Reverently he laid the flint chisel up on a shelf of the rock wall, at the same time whispering, "Little People, I want to take this."

He went to get a drink at the spring. Never had he tasted such good water! It gushed from a crack in the rock. Curiously enough, the stone on one side of the crack was different from that on the other. One side was fine-grained granite and the other a coarse pegmatite.

It struck him that this was a fault-plane. At some time the rock strata of the mountain had been squeezed together or upthrust by earth forces. The stress had folded the strata in waves. But at this particular point there had been too sudden a strain, or the rock was too brittle to stand it, and so the formation broke apart, one side slipping down below the other. Here, then, the broken edge of an upper stratum met that of a lower one which was of different composition.

Eager to see what lay beyond the Alcove, on the far side from where he had entered, Cabarrus moved on, over tumbled fragments of rock that were hard to surmount and wriggle over. They were angular blocks of all sizes up to that of a freight car, like those below the Alcove toward Nick's Run. They were a continuation of that same extraordinary barrier, here running higher up the mountain and enclosing that side of his cliff-house like a great ruined wall.

It took him several minutes to crawl over these obstacles, going circumspectly for fear of accident. A broken leg, or even a sprained ankle, would be serious to one who had vanished from man's knowledge and could never receive human aid.

At last he came to an unscalable cliff on the far side. And here the first thing to meet his eye was another fault-plane similar to the one at his spring.

"By Jove!" he thought. "This is no ordinary slip produced by folding. The whole top of the mountain must have fallen in."

Above him, high over the talus of fallen rocks, was the deep gap where he had been puzzled, that morning, before finding the way up to the outlook where the three pines grew.

Cabarrus studied the lie of the land and concluded that there might have been at one time a great cavity in this mountain, with the ridge top forming its roof; then the roof fell in, perhaps during an earthquake, and filled the hollow. In such case, the gap up yonder was what was left of the old roof.

He considered this idea for awhile. If it was right, then those big broken rocks might have been outthrust during the convulsion.

He went down to Nick's Run and brought up his pack-sack, built a small fire of dead laurel that gave off no smoke, made some strong tea and ate his lunch. Then he sat smoking and planning for half an hour.

It was a hot day, even at this altitude. There was no wind. Cabarrus fell into a dreamy reverie. Somehow once more he got to thinking of Indian Myra and the Little People. Gradually he became conscious of wild eavesdroppers round about, furtive-eyed, hidden and known only by faint rustlings here and there. Somewhere back in the inscrutable thicket were quick, gentle sounds of mice or ground-squirrels overturning leaves.

Then abruptly it all stopped, as if in hushed attention to some obtruding scent of fox or shadow of a bird of prey. Profound silence followed, save for the never ceasing clamor of Nick's Run. All creatures in the woods seemed to be listening, some tense with dread, some avid with predaceous greed. Now and again a soft sigh came from the tree-tops, or a gentle sibilant murmur of rivulets flowing underground; but all living things were quiet, until at last their strained ears were soothed by a mourning-dove cooing low.

TWELVE

A little, stoop-shouldered, weather-bitten man sidled in through the door of Matlock's store in Kittuwa. He stood apart from the bargaining crowd, hesitant, bashfully waiting till everyone else would be through. In one hand he bore a crooked stick and in the other a parcel of something tied up in an old bandanna.

His faded and ragged clothes were clay-colored and blotched here and there by darker stains, like old khaki daubed for camouflage. His ancient gray hat had long ago lost its band and it sagged down over his pate in funnel shape, resembling a clown's cap or a cowl. Long wisps of yellow hair protruded beneath the brim. Shrewd little eyes, set close together, peered from amid the thatch, alert and glittering like a jay-bird's.

One of the shoppers, a motor-camper fresh from the city, glanced doubtfully at the fellow, wondering if he were safe to be at large. The clerk smilingly reassured her, in an undertone: "It's just Sang Johnny, come down from the mountains with herbs to sell. He's odd-looking, but harmless, and nobody's fool."

The herb-hunter backed deferentially into a corner as though apologizing for being in the way. His face bore a patient and propitiatory smile.

"Sang Johnny," chuckled the woman, "What a name!"

"It's what everybody calls him. Sang is the mountain word for ginseng, a root that is shipped to China, where they use it as a cure-all and think it restores youth. The wild plant is almost exterminated now, but Johnny still knows where to find some."

"He looks like a tramp," observed the woman.

"You can't always judge by appearance, in this country: Johnny has money in bank."

"Where does the creature live?"

"He has a little hut in the woods, far off by itself. There's no one with him but his old mother, who is a character herself, a terribly uncouth old party that ignorant folks take for a witch. Her real name is Nancy Hess; but they call her Old Hex. A Jew peddler gave her that nickname. He said it means witch in Dutch. But Johnny's all right: minds his own business and is straight as a string."

The herb-hunter lingered silently in the background for half an hour while customers came and went. Finally one of the clerks, tired of seeing him standing there, called back into Matlock's office: "Sang Johnny's out here. You know how he is—won't trade with anybody but you."

Matlock laughed, dropped his papers and came out into the store.

"Hello, Johnny," he hailed. "How are you coming on?"

"Tol'able, Mr. Matlock. Jist tol'able."

"How's Mistress Hess?" inquired Matlock, politely using the ancient title of address that is still common usage in the southern mountains.

"Ma, she's poorly; thank you."

"I've got something good for her," whispered Matlock confidentially. "Good to mix yarbs in," he chuckled, adapting his speech to his customer. "I'll get it d'reckly, when nobody's lookin'."

Johnny grinned understandingly. He untied his bandanna and displayed some eight ounces of dried ginseng root. Matlock gave them expert examination. He knew how to distinguish wild roots from cultivated ones, as do the Chinese, who deem the wild ginseng more potent than what is grown under artificial shade. Then he weighed them with minute accuracy.

"Seven dollars and thirty-six cents," he computed. He took that amount from the cash-register, selecting new bills and shining coins that made an attractive display. Johnny pocketed the money and then went to buying goods with it. Such was his rule of trading: first get the money in hand, then buy, demanding a discount for cash. He lingered long over his purchases, to the great disgust of observant clerks; but Matlock knew his customer and had reason to humor him.

The transaction finished, Matlock winked at Johnny and beckoned him back into the office. From his steel safe he produced a bottle of white corn whiskey. Johnny took a good pull at it.

"Now carry that home and give it to Mistress Hess with my compliments," said the merchant. "Anything new up the creek?"

"Wall, the newest I observed was your young man a-huntin' mineral," said Johnny.

"My wha-a-at?" ejaculated Matlock, wondering what the fellow meant.

Johnny stared at him, round eyed. He had taken for granted that Matlock knew all about it.

"The spry young feller that's diggin' and pannin' in Turkey-Fly-Up," he explained.

"The devil you say! Why, that's on my property!"

"Sartin. I 'lowed you done sont him thar."

"Not by a hell of a sight, I didn't. Who is he? When did you see him?"

Johnny stroked his chin and then answered with grave deliberation: "He don't look nor act like none o' our people. Must be a furriner. Lemme see—today's Friday—'twas Tuesday evenin' that I was comin' back the nigh way from the hills, down through the holler. I heered somethin' ahead: so I side-stepped to spy it out. Thar was this young feller muddyin' up the branch and washin' gravel in a pan. He quit, by and by, and climb up the ridge side, sarchin' the rocks. Then I spied Youlus Lumbo a-sneakin' up to a quar leetle tent the feller had set in the holler. Youlus looked all round about and then he went in. Stayed jist a bit. Kem hack out with some teeny thing in his fingers. Then he went off. I doubled and slipped away, without him knowin' to my bein' thar. So I kem home. The young man has left his cyar in Terhune's yard durin' the time he's back in the mountains. Hit's thar yit. I reckon Jim knows who he claims to be. They's a license on his cyar, front and back; but I cain't read."

Matlock stroked his high forehead and silently studied this surprising news. Then he asked: "Have you seen either of them since?"

"Not the furriner; but Youlus is hyar in town today: I done seed him through the winder jist now as I was makin' up my budget."

"Whereabouts?"

"Over yander by the bank. He was havin' speech with Doc. Terry and then follered him upstairs to his office."

Matlock sprang at once into action. "I'll see about that," declared he. "Keep your tongue between your teeth, Johnny. I'll make it worth while."

Johnny gave his word and shuffled off. Matlock seized his hat and stalked out on the street.

Doctor Terry's office was across the way. Matlock went upstairs and entered the anteroom just as the doctor and Youlus, with backs turned and without hearing his footfall, went into the consulting room leaving the partition door open. Terry was saying, "Sit down awhile till I examine this."

Matlock, always brazen about butting in and with no scruple as to eavesdropping, took a seat at one side of the open door where he could overhear everything without being observed.

For some time there was silence. No patient came to disturb the scene. Matlock's eyes wandered along the walls of the anteroom, which was set with cabinets that displayed a curio hunter's hobby. There were showy mineral specimens, Indian relics, vegetable freaks, rare birds rather badly mounted, a double-headed snake in a jar of alcohol, skulls of wildcats and bears, a motley array evincing the dilettante rather than the connoisseur.

Finally Terry inquired of Youlus, "What do you think this is? Gold? Silver? Lead?"

Youlus nervously cleared his throat. "I don't rightly know; he admitted; "but it's heavy and orter be wuth lookin' into."

Matlock peeped around the door-jamb.

Terry got out some simple apparatus. He examined the specimen through a lens; he tried its hardness and its streak; he heated it under a blowpipe flame. Humming to himself and grunting and sighing, he pondered for a while, then took down a treatise on mineralogy and studied it for ten mortal minutes.

Meantime Youlus was fidgeting in a sweat of anxiety. At last the doctor scraped off a little powder from the specimen, mixed it with some chemical on a strip of platinum, and heated them together. The stuff turned green in the center of the flame.

"Quite so," declared Terry with satisfaction. "This is, as I thought, uraninite, commonly called pitchblende: one of the most extraordinary minerals in all the world. Where did you get it?"

"Up in the Smokies," gulped Youlus.

"Ah, yes: somehwere east of the sun and west of the moon," observed the doctor with a knowing smile. "Well, you've stumbled on something interesting—very interesting indeed, sir."

"What's it wuth?" asked Youlus with blunt sincerity.

"Uraninite—ahem—uraninite is a mineral of remarkably complex composition. It has, I may say, astounding possibilities, when—ah—

science has made a little further progress. For example," declaimed the doctor, striking an attitude and addressing the wide world through his open window, "in uraninite helium was first discovered. Helium, that extraordinary gas, almost as light as hydrogen but uninflammable, which makes it the ideal filler for dirigible balloons or airships, like the *Shenandoah*."

"What's it wuth?" persisted Youlus.

"A little while ago," answered Terry, "helium gas—just the gas, mind you—cost $1,500 a cubic foot."

Youlus gripped the sides of his chair till his knuckles turned white.

"But science advances so rapidly," continued the doctor, "that now it has cut the cost to two cents a cubic foot."

Lumbo's heart sank into his boots.

"And yet there is more money in helium production today, at two cents, than there was when it figured only as a laboratory curiosity at an absurd price."

"How's that?" asked Youlus.

"A triumph of science in mass production. Take the case of aluminum. Forty years ago it sold at five dollars a pound, and common folks never heard of it. Today, at twenty-some cents a pound, it is in every housewife's hands and its producers are among the world's greatest millionaires. Ahem—some of them are."

Youlus bent eagerly forward as if to receive an armful of greenbacks.

"Now, then," asked Terry of the world at large, "what else is hidden in this shiny black fragment, so insignificant-looking, that has lain for ages in some recess of the Smoky Mountains? Well, it is largely uranium, a valuable metal in itself, for which there is a world-market. But a ton of uranium is of far less value than the merest pinch of another element that this same wonderful ore contains. Uraninite, this stuff before us, is one of the chief sources of radium, and radium is by far the most costly substance in all the world. It is selling right now at $70,000 a gram!"

"H-how much is a g-gram!" stuttered the trembling Lumbo.

"About a thimbleful,"

"*What!*" cried the mountaineer, leaping to his feet.

"I mean just what I say," declared the doctor. "A gram of radium is only a small thimbleful, and it brings $70,000 in open market. Radium is infinitely more precious than gold or diamonds."

Instinctively Youlus stretched forth his hand toward the little black nodule that lay glinting at the doctor's elbow. But he never reached it.

A tornado burst into the room, Youlus was swept aside. Matlock confronted the astonished doctor with a face threatening apoplexy.

"Give that radium to me!" he thundered. "This damned sneaking scoundrel stole it off o' my property!"

The enraged bully dashed to the doctor's desk and snatched up, not the bit of uraninite, but the shiny strip of platinum that had just come from the blowpipe flame and was now resting on an asbestos pad. Instantly it burned blisters on his thumb and finger. Matlock dropped it, with an oath, and shook his fist at Lumbo.

"Who's that skulker prospecting on my place in Turkey-Fly-Up?" he demanded.

But Youlus clapped his hat on his head, dashed out of the office and thumped downstairs, two steps at a jump.

Matlock went flying after. It chanced to be mail-time and many people had gathered about the post-office next door. Youlus dove into the crowd, elbowed his way through it, slipped into a store, went out through a back door and was gone.

Matlock, thwarted, turned his rage upon an old white-bearded man in the crowd who chanced to be one of his delinquent customers. The old man saw that Matlock was in a dangerous mood; so he edged away. Matlock cried out to him: "Amos, when are you going to pay me that bill you've been owing so long?"

"Ultimately, Mr. Matlock, ultimately," answered the patriarch, slipping away from the big fellow's outstretched hand and getting well back in the crowd.

"Yes, but how long do you mean by ultimately?"

"Very ultimately, sir; very ultimately."

The crowd broke into a guffaw.

THIRTEEN

Matlock let no grass grow under his feet. Early Friday morning he departed on horseback for his place on Deep Creek. He stopped at Terhune's to make inquiry. Terhune had gone to look after some cattle in the mountains, but his wife was at home.

"Whose car is that?" asked Matlock, pointing to the old sedan.

"Hit was left Tuesday by a young man from New York who's up in the mountains," answered Mrs. Terhune.

"What's his name?"

"Cabarrus."

Matlock studied over the peculiar name and could recall no one who bore it. Well, a man from New York might be named anything, pronounceable or not.

"What's he doing in the mountains?"

"I dunno. 'Pears like he's jist projectin' around, seein' the sights."

"Know anything about him?"

"Nothin' special. He's a right peart, upstandin' feller, and he talks sensible. The childern tuk quite a fancy to him. Jim 'lows he's all right."

"When did you see him last?"

"W'y, he kem in last night from the mountains and stayed with us. He left this mornin' with a big pack o' rations and campin' gear."

"Did he say where he is camping?"

"Said fust one place, then another."

"What does he look like?"

Mrs. Terhune described in few words the man's appearance and manner. It was a swift and shrewd characterization.

"I reckon you have business with him," she added, hoping to draw Matlock out.

"Yes, I have business with him," declared Matlock severely. "He's trespassing on my property. You'd better not harbor him, for I'm going to take him with a warrant."

Without another word he rode on.

Mrs. Terhune sniffed.— "Trespassin'!" she exclaimed. "Now what harm's the young feller doin', jist ketchin' what trout he needs for hisself? Matlock's rich and needn't be so tetchious over a few fish. He's the most despisable man! I do hate the sight o' that face o' his'n. It gives me the all-overs!"

"He's a darned old skinflint," declared Kit bluntly. "I'd love to pop him in that bad eye o' his'n!"

"Take my bow 'n' arrer," offered Bupply eagerly. Bupply was fingering a new dime.

Kit spat on the ground; then, with sudden determination, he took a short cane fishpole that stood against the chimney and he started for the creek.

Bupply wanted to go along; but Kit would have none of his company. "I'll be out till dark," he announced. So away he trudged. His mother asked no questions, being used to his mannish ways. She had a well-founded trust in the lad's competency to look out for himself.

Kit watched Matlock out of sight and then quietly took after him.

"There's something dead up the branch," he averred, in the mountaineer's way of expressing suspicion. "I'll cut acrost, the nigh way, and warn Mr. Cabarrus, if I can find him."

So he took to the trail. Finding that Matlock was following the old wagon road across the mountain, Kit turned aside and sped up the Vine trail at a dogtrot.

He found old Granny Vine in her garden. From her he learned that the stranger had stopped there an hour ago and bought some eggs.

Kit had been following the fresh tracks of hobnailed boots. They led on up the mountain to Lick-log Gap. And there, abruptly, he lost them.

The boy could scarcely believe his eyes. The tracks led, as plain as print, to a big fallen log beside the trail, and there they ended. There was no trace beyond or on either side. The moss on the log itself was not disturbed.

This was unbelievable. It was as if the man had here met a flying-machine and had vanished in air.

Kit went on up the Pullback trail a short distance searching keenly but discovering nothing. He returned and took off along the side trail toward Matlock's place; and here he was worse puzzled than ever. There were old tracks made by those boots, but they came *uphill*, not down.

"Now, wouldn't this choke your goozle?" muttered the boy. "I'd say he's a ha'nt, if I hadn't more sense than to believe in the like o' that. Naw: he's side-stepped in the bushes and kivvered his tracks. But what's he dodgin' fer? Mebbe he knowed old Cock-eye was after him. And 't ain't jist fishin' he's a-doin', or he wouldn't be so sly. I wonder what game he's up to."

Kit went on, in a brown study, along the Pullback trail and descended the steep pitch to Burbank's cabin. Maybe Big Tom knew something about the stranger.

But Tom was out on patrol. Sylvia was working in the kitchen and chatting with Miss Wentworth, who was ready to go plant-hunting in the woods as soon as the dew dried from the bushes. In the Smokies there is a heavy dew and it does not disappear until about nine o'clock.

Kit "visited" for some time, after the mountain manner, talking about anything except what was on his mind. Then gradually he led up to it and told about Matlock's quest.

Sylvia had never heard of the stranger; but shrewd little Kit observed that Marian looked uneasy.

"That gal knows somep'n," he assured himself. But she was "a high-headed somebody" and he could not ask her a direct question.

Disappointed and more puzzled than ever, Kit went on down the creek and proceeded to fish its sinuous and turbulent five miles to his home.

Sylvia turned to Marian.— "I wonder what's wrong. Who can the young man be?"

"I fancy I've seen him," answered the girl. She told of her accidental meeting with a stranger at the ruined cabin. Then she asked Sylvia if she knew anything of old Professor Dale and the tragedy of his later years.

Yes: it had become a legend in the mountains, with more of fancy than of fact embodied in it. Many folks thought the old cabin was haunted. Sylvia herself would not like to pass it at night, particularly if she were alone.

Marian told her the true story, as she had heard it from Colonel

Fielding, and she added: "I believe that this young man whom Matlock is after is no other than little Jack Dale grown up."

"Then there'll be a killin'," declared Sylvia with emphasis.

"Oh, no—surely not!" exclaimed Marian.

"Yes, indeed: you can jist put it down that Bill Matlock never forgits nor forgives. He's a bad man to cross. He won't fight fa'r and squar' when there's a chance to layway. He's sly. But, of course, he'd fight a rigiment if he was cornered or driv into the open."

"Do you mean he would commit murder?" asked Marian anxiously.

"You needn't say I said so," answered Sylvia calmly; "but there's them that believes Matlock hired a murder done, oncet. He kem clar in court; still they's lots o' things cain't be proved that we know good and well."

Marian was troubled. Her fingers drummed nervously on the table. Presently she said: "That boy seems sure that Mr. Cabarrus is camping somewhere in this neighborhood."

"Then Tom'll find him," said Sylvia confidently. "Mebbe he knows about him a'ready."

"But he would have told you."

"Deary, you don't know a mountain man's ways. He don't tell his wife nothin' he thinks ain't good for her. He loves to harbor a secret, anyway. Then he feels he knows more 'n anybody else."

"How about the mountain woman?" asked Marian shrewdly.

Sylvia laughed.— "Well, she is liable to talk too much, sometimes. But she can play shet-mouth as good as ary man, when she wants to."

Marian looked out through the open doorway and saw that the dew was off the bushes. She arose and gathered up her botanizing kit.

"Don't you go fur away," warned Sylvia. "You might git lost,—or run into that young man, and he'd eat you up," she added mischievously, "If I was a man, I'd be tempted to."

"Then you'd get slapped over," laughed Marian. "I'm only going into those pretty woods beyond the branch," she said, pointing southward toward a ridge that rose above a bit of level woodland, three or four hundred yards away. Even Sylvia did not know what lay on the farther side of that steep and laurel-covered ridge. It was the northern wall of Nick's Nest.

Marian crossed the old field where Tom had sung his ballad of "Sourwood Mountain" and had felled the dead chestnut tree. She came to a small branch of gurgling water, sprang lightly over it, and came out into a wild garden embowered in all the verdure and shade of noble woods.

Here she rambled hither and yon, gathering and pressing one species after another; and so gradually she came to the base of the ridge, where great ledges and detached rocks stood covered with mosses and flowering plants and ferns.

Out of a tall tree flew a log-cock, or pileated woodpecker, filling the forest with a shrill, startling cry of *whicker—whicker—whicker*—that warned every creature within half a mile that an intruder had come. It was a bird tall as a pheasant, very wary of mankind and seldom seen anywhere but in the deep, ancient woods. It settled on a dead tree somewhere on the mountainside and went to drilling after insects, striking terrific blows on the wood with a steady rat-tat-tat.

Presently Marian became aware of another sort of pecking, seemingly near by. It was at longer intervals and had a clinking, metallic sound. Wondering what it might be, she arose from her gleaning and looked about.

Again it came to her ears. And there on a great cloven rock, above her on the side of the ridge, she descried a man in tan-colored duck, vigorously pounding stone with his prospector's pick. As he turned, facing her, she saw that it was Cabarrus, and her heart leaped at the recognition.

Early that morning Cabarrus had set forth to trace the course of the fault-planes and to study the great slip of rock that had split the mountain. Not satisfied with examining this freak of nature on his own side of the ridge, he proceeded to the other, which faced toward Burbank's cabin. After struggling around cliffs and down through mazes of laurel, he came at last to where there were detached masses of rock similar to those that fortressed his Alcove, but much less in number and magnitude. Here was evidence that the slip extended clear through the mountain spur.

So, as he was breaking up samples of rock to determine their nature, he chanced to look down into the flat woodland below him, and there he beheld the flushed face of Marian Wentworth.

At once he jumped down from the rock and came swiftly to her. Lifting his battered hat and bowing low, he greeted her:

"Welcome, fair Rosalind! This is the forest of Arden."

"But I'm not Rosalind," said she. "My name is Marian."

"Maid Marian, by all that's blest! Then this is Sherwood forest and you seek Robin Hood."

"But who, good sir, are you?" asked Marian, catching his whimsy and returning it like a tossed ball.

"I am his henchman, one Little John."

Marian regarded him quizzically. Then impulsively she thrust: "Are you not, rather, Little Jack, grown up to be Big John?"

The words had scarce left her tongue before she blushed at her own audacity. What right had she to intrude into this man's private affair?

She saw Cabarrus flinch as though a missile had struck him unawares. He lifted his eyebrows. For a hushed interval he searched her countenance. Then, nodding to her challenge, he said: "I'm glad you have found me out. Won't you sit by me, here on this mossy rock, and tell me how you learned about that Little Jack?"

"For your own safety's sake, yes," answered she. "It is not the high sheriff of Nottingham that's after you, but the very real sheriff of this county of Swain."

"Are you serious?" he asked.

"Quite serious," she assured him. Then, sitting with hands clasped in her lap, eyes gravely regarding him, she told Cabarrus the ill news that Kit had brought to the Burbanks.

The young man listened, his eyes half closed, his lips pursed in study of the situation. When she had finished, he made a gesture of quick decision.

"I had well-laid plans, or thought I had," said he; "but now I'm rather pleased that they have 'gang a-gley.' You wouldn't have done this for me if you had thought I was a skulker looking for something to steal."

"No."

"Then I have lost nothing, and gained a friend. May I tell you what I'm really up to?"

"You think I may be trusted?" she asked, smiling.

"I know it. You have honest eyes."

"So has a sheep; but have I discretion?"

"You have keen eyes."

"So has a fox; but it is tricky."

"You have kind eyes."

"So has a puppy; but it is foolish."

"You have lovely eyes."

"Oh, really!" she mocked. "Now go on with your story."

"All right. But if you'll first tell me what you already know, I can sooner get to the gist of the matter."

Marian repeated her uncle's narrative of Professor Dale, the cabin in the woods, Matlock's chicane, and little Jack's disappearance.

When it was told, Cabarrus took up the story.—

"It is all true, as far as it goes," said he; "but folks hereabouts never knew my real name. I was an orphan and was brought up by my mother's father, Professor Dale. People got to calling me Jack Dale and the name stuck to me. But my father's family name was Cabarrus."

"Is it English?" asked Marian.

"No. My father's ancestors were French. One of them moved to Spain, where he became a banker and financial adviser to the king, who made him minister of finance. His daughter, Madame Tallien, afterwards princess of Chimay, won a certain fame in the French Revolution as 'Our Lady of Thermidor.' During that troubled period some members of the family moved to America. One of them became a planter and politician in North Carolina. So far as I know, I'm the last survivor of that branch.

"You have heard how I came away from Kittuwa. Well, I saw some pretty pinching times until a country doctor in Missouri took a fancy to me, picked me up off the village streets, and gave me an education. After college, I became a chemist and settled in New York.

"Grandfather Dale was a naturalist. Among other things, he collected minerals. He tried to teach me something about them. Among his finds hereabouts were many rarities. They interested scientists because they contained elements that were little known at that time. In recent years these same rare elements are sought for industrial purposes. They may find use on a large scale if sufficient deposits of the minerals that bear them are discovered.

"For instance, there is beryllium. It is a metal derived from the mineral beryl, which, by the way, in its perfect state, forms gems grading up from plain beryl to aquamarine and the precious emerald. The metal beryllium itself is remarkable stuff. It is very strong, very hard, has a high melting point; yet it is four times lighter than steel, one-third lighter than aluminum. You can readily see how valuable it would be for air-ship building and other construction, if it were not so very costly to produce. Well, I have perfected a process by which it can be turned out at a reasonable price, if I can locate a big deposit of crude beryl—and right here is where I hope to find it."

"Oh!" exclaimed Marian. "That would be wonderful! But—"

"But what?"

She was suddenly struck with something still more wonderful: that John Cabarrus, who knew nothing of her, should trust her so implicitly with his secret. Instinctively she placed her hand on his.

"Does Matlock suspect what you are after?" she asked.

"What could he know about beryllium? If one spoke to him of the 'elements' he would think one meant the sky and the air, fire and water. Haven't you heard the mountaineers say: 'The el-e-ments looks like rain—hit's goin' to weather?'"

Marian smiled. "Go on with the story," she bade him.

"Well, there are other rare chemical elements to look for, here, if beryllium doesn't show up. Zirconium, molybdenum, titanium, uranium, and so on. All of them are wanted in industries and they command high prices. All of them have been found in the Carolina mountains, though little has been done in prospecting for them. The quest, to one scientifically trained, is more fascinating than hunting for silver or gold."

"I hope—I do hope you'll find them, Mr. Cabarrus."

"Thank you. But here's the rub: Matlock owns this land. However, my grandfather, in deeding it to him, expressly reserved all mineral rights. At that time Matlock had his greed excited by the strategic position of this tract of land with reference to railroad building. He did not believe there were any mineral deposits on it that amounted to anything. He thought my grandfather was a pottering old fool to spend his time prospecting here. He came right out and said so, in my hearing.

"A short time before the old professor died, he made a will. He read it to me. By that will he made me his sole heir. It was witnessed, but never recorded. The document itself disappeared when the old man died and I fled the country. Without the will I can not establish my legal right to dig mines here, or even to prospect on this tract of land.

"That is the whole thing in a nutshell. You can now understand why I am scouting in secret here."

Marian spoke up at once: "You have a perfect moral right to do so. Do you think the will still exists, hidden away somewhere?"

"Yes: I believe Myra knows what became of it. But I have no object in seeking it until I positively know that there is something here worth mining."

"I see," said Marian. "But Matlock is already searching for you. How can you remain hidden?"

John's eyes twinkled as he answered: "Robin Hood and his merry men dwelt in a cave. So, too, do I. But please don't tell anybody."

"I won't. Is it near here?"

"On the other side of this very ridge, but in a secluded place hard to find. The glen over there is one of the roughest places I have ever been in. The approaches are difficult and my refuge is well masked."

But Marian was not reassured.— "This Matlock is a hideous beast," said she. "They say he would not stop short of murder."

John's only comment was an indifferent toss of the head.

"I'm told he is treacherous," she persisted. "He would stab in the back, shoot from ambush, or hire some gunman to do it for him."

"That may be so; but forewarned is forearmed."

"Why don't you go to Myra at once?"

"Do you know if she's still living?"

"I think so. She's half-sister to the old chief Degataga, whom my uncle knows very well."

Cabarrus studied the suggestion. Finally he answered: "As things are turning out, I believe I'll go and look for her."

Marian arose.— "I must be getting back to the house," she said. "Won't you come over and meet the Burbanks?"

"It would hardly do," decided Cabarrus. "For the time being, it's well they don't know I'm so near a neighbor. Matlock will soon make inquiries. For their sake, as well as my own, it's best that they can honestly say they know nothing about me."

"You're right," agreed Marian. "But this hiding out must be—"

"It's hell!" he broke in. "Makes a fellow feel like a sneak. But when I find the will there'll be a showdown."

"Good luck to you, Mr. Cabarrus," said Marian heartily.

"Why not plain John?" he asked. "We met without formalities—let's keep it up."

"All right, John," she laughed. "Come and see us in Kittuwa when I get back to town. My uncle will do everything he can for you."

"I'll come, Marian," he promised. "Meantime remember that this is Sherwood forest in the time of Robin Hood." Suiting the action to the fancy, he bowed low, with old-time courtesy, and kissed her hand.

She waved him a salute as he stood watching her go with light and nimble steps through the ancient wood.

FOURTEEN

When Marian returned to the cabin she found Tom just coming in from the woods. Sylvia had taken little Margaret down to the creek and was fishing. Marian went into the back room and busied herself with her plant collection. By and by she heard Tom's hound bay warning of someone's approach down the road. It was Matlock, riding a big black horse.

Tom met him in the yard. Matlock on horseback was a pompous figure, like an old-time colonel of militia. He spoke in a loud tone of command, as though addressing an inferior. Tom instantly resented it, giving curt answers. Marian heard every word they said.

Matlock had found no trace of his trespasser in Turkey-Fly-Up except the dead embers of his camp-fire. He wanted to know if Tom had met him or knew anything of his whereabouts.

No: Tom had not even heard of him.

That was queer. Tom ranged the woods; didn't he?

Yes: for the Unaka Company but for no one else.

"Now, see here," said Matlock, more considerately: "this fellow is dodging and hiding out. I'll give you five dollars to find him and keep an eye on him while you send me word."

"Humph," grunted Tom, "if I find him on Unaka property I'll ask to see his permit; but I ain't got no call to mix or meddle in other folk's business."

"But I'll give you ten dollars," persisted Matlock.

"Keep your money," answered Tom bluntly. "I ain't that hard pushed yit."

Matlock angrily jerked his horse's head and dashed off at a hard trot. He was a man of quick inferences and he at once suspected that Tom Burbank was lying—that he did know where the stranger was, and that he was in cahoot with him.

Tom stood scowling after the retreating figure as Marian came out on the porch. To her he said: "Yon's a man I won't have no truck with. If he has polecats to skin, let him do it himself."

"I'm told he's a sharper," said Marian.

"He ain't sharp enough to trim me," declared Tom.

Matlock urged his horse to a faster pace than the rough road warranted. He was in a hurry to get to town and set the hounds of the law after John Cabarrus.

When he came out of the woods into the old field below the ruined cabin he was espied by Youlus Lumbo from one of the near-by ridges. The woodsman gritted his teeth.

Youlus was in no happy mood. Things had gone wrong. All signs had failed. Some evil thing was haunting him with malicious zeal to thwart every move he made. The charms he had used to gain his ends were impotent. Some stronger magic was at work against him.

That prospector, now—the devil was in him. Youlus had watched him cooking supper after his cruise in the woods; had heard him contentedly humming to himself and mocking the owls and gathering wood for a three-days camp. He had seen the fellow go to bed. He knew just where to find him in the morning.

But when morning came, the prospector had decamped. He had taken alarm and fled by night. He had discovered that someone was spying on him.

Youlus hunted hard before he found which way the stranger had gone out of Turkey-Fly-Up. He found the tracks in an old trail to Licklog Gap. He followed them down to the Vine place, and there he lost them in the rocky sled-road.

Naturally assuming that Cabarrus had gone on to where his car was parked, Youlus still followed. But those damned Terhunes denied that the man was anywhere about, and they grinned in Lumbo's face. They actually favored a furriner before and against their own neighbor, who was mountain-born and had mountain rights. A witch's curse be on their heads!

Then Youlus went to Kittuwa, saw Doc. Terry, and, just as an immense fortune came within his reach, Matlock, the misbegotten beast, broke in and ruined everything!

Now the whole country would know there was treasure to be dug in Turkey-Fly-Up. The woods would be full of sneaks, prowling and snarling at each other. Lumbo's own cousins would be among them.

And Matlock, having turned against Youlus, would run him out of Turkey-Fly-Up if he showed his nose there.

But what had become of the stranger? His car was still at Terhune's. He must be back in the woods, somewhere.

Youlus had scouted hither and yon. He detected at once that Cabarrus was in the habit of covering his tracks, and that he had the devil's own knack in doing it. But shucks! the man didn't live who could keep hidden from a Lumbo by any such silly trick.

Nobody can stay in one place three days without wearing a plain track from his hide-out to where he gets water, even though he goes barefoot. And a man in the woods is bound to do some cooking. That means a wood fire, which means smoke, and smoke will rise to the sky and betray the most secret hiding-place for miles in every direction.

So Youlus took to lying out at night and going, at peep of day, to some ridge-top that gave a good outlook over the surroundings. Thence he scanned all the country—but never a wisp of smoke did he detect, other than from Tom Burbank's home.

There was something queer about all this. Did the fellow live on cheese and crackers? If so, what sort of innards had he?

Youlus had prowled over every ridge, down every branch, up every cove and dell, within a mile or so of the old cabin. He found, for his pains, not a single footprint, not a chip from the stranger's hunting axe, not so much as a clipped twig.

Yes: he had searched everywhere save in Dog-eater Hollow. Ugh! that place. Nobody ever went there, even on the sunniest day—not even the sang hunters. The place notoriously was haunted.

Once, indeed, a crew of surveyors traversed Dog-eater Hollow, because they had to, in retracing a property line. They reported that the place was a devil's nest: so steep on all sides that one could mighty nigh stand up straight and bite the ground. It was jam full of brush and thorny vines, littered with broken rocks, impassable save by cutting one's way, foot by foot. Nobody but the devil himself could camp there.

Anyway, no smoke ever rose out of Dog-eater Hollow.

So all his skill in woodcraft, of which Youlus was inordinately vain, had been set at naught. The stranger might have been a wraith, for all the traces he left behind him.

The strain of perplexity was beginning to tell on Youlus. He no longer slept well in the woods. He would start up from uneasy slumber and come wide awake with a horror clutching at his vitals. In broad day he was forever casting quick glances from side to side, as if in a snake-infested place. Often, when on the march, he would, whirl and look backward, fearing something evil that might be sneaking up behind. He was jumpy at sudden noises, as when a dead branch cracked overhead. His face was haggard. His left eye got to twitching all the time and nothing he could do would stop it.

One morning, as he perched on a hill-top looking for smoke, a solitary raven, like a prodigious crow, flew over him and lit on a tree two hundred yards away. That was odd—it was ominous—for ravens are seldom seen below the 5,000-foot level, in the Smokies, or where the spruce and balsam zone begins. The raven squawked and scolded Youlus from afar and cackled with shrill mocking laughter, as though taunting and daring him to shoot.

That was a bad sign—very, very bad!

Last night, in a series of troubled dreams, Cabarrus had appeared to Youlus. It seemed the prospector was hiding in the woods near Tom Burbank's place and there was a girl carrying him rations. She was the same girl whose horse Cabarrus had caught below the old ruined cabin.

That seemed plausible enough. It would explain the absence of telltale smoke; for evidently the girl was carrying cooked rations to her lover and so he had no need of a fire.

The more Youlus studied this message from dreamland, the more he became convinced that his good genii had returned and were pointing out the way. Let him watch the girl and she would unwittingly lead him to the man.

So he got to haunting the woods in the neighborhood of Tom Burbank's cabin. But on the morning of the second day he saw Tom saddle old Jaybo. The girl came out, chatted a while with Sylvia, kissed little Margaret, mounted the mule and rode off down the creek, with Tom striding on ahead.

"They're gwine to Kittuwa," thought Youlus. "But she ain't tuk her yarb box nor nothin' with her: so she's aimin' to come back agin. There's a rat in the meal. Begod, I'll foller and see *now* what they're up to."

Tom and Marian traveled the old road along the creek. Youlus cut across the mountain to the Vine trail and so got home half an hour before

Jaybo came splashing through the ford at the Lumbo settlement. He watched Tom and Marian out of sight, then saddled his own "ridin' critter" and followed them on to town.

Marian had decided to prolong her visit with the Burbanks. So she went to Kittuwa for more clothing and to make other arrangements for the purpose.

As soon as she got back to the Fieldings she told her uncle and aunt what she had learned from John Cabarrus. The old colonel stalked back and forth, talking rapidly with both hands and tongue, chuckling over his "little Jack" who had turned out so well.

"That boy's all right! Ay gad, he's got it in him! He'll make good! But he must drop that prospecting at once and get busy seeking the will. I'll send word to Degataga and find out where Myra Swimming-Deer is to be found."

As it turned out, he was saved that trouble. The next morning an old sedan drew up at the curb before the Fielding home and John himself inquired for the colonel. The old man seized John's hand in both of his own.

"Lord bless us all!" he cried. "If here isn't that runaway scamp come home again. Take that arm-chair, you prodigal, and we'll kill the fatted calf! They say you've been out in the Smokies eating your own cooking. That's enough punishment for any sin, by Jove, and you've got to stay here, now, for a square meal!"

And so he rattled on, clapping the young man on the shoulder, asking questions faster than John could answer, cheering him on, promising every assistance in his power. The two had been in close conference for an hour when Marian came in from a shopping trip and found her uncle and Cabarrus cheek by jowl. John had changed from his rough woodland garb and he was quite presentable.

After a midday dinner of rural amplitude, John invited Marian to go with him to Degataga's home.

"Good luck!" she cried. "I've been wanting to see the Indians. Hope they're not distressingly civilized."

"Don't worry," advised the colonel. "Two-thirds of those Cherokees on Lufty are full-bloods. Some of the older ones can't speak English. But Degataga himself is well educated. He uses as good English as I do. He ranks as a statesman among his people and is well thought of in Washington."

Marian's aunt, sensing a change of weather, insisted that she take a raincoat. All morning there had been billowy white clouds drifting high in the sky, with soft airs and every indication of fair weather; but now there came darker masses, marshalled from the horizon in the north, east and west, slowly making toward each other like armies converging from three directions.

Little streamers and wisps of spindrift clouds, detached like scouts, went scurrying on ahead, shifting hither and yon as if uncertainly seeking something. Gradually the heavy battalions drew together, merged and became denser, changing to a dull gray. The earth fell into shadow.

The car sped on up the highway to the Lufty River and there turned north on a dirt road that led to the Indian school. Degataga lived off to one side, on Soco Creek, a tributary of the Lufty. The car turned east over a bridge to gain the Soco road.

Then, out of a gap in the mountains to the northward, came a dark and sullen cloud, charging down upon the Lufty valley, with curling edges of white frothing along its margin. The air chilled and the woods awoke with sound of leaves aflutter. All else was ominously still.

"I hope we may reach Degataga's house before the rain comes," said John. "Your uncle told me that I can't drive the car up the rough by-road that leads to it. We must walk nearly half a mile."

Presently the dark cloud spread around and overhead, covering all the sky, save that in its rear loomed the dead gray of far-off driving rain. The wall of mountains in the west was blotted out of the picture. Still the heavens were hushed and there was no wind.

At a stony lane that ran up along a brawling brook John parked the car. They climbed out and started afoot for Degataga's home. They were within sight of it when suddenly out of the southwest there came a huge ball of cloud, wickedly green and charged with fury. There was a blinding flash, an ear-splitting thunderblast, and they were almost thrown to the ground by the violence of a great surge of wind. Then the rain came down in sheets and they were drenched and buffeted about as though the cloud had burst overhead and dropped all its water at once.

Staggering and almost breathless, but still gaily cheering each other, they waded ankle-deep through a muddy torrent that swept down the pathway. At last they gained the porch, stumbled up its steps, and beat upon the closed door of Degataga's cabin.

For a space they were not heard above the uproar of the storm; but presently the door opened. A startled Indian maid stared at them as if they were apparitions. Then she bade them come in, closed the door tightly against the tempest, and gave them chairs while she went into the kitchen and called to an old squaw to hurry and build a fire to dry their clothes.

Marian had to take off her shoes and stockings, and Cabarrus his coat. So there they sat, dripping water all over the floor, and barefoot Marian laughed as if it were the greatest sport in the world.

Soon the wind and the roaring ceased and they could hear each other without shouting. The Indian girl came back to the front room and Marian told her who they were and whom they had come to seek.

"My grandfather, he will be here soon," said the girl. "He can find Myra."

"What is your name?" asked Marian.

"Kamama," answered the girl, with soft vowels sounding like a lullaby.

"That is so musical, Kamama! What does the name mean?"

"Butterfly," she interpreted, posing airily. She was a pretty maid, a rare type of Indian beauty, and she well knew it.

"Exquisite!" declared Cabarrus. "The name fits you."

"But it means elephant, too," laughed Kamama.

"Elephant!" quoth he. "In the name of absurdity, where's the connection?"

"I don't know; but here comes my grandfather. He knows all the old things and he can tell you."

An aged Indian, tall and dignified, dressed in neat black, came toward them from an inner room, peering quizzically at the bedraggled visitors, but with a pleasant smile of welcome on his lips.

Cabarrus introduced Marian as a niece of Colonel Fielding of Kittuwa.

"I'm glad to meet a relative of Colonel Fielding," said the chief. "He's an old and very dear friend of mine. And you?" he asked, turning to Cabarrus.

"My name is Cabarrus," said the young man, shaking hands.

"Mine is Degataga," said the Indian. He pronounced the syllables slowly and distinctly, *Day*-ga-*taw*-ga, accenting the first and third, giving the *aw* a deep sound, as a white man would pronounce "law" if his mouth were opened as widely as it can go in that position.

"Kamama has puzzled me," said Cabarrus. "She says her name means butterfly, but that it also means elephant. How do you explain that?"

"Very simply," replied the chief. "The Indians never saw an elephant till a traveling circus came this way. An elephant stopped at a ford and sucked up water in his trunk. He squirted the water into his mouth and then flapped his big ears. The Indians cried *'kamama'* because a butterfly has a trunk that it sucks up honey with, and the elephant's ears are shaped somewhat like a butterfly's wings. They knew nothing else to compare this big thing with."

"Who but an Indian ever would have thought of that?" exclaimed Marian. "But all your names are so interesting! My uncle tells me that your name means Two-in-One."

"It is more than that," explained the chief. "Degataga means Two-persons-stand-together-but-their-hearts-are-one-as-if-they-had-but-one-body."

"All that sentence compressed into a word of four syllables!" cried Marian in astonishment.

"Yes. In Cherokee, much can be said with little breath. But the whites get such things badly mixed. There was Wasituna, the boy who was spared from execution when his father, Tsali, and his uncles, were killed by General Winfield Scott to cow the other Cherokees at the time they were driven west. The whites called him 'Washington,' thinking that Wasituna was the Indian way of saying Washington. But it is not so. Wasituna is Cherokee and it means Log-lying-on-the-ground-pointing-straight-away-from-you. The whites, when they try to use Indian names, make a mess of sound and sense. In history we read of a Sioux chief called Young-man-afraid-of-his-horses. That would be a coward. Anybody would laugh at such a fool name. But the real meaning is Young-man-whose-very-horses-are-feared. So he himself must have been a terror."

Cabarrus now announced his mission, first explaining who he was and how he had known Myra in the past; but for the present he did not mention the will.

He had no sooner stated that he was a grandson of old Professor Dale than Degataga sprang to his feet, with eyes glistening. The chief placed his hand on the young man's head, softly stroking his hair and looking him intently in the face.

"Then you are doubly welcome here," said he with a touch of

fondness. "Abelard Dale was a kind and understanding friend of the Cherokees. Any kin of his is our friend, and particularly the little Jack of whom Myra was so fond."

With much feeling, Cabarrus inquired if Myra still lived among the Cherokees.

"Yes," answered Degataga: "far up in the Big Cove; where no car can go. I will send a message to her. She will come to see you. Myra lives high up on a mountainside, with only a foot-path leading to her cabin. She and her crippled son stay there by themselves. They have no horse. But she would walk three days to see you."

"No," decided Cabarrus: "I will get a horse and go to her myself, tomorrow morning, if you will find me a guide."

"Let me be your guide," offered the chief. "I have two horses and you need not hire any."

"So much the better," agreed John, "if you can spare the time. Shall we say nine o' clock."

"Yes," agreed the chief. Then turning to Marian, he told her he was very sorry they had got so wet.— "But I hope you'll stay and have supper with us. I think my wife is a pretty good cook."

Degataga called the old squaw from the kitchen. She was a short, stout woman in bright calico, with the inevitable apron, and a scarlet bandanna bound round her head, not as a turban such as old negresses wear, but with one doubled end hanging free down her back. She had a grave but amiable expression.

He spoke to her in Cherokee and she answered in a crooning tone. Their lips were but slightly parted and seemed not to move. They spoke so low that it was almost a whisper. That seemed odd to the whites; but Indians habitually converse in an undertone, unless excited by some emotion. Their ears seem to be keener than ours.

The old squaw smiled at her visitors and said "How do?"

"She does not speak much English," explained Degataga.

"Huh!" interrupted Kamama. "She can talk it better than she lets on. She's bashful." And Kamama laughed.

"You have a comfortable home here," remarked Marian, "and it is so quaint!"

It was a log house, better built than the average, with stone chimneys showing neat handiwork. The floors were bare but clean. The simple furniture was all home-made out of trees that had grown nearby. The low chairs had seats made of white oak splints. A bed in the corner was spread with blankets woven on an Indian loom and a coverlet gay with native needlework. On the wall were crayon enlargements from old portraits. In another frame was an engrossed parchment, yellow with age, which Marian read aloud. It was a testimonial from President Van Buren to the Chief Yonaguska or Drowning-Bear.

"My great-grandfather," explained Degataga simply.

The storm had settled into a steady rain that beat upon the house with dull monotony. Degataga whiled away the time with stories of whites and Indians in the olden time. They were historically true, yet strange and thrilling as any romance.

"What a shame," exclaimed Marian, "that the two races should have so misunderstood each other!"

"Yes," sighed the chief. "It seems so hard for the whites to tell one kind of Indian from another. There are all sorts of characters among us, good and bad, just as among yourselves. It has always been so. We Indians are neither all-devil nor all-saint: we are just human."

"It seems to me," said John, "that some of our myths run back to a common source. Anyway, the tales that Myra used to tell me appealed to me just as Mother Goose and Uncle Remus stories are loved by children everywhere."

"O Degataga!" cried Marian, "won't you tell us some of those Indian stories?"

"After supper," he agreed, smiling. "It is ready now."

They went out into the kitchen and sat around an uncovered oaken table that was set with simple white crockery and steel table ware. A platter of fried chicken was flanked by dishes of potatoes and beans and squash and sweet corn. Kamama had added a touch with a salad of crisp watercress fresh from the spring branch.

The corn bread was excellent, the butter sweet and firm. There was a surprising variety of jellies and preserved fruits, not less than a dozen kinds, some of them strange to the guests and of piquant flavor, made from service-berry, wild gooseberry and wild plum. For dessert they had a pie or cobbler made of tart and juicy buckberries.

Neither the old squaw nor Kamama sat at table with them. Marian tried to get Degataga's wife to eat with them and let the girl wait on the table; but the red dame only laughed and said, "Na, na," in a way that meant it was good manners for her, too, to serve and wait.

The guests lingered over the meal in keen enjoyment. When finally they arose and went into the front room it was growing dark.

"In an hour or two," said Degataga, "the rain will cease. It is the time of the full moon and you may yet have a pleasant drive home."

He did not begin his story-telling until the women had finished in the kitchen. Then Kamama came and sat beside the guests, but the old woman retired to a corner.

FIFTEEN

The violence of the storm was spent. All was quiet once more save for the beating of the rain and the eddying of wind among the trees. Night was falling. Degataga lit a pine knot and stood it against a backlog in the fireplace. The resinous wood blazed like a torch, casting a ruddy glow over the group of four who sat by the chimney; but the rear of the cabin room, where the old squaw sat in silence, was still a murk of weird shadows shifting as the hearth-fire danced.

Degataga spoke.

"When I was a boy, this is what the old men told me.—

"In the beginning there was no fire, and the world was cold, until the Thunders sent their lightning and put fire in the base of a hollow tree. Then men had fire to warm themselves in winter and to cook their meat.

"There are little Thunders in all the cliffs and mountains. At the waterfalls you can hear them always talking for such as can understand. But they are not the ones who sent the fire.

"The great Thunders are Kanati (Kah-*nah*-tee) and his two sons, who live far in the west above the sky vault, in the Darkening Land. It is Kanati who rules the whirlwind and the hurricane. He is kind when we pray to him, but when he is angry the earth shakes with uproar and the lightning flashes.

"His sons are the Little Men, though some call them the Thunder Boys. They are magicians and full of mischief. When we hear low rolling thunder in the west we know it is the Little Men conjuring and plotting together.

"Long, long ago, when the Sun climbed every day up along the sky arch on her way to the west, she used to stop for dinner at her daughter's house in the middle of the sky.

"The Sun hated the people on the earth because they would not look straight at her. She said to her brother, the Moon, 'Those men are mean and deceitful: they can't look me in the face.' But the Moon laughed and said, 'I like them: they always smile pleasantly at me.'

"This angered the Sun all the more; for she was proud of her brilliant rays and despised the mild glow of the Moon. So she said, 'I will send a sickness to destroy those squinting creatures.'

"Then the Sun sent down burning heat from a sky that was cloudless and bright as brass. Every day it continued so. The forest withered and the fields parched. All the cold springs in the hills dried up. The people were stricken with a great fever, but there was only warm river water to wet their lips. So they died by hundreds, till every man had lost a friend and feared that his turn would come next.

"Then the people held a council of all the clans. They besought their shamans, the priest-doctors, to save them from the Sun's wrath.

"But the shamans could not make medicine strong enough to prevail against the great enemy in the sky. So they said to the people, 'The greatest magicians of all are the Little Men. We must ask them to help us.' And they did so.

"Then the Little Men answered, 'The only way to save yourselves is to kill the Sun.' So the Little Men changed a certain man into a spreading-adder and another into a copperhead. They sent them up to the midday point in the sky, where they were to lie in wait and bite the Sun when she stopped at her daughter's door.

"But the spreading-adder was blinded when the Sun drew near, and the copperhead got scared and ran away. So they came back with nothing done.

"Still the people kept dying from the heat, and once more they prayed to the Little Men. This time the Little Men turned a warrior into the great Uktena (Ook-*tay*-na), which is an enormous snake with horns on its head and terrible strength in its coils. They changed another man into a rattlesnake. And they sent these two against the Sun.

"Everybody thought the Uktena was the champion to do the work, for he was the awfulest looking thing in the world. But the rattlesnake was so eager to distinguish himself that he hurried ahead and coiled up in front of the house before the Uktena could get there.

"When the Sun's daughter opened the door to look out for her mother, who was still in the distance, the rattlesnake got excited and sprang and bit her, and she fell dead in the doorway. The rattlesnake, all puffed up with pride, forgot to wait for the Sun but had to run back and tell everybody what he had done. And the big Uktena was so angry at the way his chance had been spoiled that he went back, too.

"When the Sun found that her daughter was dead, she clothed herself in dark clouds and mourned for a long time. So the heat was dispelled and the people were well and happy again.

"But the Uktena sulked and was jealous because the people revered the rattlesnake as their deliverer. His grudge festered within him till he became so venomous that if a man so much as looked at him it was death— not to the man himself but to his family, and that made it all the worse.

"So they prayed again to the Little Men that they should remove this curse from them. And the Little Men carried the Uktena far away to the Darkening Land, where, some say, they use him to conjure with.

"But the great Uktena left behind him a brood of his own kind that are almost as big and dangerous as himself. These hide in deep pools of the river, and about caves and lonely passes of the mountains. Such places the Cherokees call by a name that means Where-the-Uktena-stays. No one will go near those spots without first making medicine, and then only in fear and with great caution."

Degataga ceased and stared silently at the embers.

Marian sighed, as a child might do at the end of a breathtaking fairy tale.

But Kamama broke out in startling rude laughter.—

"Applesauce!" she exclaimed, turning to her grandfather. "So that is one of the *old things* you think so much of!"

She meant only to show off her disdain of old-fogyism; but a curse would have sounded less profane than her impudent slang.

Cabarrus had been in a brown study: but now, shocked out of his meditation, he turned to rebuke the girl. Before he could frame words there was a cry out of the darkness behind them. The old squaw, hitherto mute and unnoticed, was advancing on Kamama with menace in her eyes, shrilling something in Cherokee. The girl, scared by what she had thoughtlessly evoked, but bound to hold her own before visitors, arose in defiance.

But Degataga raised his hand, palm outward, and the old woman backed into her corner, silenced. "*Kamama* has been to school," said the chief, "and she has learned much. She is a flapper Indian." And he laughed. But there was a queer glint in his black eyes and the visitors wondered what it betokened.

Cabarrus, to relieve the tension, asked an abrupt question: "What does Uktena mean?"

The chief answered: "It is from *akta*, eye. *Aktati* means to examine closely. Uktena is the Keen-eyed-One."

"Has anyone ever seen an Uktena here in the mountains or in the pools?"

"Yes: men have blundered on them at times. It was their evil fate. They did not die, but some of their kinsmen did."

"What does the thing look like?"

"Those who know say that it is a monster snake, as big around as a tree trunk. It has horns on its head, and a bright blazing jewel in its forehead that we call Ulunsuti (Oo-lun-*suh*-tee), which means transparent. The snake has spots of color along its whole length. It can not be killed except by shooting in the seventh spot from its head, because its heart and life are under that spot."

"Did any man ever kill an Uktena?"

"Many daring warriors have tried; for he who should get the blazing jewel from the snake's forehead would become the greatest wonder-worker of the tribe. But all who attacked the Uktena were so dazed by the brilliant light that they were drawn to the monster as by a charm, and they were killed and eaten. All of them but one."

"Ah, then one man did succeed? Tell us about him."

"That is just one of those old things again," evaded the chief. He shot a shrewd glance at Kamama, who now sulked by herself, with her chin in her hands.

"So is the *Iliad* one of the 'old things,'" answered Cabarrus; "but to my taste it is better than jazz."

Kamama bridled at the reproof. Marian put out her hand and stroked the Indian girl's hair.

"Who was the man?" persisted Cabarrus.

"It was a long time ago," said the chief, "when the Shawnees roomed in the Great Valley to the west of the Smoky Mountains. All of the Shawnees were magicians, and some of them excelled all other tribes in the power of their medicine. It was the Shawnee Prophet, you remember, who preached all the northern tribes into that fierce war with the whites in which his brother, the great warrior Tecumseh, distinguished himself.— But this that I tell you about was long before that.

"We Cherokees were at war with the Shawnees. In one of our battles we captured a great medicine-man of the Shawnees whose name was Agan Unitsi. They had tied him to the stake for torture when he said that if they spared his life he would go and slay the Uktena, take the great shining jewel from its forehead, and bring this wonder-working charm to our people, so that we should have a magician even greater than himself.

"They warned him that it was certain death to meet the Uktena in battle; but he only answered that his medicine was strong and he was not afraid. So they untied him and sent him forth, with runners to watch and report what might befall him."

Degataga paused and wiped his brow. The strain of translating was severe. Marian wondered at his facility. She did not know that Degataga had often served as interpreter in court. He was a professional "linguister," as the old-fashioned mountaineers call it.

"The story of the Shawnee magician's adventures in trailing the Uktena is too long to tell now. It is enough that he finally surprised it asleep, and killed it, and brought the magic jewel to the Cherokee council, and offered it to them as the price of his life. They were awed by his mighty deed and by the proof that he held in his hand. So they took him into the tribe. He became the greatest medicine man of the Cherokees. He has descendants here to this day."

The chief had finished. For a time the four of them sat brooding before the fire. Then Cabarrus lit his pipe and spoke.—

"Strange," said he, "how the serpent or dragon figures in all mythologies: Chaldean, Assyrian, Phoenician, Egyptian, Hebrew, Greek, Roman, Teutonic, Norse, British—all over the world, and in all times, from the beginning. The slaying of the monster was the crowning achievement of heroes: Perseus and Hercules, St. Michael and St. George, Siegmund and Siegurd, Beowulf and Arthur, Tristram and Lancelot, all were killers of dragons. And the jewel in the serpent's head—how it persists as a talisman in myth and fable! We are all one under the skin."

"Yes," answered the chief. "I can see points in our old Indian religion that resemble some things in the Bible. But the whites will not have it so. Their missionaries never tried to understand us. We were just heathen in their sight."

"I like pretty fables," said Kamama, seeking to win back her footing, "but these snake stories give me the creeps. There's one thing, though, Grandad, that you haven't told.— What became of the Ulunsuti? Did you ever see it?"

All felt the challenge in her words.

Degataga arose as with sudden determination.— "I have seen it," he answered. "And now, my friends, if you can amuse yourselves for a little while in my humble home, I will attend to some business. It will not take me long."

He opened the door and strode out into the night.

The rain had ceased. A round moon gleamed through a break in the clouds for a minute; then again it was overcast by the followers of the storm.

SIXTEEN

When the chief was gone, Marian turned to Cabarrus as if to a referee.—

"Did you notice how earnest and even reverent Degataga grew when he warmed up to his story? I wonder—" She hesitated, then continued: "He was educated in a northern college. He uses as good English as I do. He's a member of the Baptist church and sometimes preaches to the Indians. Surely it can't be that he *believes* in this Uktena thing!"

"Why not?" asked Cabarrus indifferently. He tilted back his chair and blew a ring of smoke into the air.— "You've heard of John Wesley, founder of the Methodist church," he suggested. "Well, he was a classical scholar, an Oxford man; yet he believed in ghosts. He taught that nightmare, epilepsy, insanity and other ills were caused by devils, real devils, that entered into men to possess them, and that these devils were the gods of the heathen. He declared, in so many words, that to give up a belief in witchcraft was to give up the Bible."

"Oh, but that was long ago."

"It was as late as the American Revolution. And today I know Harvard graduates who would go without dinner rather than sit thirteen at table. Lots of educated whites are spiritualists. Many have faith in portents and divination. Let's not take our own up-to-dateness too seriously. 'All the world's a stage,' and we are only in the first act."

"But this is all so silly!" cried Kamama.

"I don't find it so. This Indian belief that everything around us is alive, that rocks and stars have souls, takes hold on the imagination. It's not science, but it's darned good poetry, for all that."

Kamama touched Marian's hand and sought to divert her with light prattle. For a time the white girl was rather grateful, not relishing the spooky atmosphere of the place. But she could not rid herself of a feeling that something uncanny was in the air. Degataga must be up to something.

Twenty, thirty, forty minutes passed. Cabarrus was tilted back in his chair, deep in reverie, his hands clasped behind his head. Marian, with wits gone wool-gathering, was unresponsive to Kamama's efforts. So the Indian maid herself fell silent, bored but nervous, yawning and fidgeting by turns.

A lonesome dog howled on a nearby hill. A horned owl hooted in the deep woods. The old squaw crooned to herself in a low moaning tone. A cold wind came in through cracks between the floor boards. Marian shivered and studied her finger nails.

It was nine o'clock when a fice that guarded the porch let out a yap or two announcing his master's return. Degataga entered, bearing a small parcel, something wrapped in folds of soft fawnskin that was old and stained. As he closed the door, the little dog sprang off the porch and ran toward the stable, barking.

Degataga was wan. Sweat stood on his brow as if he had been climbing or going at a run. He took position in the middle of the room, as if to address them. When he spoke, it was without prelude, as though he were continuing a discourse.—

"Through all the troubles of the Cherokees, through defeat and exile, the sacred Ulunsuti has always been preserved by our Eastern Band. The chief medicine-man of his time was its custodian, and none but he knew where it was hidden, save only the one appointed to be his successor.

"It was supposed to have been lost at the time of the Removal, when most of the Cherokees were driven out of this country into exile in the wild country beyond the Father of Waters. That was when my own ancestors and a few hundred of their neighbors fled before the American army and hid out in the roughs of the Great Smoky Mountains, where many starved to death, rather than give up their old home.

"Long years passed. The Eastern Band of Cherokees, as we are called, was reestablished here. Once when a ball of fire fell from the sky upon a high peak of the Smokies our people said, 'It is the Ulunsuti of the Uktena come again!' And many went seeking it; but it was not there.

"When my grandfather, a great shaman, felt his last sickness coming, he led me, a youth, to a rock-house, a shallow cave, in the wildest and most lonesome part of the Smoky Mountains, and there, pointing to a spot where something was sealed away in a dry pocket of the rock, he told me what was to be found when the proper time should come."

Degataga paused. He looked over and beyond them as to something far away. Then, in a high-pitched monotone and with sudden vehemence he exclaimed: "It is death to uncover the Ulunsuti until the ceremony has been performed.—

"Yu! Sge! Usunuli hatunganiga..."

He began a sacred formula in the Cherokee tongue, speaking earnestly as to some personage invisible but present in the room.

Cabarrus leaned forward, listening intently. Kamama shrank back into a corner. The old squaw, silent in the rear of the room, followed the performance with keen beady eyes.

Marian heard faintly the little dog barking in the stable yard. Then it yelped as if hurt.

The conjuration went on. All eyes were riveted on Degataga who had passed into a state of ecstasy in which he seemed unconscious of his surroundings. At times he spoke sharply, emphatically, in a commanding tone; again, pleadingly in a weird minor. Then he would chant, using the same word over and over, accenting it strongly on the last syllable, with an explosive issue of his breath that seemed to start from his midriff.

"Yu-ha-HI, yu-ha-HI, yu-ha-HI, yu-ha-HI—YU!"

Marian sat facing the one small window of the room. Degataga's head chanced to be between her and the window. As she watched the old chief, her eyes gradually registered a shadow that moved at the window. Startled, she looked now beyond the chief and saw a face press up against the glass. It was very dark outside and she could not tell whether the face was white or red; but it was a man's.

Then quickly the face withdrew. Yet Marian was sure that someone was still spying on them from the dark background, where he could see through the window without being seen. Tensely she sat watching the window and she was on the point of giving an alarm—

Then something befell so startling that it erased all thought of a spy from the girl's mind.—

Degataga removed the wrapping from the object he had in his hand. He held the thing forth.

It was an egg-shaped orb of crystal, so large as to fill the palm of his hand, and it stood full four inches high. From its center there blazed a pure white light of dazzling radiance. Then, as the chief lifted the crystal on his fingers and slowly revolved it, the light changed in rotation to every color of the rainbow and a thousand arrows of prismatic fire shot from the glowing orb.

"My God, what a diamond!" exclaimed Kamama under her breath.

"Oh! Oh!" cried Marian.

Cabarrus strained forward in his chair, eyes staring, mouth pursed in critical inspection. He had divined that some curio would be revealed: an odd-shaped stone or a colored one— a geode of agate, for instance, or perhaps a garnet or a sapphire— but he was struck dumb by this amazing spectacle.

Degataga bade the squaw clear off the top of a small table. He set it near them, facing the firelight. Then he covered the stand with a black cloth and reverently laid the crystal on it.

"Look, but do not touch," he commanded.

Cabarrus, recovered from his surprise, arose and went round and round the Ulunsuti. He saw that the stone had no facets to reflect brilliant light, no angles to account for its prismatic fire. It was smoothly rounded, as if cut *en cabochon* like a cat's-eye gem or a moonstone.

Plainly the body of the great stone egg was of rock-crystal; but it was shot through, in all directions, with long hair-like crystals of brilliant color, varying from deep red to reddish-brown.

Fleches d' amour," said he to himself.

But what puzzled him was something in the center of the orb. It seemed to be a cavity, about an inch long, but not empty—nay, filled with some liquid that was colorless and perfectly transparent. It was from this center that the chief radiance emanated when the Ulunsuti was viewed at certain angles with reference to the source of light. And distributed in other parts of the stone were tiny spots of a like nature, from pinhead size to that of birdshot, and each of these glittered with varying colored fires, changing from one hue to another as one walked around the orb.

Often Marian had noticed on their lawn at home, when the morning sun struck the dewdrops that clung to the blades of grass, that the drops sparkled with intense light—white, green, yellow, red—changing color as the angle of the sunlight shifted. And so did these spots in the Ulunsuti.

Degataga now went to talking in English, low-toned and reverent.

Marian did not know what the man was saying, for she was fascinated by this wondrously beautiful and awe-inspiring thing. If Cabarrus listened, he gave no sign. As for Kamama, she sat rigid, spellbound, gazing into the crystal's depths.

So for ten minutes; and then the Indian girl strangely drew their attention.—

"I see little people moving!" she exclaimed.

"Where?" asked Cabarrus.

"There—there, in the Ulunsuti!"

"You mean around it?"

"No, no: inside it."

"Why, Kamama, there is nothing there."

"But, I tell you, there *is*. I see them as plain as I do my own fingers."

"You imagine it."

"I do *not* imagine it. They are *real*. Look at them: there they go!"

"Kamama, look at me," commanded Cabarrus.

The girl turned and looked him straight in the eye. Her own eyes were frankly puzzled, but they were as bright and intelligent as ever. Plainly she was in her proper senses.

"Don't you believe me!" she asked.

"I believe you thought you saw those things, but it was a hallucination,"

"Oh, you think I have no sense!" said the girl, frowning.

"Look again," suggested Marian.

Kamama again peered into the crystal. She was no whit afraid. She was evidently sincere. In a moment her eyes glistened with excitement. "There they are, still moving about!"

"Like pictures at the movie show?"

"No: all in their real colors. They are real people."

"Do you know any of them?"

"No."

"What do they look like?"

"They are Indians, men, dressed for hunting—no, for war! They are half-naked, with feathers in their hair and moccasins on their feet. Some have guns and some bows and arrows."

"You must be dreaming."

"I am no such thing! I'm as wide-awake as you are. Look and see for yourselves."

Marian looked over the girl's shoulder into the crystal. All she beheld was a clear white light in the center of the orb and scintillations from the colored hair-crystals that radiated outward from the pellucid core.

"I see nothing, Kamama," said Marian rather severely.

"But I still see the little men as plain as day. They are marching. It is a war party....Now they've gone, and there's nothing but a rock-cliff and trees and ferns....No: here come others. There's an old woman with a basket that has something alive in it. And a naked man with a spear strung with scalps. And a wolf following. And a big black bird in the air."

Kamama sat with her back to the fire, which had died down till it cast only a dim light, and the Ulunsuti, instead of flashing, as it had before, was now like a globe of glass with fine striae of bright color glittering around the core.

Marian turned away, shaking her head. "Imagination!" she murmured to herself. But Kamama's quick ear caught the sarcastic word, and she picked her up on it.—

"You think I'm making this up; but I'm no such fool! I'm as much surprised at what's going on, in there, as you are."

"That doesn't sound like hypnotism," said Cabarrus openly. "And I'll be hanged if she isn't chewing gum!"

Degataga had been standing aside, silent, with arms folded across his chest. He now pressed close to Kamama and laid a hand gently on her shoulder. His face was radiant, as with beatific vision. It was the old man, and not the girl, who looked like one in a trance. He had been under intense mental strain. His face and his bearing showed it. He had worked himself, with his conjurations, near to a state of ecstasy; as many white devotees do at their religious revivals.

Cabarrus naturally suspected that there might be some reality in thought transference. He speculated, half skeptically, on the possibility of waves, vibrations, maybe rays, of thought, and of minds "tuning in" together, like radios. In such case, Degataga's trained and powerful intellect might dominate the girl's and "turn her eyes inward" so that she saw whatever visions the old chief willed her to see.

And yet, was there ever a less receptive mind than Kamama's? All through the chief's story-telling she had been coldly indifferent and frankly bored. Her flippant mind, skipping like a grasshopper from one trifle to another, could fix seriously on nothing. When the Ulunsuti was actually produced, she was excited, of course; but only by the novelty and beauty of the thing. Even the vision in the crystal was, to her, only a sort of super-show, wonderful, but soon to be forgotten among other diversions. There she sat, now, lustily chewing gum!

No: Cabarrus could not bring himself to believe that telepathy had brought this thing about. Was it not more likely that her own subconscious mind was playing her some strange trick?

The girl was sincere; he had no doubt of it. The vision in the crystal was no play of her own fancy. Her conscious mind had nothing to do with framing it, but only reported what it observed. Imagination, no matter how powerful, can not create a picture so vivid, so correct in all the minutiae of reality, as to deceive the individual himself and make him believe that the thing he sees is real. But the subconscious?

Well, what is it we actually see with? The eyes? No: they are only lenses to transmit rays of light along the nerve channels to the brain. The brain is the sensitized plate in the camera where the picture is received and developed, visualized. Might it not be, under certain unusual conditions, that the optic nerves were excited by something other than light rays coming through the eye, and that real pictures of unreal things were developed in the sensitized brain cells? What do we know about the subconscious mind?

He was aroused from this queer speculation by Degataga's action. The old man was bending over Kamama and whispering something to her in Cherokee. She murmured an answer without moving her lips. The grandmother drew near. The three of them joined in susurrant council.

A change came over Kamama, as she still peered into the crystal. Her airish pertness was gone. She was awed and humble now. They kept on whispering together. Then suddenly the girl screamed, sprang upright, cried out something in her native tongue, and ran and cast herself face-downward on a bed, covering her eyes and sobbing with the vehemence of hysteria.

The old squaw followed, throwing her arm around the girl and crooning to soothe her. Degataga took the crystal from the table and wrapped it up in the fawnskin. Then he turned to his guests, without any explanation, and simply said: "I must go back, now, to the mountain."

Cabarrus answered with quick decision: "We, too, must be going." He opened the door. "The clouds are near all gone," he announced, "and it is bright moonlight. Marian and I can readily find our way down to the car."

Marian said a few gentle words to the old woman and Kamama. Then she spoke to the chief: "This has been a wonderful evening. We thank you so much for our entertainment, and we trust all will go well with you."

Degataga was outwardly calm, but there were new lines in his face. "I will be ready to go with you, Jack, in the morning at nine o'clock. Be sure, both of you, to come and visit us again."

The three of them went out, Degataga quietly closing the cabin door behind them. They shook hands in parting and the chief took to a side trail that led up the mountain behind the house.

The young couple went down the lane, passing on the way the stable where Degataga kept his cow and horses. On a bare spot of ground, on the far side of the stable, was a pitiful object that they did not see. It was the body of the little dog, lying stark in the moonlight, with its head crushed in.

SEVENTEEN

The wet path glistened in the moonlight. The lonesome lane was hemmed in by black masses of trees that shut off all but a strip of sky overhead. Their diffused outlines seemed to shift and reform, advance or retreat, like silent, creeping, ghostly things. Beneath the trees were still deeper shades that might conceal anything, natural or supernatural, that a strained fancy feared. A mouldy smell came from the decaying litter of the woods. An intense listening silence was over all the hills and vales.

Marian clung tightly to John's arm as they trudged down the lane. It was not simply from the risk of slipping and falling on the sleek wet clay. Her nerves had been overstrung by the unexpected turn of events in the Indian cabin. They were racked by the eeriness of the tales she had listened to, the mysterious departure of Degataga, his return with the Ulunsuti, the spying face at the window, the awesome exhibition of the magic crystal, the sudden reversion of the civilized chief to barbaric mood and conduct, the overwhelming of Kamama's pert irreverence and the hysteria of her conversion.

John felt her shivering as with cold. He pressed her hand and laughed gently with the reassurance, "Just a hop, skip and jump, now, and we'll reach the car."

"What is the Ulunsuti?" she asked, with a brave show of composure.

And John, eager to divert her mind to practical things, answered: "The body of it is colorless and perfectly transparent quartz, of a kind that we call rock-crystal. Merely as such it would not be remarkable. Fine specimens of rock-crystal have been found in these Carolina mountains; some of them huge, weighing two or three hundred pounds. But this Ulunsuti is peculiar: it has inclusions."

"What are inclusions?"

"Other substances enclosed in the quartz. You noticed the brilliant red streaks that run through a good part of the crystal."

"Yes. What are they?"

"I think they are rutile."

"What is rutile?"

"A valuable gem, for one thing; but it is more than a gem: it's an adventure that I've been hoping to meet."

"What do you mean by an adventure?"

"Rutile is a pure oxide of the rare metal titanium. It would be an exciting adventure to find titanium here in the Smoky Mountains."

"Then I hope you will find it, John. Don't you suppose the Indians picked up this Ulunsuti somewhere in the Smokies?"

"Quite likely they did. I noticed a queer thing on the buckskin wrapper when Degataga took the Ulunsuti from it. The skin had a symbol painted on it: the crude figure of a dragon. I nearly jumped out of my own skin when I saw that thing; for precisely the same figure is graven on the wall of the cave where I am camping; and the flint chisel used in carving it lay half-hidden in the dust beneath it."

"Why this is growing positively uncanny!" exclaimed Marian.

"It is sorcery for the Indians," chuckled John; "but for me it may be a bonanza. Suppose I should find a good bed of titanium ore in Nick's Nest!"

"What do you call Nick's Nest?"

He told her.

"What a romantic place it must be! I hope the sequel of your adventure will all come out like a story-book. You will be a hero, John!"

"In story-books, you know, the hero—"

"Becomes rich and famous."

"Fudge! He marries the heroine."

"Now you are getting humorous."

"Well, no spectre can daunt a humorist. I'm going after the Uktena and bushels of Ulunsutis."

"Good luck to you! And here is our car. I'm glad to be out of those shivery, ghostly woods."

They drove on down the Soco in enforced silence for a time, owing to the roughness of the road. Then, coming to a smoother stretch, John asked "Did you notice something queer in the heart of that crystal?"

"Y-yes. From some directions it blazed like a little sun; but when I stood and looked over Kamama's shoulder, the way she was looking when she saw the 'little men,' it was just a clear, colorless core, something like a lens."

"Precisely." said John. "Now Kamama happened to be sitting in such position that there were none of the red streaks between her and the core of the crystal. And the firelight had died down to an even glow. Her back was to the fire: so there was a dark background beyond the crystal and she had a clear view of the pure colorless center of the Ulunsuti. That center is hollow."

"Hollow!"

"Yes; but filled with fluid, probably water charged with carbonic acid."

"Why, that couldn't be. Water could not get inside that rock-crystal. It could as easily go through an inch or so of solid glass."

"It never got in from outside: it was always there. I fancy that the material of the crystal was originally all fluid—what we call a saturated solution. In the course of time the mineral content crystallized out, like rock candy from a thick solution of sugar. Then it formed a solid mass within the pocket of the rock bed that held the liquid. So it took partly the form of that matrix. Probably the Indians ground off any angles on the outside and then polished the orb. Well, some of the water of crystallization was left inside, free from mineral."

"Did you ever hear of such a thing before?"

"Yes. Here in North Carolina. Some countryman plowed up a stone that he thought was an emerald with small diamonds set in the midst of it. But when he took his treasure to an expert, the thing turned out to be just a chunk of greenish quartz filled with thin byssolite crystals on which were strung out small liquid-cavities that glistened in the sun like diamonds."

"Poor man! And so our Ulunsuti is scientifically explained, and *puff* goes its romantic interest! But can your coldblooded science explain Kamama?" asked Marian. "Was she just acting?"

"No: she was sincere. She told the truth, or what she took for truth."

"But she was 'seeing things.'"

"Of course she was seeing things—she didn't invent them."

"Heavens! You don't think they were real?"

John wrinkled his brow, searching for words, but finding none that would make an abstruse point clear. The best he could say was, "They had visual reality in her brain. I don't mean just a thought: I mean that in her brain a moving picture was formed that was precisely like what we see with our eyes—she couldn't tell the difference."

But Marian did not grasp that.— "I think," said she, "that Degataga put it all in her head by suggestion—call it thought-wave."

"I doubt it," objected John. "The crystal, after all, had something to do with it."

"How?"

"You've heard of crystal-gazing?"

"Oh, yes. I 've seen a back-street scryer dupe credulous people by looking into a crystal and pretending to unveil the past, foretell the future, find missing articles, and all that sort of stuff. Are you so easily taken in?"

"Bunk!" exclaimed John. "But this marvel we witnessed tonight was no common humbug. In my college we had a professor of psychology, Topping, who employed crystal-gazing in his studies of the subconscious mind. There was nothing credulous about him: he was a hard-boiled old party. The boys used to say that if Old Top could get hold of Satan's liver he'd dissect it, to see how he got that way."

"Well, what did Old Top think of crystal-gazing?"

"He said we have two minds: One, the conscious, is active only when we are awake; the other, the subconscious, never sleeps. The one is subject to our will; the other is not. Dreams are the work of the subconscious mind. It is quicker than conscious thought, being automatic. It moves instantaneously, like a released spring, in time of sudden peril, as when one jumps back from a rattlesnake. The subconscious cannot plan or invent anything; neither can it perpetrate a fraud. It has no moral restraint and no sense of the ridiculous."

"Yes: I have read that sort of thing."

"Well, once in a while, under abnormal conditions, the subconscious may play strange pranks with us, when the reasoning mind is off guard. Or the 'sub' may even overwhelm the conscious, when we are awake; and then sane people do irrational things, as, for instance, in the ecstasy of a religious revival. All humanity is subject to such disorders, in proportion to strength or weakness of mind and nerves."

"Yes; but what has crystal-gazing got to do with it?"

"Just this, and no more: it helps to lull the conscious and bring the subconscious into play. Some people—not all—can see vivid moving images in the crystal, not dreamy but real as life. Such a person can't foresee what comes next, and he is honestly surprised at what goes on in the crystal."

"I don't get you," said Marian, shaking her head. "If the pictures were not really in the crystal, then Kamama simply *must* have imagined them."

"Do you imagine your dreams?"

"Well, no."

"Can you control them?"

"No."

"Crystal-visions are like that; only they are more vivid and realistic than dreams. That may be because the conscious mind is active at the same time—looking on, as you may say. That's something altogether different from imagination."

"Very well," granted Marian. "Kamama was honest about the visions she had. But what happened to her after the old man opened up to her in Cherokee? She wasn't herself after that."

"No, she was not. When Degataga began to whisper to her, he did put things into her head. Of course, I don't know what he said; but it seemed to be something that convinced her, suddenly, that those pictures were supernatural. The moment she believed that, her good sense forsook her. Thereafter she was nothing but a tool in his hands. But that is something quite apart from crystal-gazing. That is where science stops and superstition takes control. I'm sorry it happened."

"So am I, declared Marian. "It made a fool of her."

"That isn't the worst of it," said John. "None of the Indians know what the Ulunsuti really is, as we know it. And it is not strange that even such a man as Degataga, for all his education, but with all his heritage of tradition, should believe that the Ulunsuti has some occult, supernatural power. No doubt the Indians have faith that miracles may be performed by it."

"What nonsense!" exclaimed Marian.

Cabarrus shrugged.— "Let's not be too superior," he advised. "Aren't there millions of whites who have the same faith in their own sort of sacred relics?

'Strange all this difference should be
'Twixt Tweedledum and Tweedledee.'"

"But that sort of thing is capable of stirring up trouble," observed Marian.

"Yes; but we can't help it. If we should tell the Indians the truth about their Ulunsuti, they would take us for blasphemers. That is human nature."

Marian gave a startled exclamation. In a flash there had come to her the recollection of that evil face at the cabin window. She told John about it.

He stopped the car and stared strangely at her.

"How could a spy have been there on the porch and no housedog sounded the alarm?"

"They have only one dog. It did give the alarm. You were too busy to notice it; so were the others." Then Marian told how the little dog started off into the night, barking; how it yelped as if hurt; how Degataga revealed the Ulunsuti at that moment; and how the dog was heard no more.

John bit his lip, saying, "I don't like that!"

"Nor I," said Marian.

"You are sure you saw a man's face?"

"As surely as I see yours right now; but it wasn't moonlight then: I couldn't tell whether he was a white man or an Indian."

"A redskin, doubtless," said John. "More than one Indian must know that Degataga possesses the sacred crystal. Who can tell what morbid fancies may sway them, now that he has been caught displaying their holiest magic to the whites?"

"John, he wouldn't have done that for anyone but you."

"Why just for me?"

"Because the Indians revere the memory of your grandfather. He never made fun of their old religion or tried to convert them from it. He enjoyed it as good poetry. And Degataga saw at once that you were of the same mind. You listened to his tales with respect and you told how they agreed in some ways with our own myths."

"There may be something in that; but Degataga had a more serious object."

"Meaning?"

"Don't you see? He was stung by Kamama's airs, by her ridicule of the ancient faith. She was eager to show us whites that she was up-to-date: that she was no such simpleton as to be taken in by his old-fogy mummery. So Degataga was in precisely the same position as many a fundamentalist father, nowadays, when his daughter comes home from college. Well! Was the old man to be mocked before visitors in his own house, by one of his own blood? He would show her. He would crush her infidelity. He would even show the whites, her tutors in modernism, that they still had something to learn. So he went for the Ulunsuti. And, by Jove, it worked!"

"True," agreed Marian. "But did Degataga know in advance that Kamama was susceptible to crystal-gazing?"

"No: she had never been tried. But he did know that the amazing beauty of the Ulunsuti would at least awe her into respectful attention. Then, to his astonishment and rapture, there came the miracle of Kamama's visions. For Degataga and the old squaw it could have been nothing short of a miracle. It was a direct interposition of the old Indian gods. The Thunders had come to his aid with overwhelming magic!"

"Then," said Marian— "then he went wild. That is the very word for it: wild! He stripped off his civilization in a twinkling. He flew back— back to barbarism. Oh, it's discouraging; it's shocking!"

"I don't know," demurred John lazily.

"You don't know?"

"Humph! Who are we to call it shocking?"

"Why, John Cabarrus!"

"Well, the Indian only reverted to a bit of his old-time religion, in which he had been fostered as a child. But we—the whole civilized world—we have gone back to the jungle for our music and our dances. Which is the more respectable?"

Marian bridled.— "You are always finding excuses for the Indians. Are you a pagan yourself?"

"I don't worship false gods, if that's what you mean," answered John gently. "I'm just a scientist. And yet I love poetry." He mused for a long minute and then said: "Perhaps the two traits don't go well together. Perhaps the blend makes one foolish now and then. There are times when I believe in fairies. Somehow I seem to feel that they are not far off now."

He dwelt upon her with a look of tenderness that the girl did not fail to note, for all the dimness of the moonlight. She glanced up at him with a questioning light in her eyes; then, smiling, she said: "I hope you'll always believe in them—but watch the road, John; the fairies can't steer your car."

"They may steer us both into strange new ways," he forewarned her. "'The day of high adventure is not past.'"

"It has begun," said Marian. "This trip to Degataga's: how weird and thrilling! It's more than I thought could ever happen. Just think: it's only ten days since I came to Kittuwa. I'd no thought of anything more exciting than to poke around after plants for a college herbarium. Just a commonplace girl doing prosy things. Then, out in the big woods, I stumbled on you, mooning over ruins and hunting fairies, pounding the rocks and seeking your fortune, one minute lecturing like a big wig and the next minute prattling about Robin Hood. And now, see what you've got me mixed up in! Consorting with Indians and spooks!" She gave a purling little laugh and clapped her hands.

Seriously John answered: "No commonplace girl ever would have dared go up into the wild Smokies, all alone."

Marian tossed her head as if that were nothing.

"Ever read Disraeli?" he asked.

"No. What did he know about it?"

"Everything.— When Ixion was in Heaven, the Goddess of Wisdom invited him to inscribe a stanza in her album. And he, the king of Thessaly, wrote this:

> 'I have seen the world, and more than the world:
> I have studied the heart of man, and now I consort
> with Immortals. The fruit of my tree of knowledge
> is plucked, and it is this:
> ***Adventures are to the Adventurous.***'"

EIGHTEEN

Cabarrus spent the night at a hotel in Kittuwa. In the morning he had an early breakfast, then got his car out of the garage and drove to the post-office. As he stood in the corridor reading a letter, he became aware that someone was giving him close scrutiny.

John looked up from his letter and straight into the eyes of a burly man who had planted himself directly before him. Rather he looked into one of that person's eyes, the other being cast aslant by a defect of the optic axes. Instantaneously John recognized his ancient enemy.

Matlock was about to speak, but he checked himself when John looked up, being puzzled by something in the stranger's appearance that it seemed he ought to recall but yet could not.

John regarded him with a cool stare.

"Excuse *me*," opened Matlock, with the inflection of one about to challenge or command; "but is your name Cabarrus?"

"It is," replied John.

"Have you been camping on Deep Creek?"

"I have."

"Whereabouts on Deep Creek?"

"How does that concern you?"

"You'll soon find out how it concerns me," flared Matlock. "I own the property where you've been trespassing."

"Indeed! So you think I've been committing trespass."

"I don't think. I know. You've camped in Turkey-Fly-Up."

"Is it forbidden a stranger to camp where night finds him, in that wilderness?"

"You have eyes, haven't you? Any passing stranger can see that my land is posted."

Matlock had raised his voice so high that a curious crowd was gathering. It needed only this audience to stimulate the big man's bluster.

"Right now I give you public warning," cried he, "to keep off my property. You've been digging mineral there, on the sly. I have witnesses to that effect."

Bystanders began to nudge each other, hoping to see a fight.

"I dug no mineral," answered Cabarrus smoothly; "but I did wash out some gravel to determine the geological character of the place where I spent a night."

"And you saved specimens," declared Matlock.

"Certainly. That is the habit of all geologists."

"It's a damned bad habit to practice on my land, without a permit. Now I demand every speck and grain of specimens that you took from there," shouted Matlock, shaking his finger in John's face.

"Not quite all is available," answered the young man coolly. "A spy slipped into my tent while I was gone and he stole some of it. Do you know who he was?"

"Answer me," roared Matlock. "How quick are you going to give back those specimens to me?"

"Never."

"What! You defy me!" Matlock turned to the bystanders and cried out, "Has anybody seen the sheriff?"

Someone answered: "He's gone up on Lufty. Had a hurry-call from the Indian superintendent, an hour ago."

"Young man," thundered Matlock, "I'm going straight to a magistrate and swear out a warrant for you!"

Cabarrus laughed in his face.— "Suit yourself," said he. "I'm going up Lufty now. If I meet the sheriff I'll tell him you want to see him, sir."

Several men grinned at the stranger's easy effrontery, but others looked serious and shook their heads.

Matlock dashed off to the court-house, swinging his arms with the vigor of a strong man bent on destruction.

Cabarrus pocketed his letter, walked leisurely to his car, entered it and drove away toward the Indian reservation, chuckling to himself at Matlock's failure to recognize him. He would prick that bubble of self-importance when the proper time arrived.

The road up the Lufty was strangely deserted. He passed several Indian cabins but saw no one about them. The front doors were closed. At the wayside post-office of Birdtown, kept in an isolated little store, there were none of the usual hangers-on. That was queer, thought Cabarrus, and a vague uneasiness stole over him.

Farther up the road he saw two Indians coming, but as quickly as they glimpsed his car they stepped aside into the bushes and disappeared, as though fearing to be stopped and questioned.

Within sight of the Government school grounds the road forked. He crossed a bridge to the Cherokee railway station. A few white men were clustered about a store, conversing in low tones. They stopped talking when he approached and stared curiously at him. There was not an Indian in sight.

Evidently something serious had happened—something that the local people would not discuss with a stranger.

Filled with foreboding, Cabarrus drove down the east side of the river to the Soco road and on toward Degataga's home. He found three empty cars parked where he had left his own the day before. Leaving his sedan beside them, he jumped out and hurried up the lane, anxiety spurring him on.

As he neared the house he saw a few Indians grouped about the place. Silently they moved aside as he came near, three white men were coming out of the house. One of them wore a badge on his breast and was evidently the sheriff. Another was the Indian superintendent, a Government official. They looked keenly at Cabarrus, as if wondering who he was and what he wanted.

"My name is Cabarrus," said the young man to the sheriff. "I'm a friend of Degataga. Has anything happened to him?"

"He was assaulted last night and seriously hurt."

"Is he conscious?"

"Yes; but he's very weak."

"May I see him?"

"There's the doctor: ask him."

A man with a medicine case had come out on the porch. John went to him.

"Is Degataga dangerously wounded?" he asked.

"I think he'll pull through," answered the physician. "He got a bad crack on the head from a blackjack, or something of the sort, but I don't think his skull is fractured."

"May I see him for a moment? I won't excite him."

"Yes, if it's important, but don't stay more than a minute." Cabarrus went in. Several Indian women were in the front room. Degataga lay on a bed that filled one corner of the room. His head was bandaged and his eyes were closed. As John approached the bedside Degataga opened his eyes and gave him a faint sign of recognition.

"I'm sorry you're hurt, chief," said the young man. "Do you feel much pain?"

"Not so bad now," answered Degataga weakly. "I can't go with you today, as things have turned out."

"Of course not. Do you know who attacked you?"

"No. I was struck from behind and knocked senseless, just after you folks left."

"Were you robbed?"

Degataga groaned. In a whisper he answered, "They got the Ulunsuti."

"That's bad. Did you tell the sheriff?"

"No, no. We Indians must manage this ourselves. The whites would make a mess of it. Keep it to yourself, John."

"I see. But maybe I can help, after I have talked with Myra. I shall go to see her at once."

"Stop at the boy's dormitory, up at the school. Ask for Taywa, Flying-Squirrel. He will show you the way. But don't talk about this. The Indians are scared. They think some calamity is coming."

"All right. I will go now. Soon I will come to see you again."

"Good bye, John," said the chief. "I can rest better now."

Cabarrus spoke a few words to Degataga's wife, asking her for a list of things they needed and promising to send them to her. Then he went out into the yard and overtook the sheriff as he was starting down the lane.

"There's a matter that I wish to speak to you about," said he to the officer.— "When you get back to Kittuwa you will probably hear a complaint about me from Bill Matlock. He may even have secured a warrant for my arrest. Matlock claims that I have been trespassing on his property on Deep Creek. I deny the charge. Just now I have important business to attend to, up in the mountains, and I may not be easy to reach at a given time. But I will be back in Kittuwa now and then. I am not dodging anybody. Colonel Fielding will vouch for my presence when needed."

The sheriff did not reply at once. He studied the matter, but asked no questions. Finally he said: "Well, if Matlock gets a warrant, of course I'll have to serve it. But Fielding's word is good with me; so I'll wait a reasonable time for you to show up, instead of sending deputies to scour the woods for you."

"Thank you, sheriff. There's a legal matter to be settled between Matlock and me, and I'm as keen to have it adjusted as he is."

Then abruptly the sheriff asked: "Haven't I seen you somewhere, before?"

"Not in a good many years," replied John; "but I sold papers and shined shoes in Kittuwa when I was a boy."

"I don't recall anybody by your name," said the sheriff, puzzling.

"Cabarrus is my name, all right; but here I was known as Jack Dale, after my grandfather."

"Hell's bells!" exclaimed the sheriff. "You were the kid that busted Bill Matlock's nose with a rock."

"With an axle-nut that lay in the street."

The sheriff broke out into a hearty guffaw.— "No wonder Bill wants to have you locked up."

"He hasn't recognized me; but of course he will, before long."

"Well, mind your step when he does realize who you are."

John chuckled.— "I'm letting him find out for himself. I wish you'd do the same."

"You bet I will," laughed the sheriff. "Cripes, what a joke on Bill! Going to sue you for trespass instead of for a flat nose." The officer kept on laughing till they came to their cars and drove away.

John turned northward after crossing the Lufty bridge and drove into the campus of the Cherokee school. It was vacation time and there were few children about. Amid a group of neat buildings he found the boy's dormitory and inquired for Flying-Squirrel. Someone shouted "*Tay*-wa!" and soon a good-looking full-blooded Indian of sixteen came out, walking with the elastic step and erect carriage of an athlete. He wore a pleasant smile.

"I have come from Degataga," announced Cabarrus. (Instantly the lad's face fell and became an inscrutable blank.) "He was to have taken me to Big Cove to see Myra Swimming-Deer on a matter of business; but the old man has been hurt and can not go. He recommended you as a guide. I'll hire saddle horses, if you show me where to get them, and I'll pay you two dollars for guiding me. How about it?"

"I'll go," said Taywa. "You can get horses at Morley's, a mile above here."

"Then, if you're ready, hop in," said Cabarrus.

The boy jumped in beside him and they drove off. At Morley's they got a pair of horses and left the car.

They rode ten miles up the right prong of the Lufty and then took to a narrow trail that wound and zigzagged up the steep face of a mountain, through thick woods, to a small clearing five hundred feet above the river. Here, amid some fruit trees, at the lower end of a cornfield pitched at an angle of forty-five degrees, was a log cabin of but a single room, with a narrow porch in front.

Taywa gave a signal cry, the Cherokee equivalent of "Hello."

A short, stout, middle aged squaw appeared in the doorway.

John leaped from his horse and went to her with extended hand, asking "Do you know me, Myra?"

The squaw looked him long and earnestly in the face, cocking her head first to one side, then to the other, like a bird. Then her eyes flashed recognition, she smiled, crooned softly to herself, took the proffered hand and wrung it warmly, saying, "Little Jack come back—Little Jack!—what a big man now!"

"Yes, I'm Jack. How are you, Myra?"

"I'm well, but much shamed."

"What are you ashamed of?"

"Shamed you see my place so dirty. Hard work here. Not much time clean up."

"I know. Have you any help?"

"My boy. He cripple."

"How do you cultivate that cornfield? It's too steep to plow."

"Dig with mattock; then hoe."

John shook his head at the enormity of the task, to make a few bushels of corn on such a place. And the isolation! Myra had once spoken good English; but here on a remote mountain she had been immured for years, out of contact with the whites. Although she still understood English as well as ever, facility in speaking it had left her… Well, he must get at once to the business of the hour.

"I have come from Degataga," said he. "Have you heard that he has been hurt?"

"Yes," answered Myra. "Runners they go last night all over reservation. Degataga, mebbe so, he die."

"No," John assured her: "the chances are he will get well. But he does not know who hit him. I was at his home yesterday until long after dark. There was a young lady with me, Miss Wentworth, a niece of Colonel Fielding. She saw a spy looking in at the window when Degataga was telling us Indian stories, and just at the time when he showed us the Ulunsuti. I have no doubt it was this spy who assaulted Degataga when the old man parted from us in the yard. Of course, it must have been an Indian."

"I think not so," declared Myra. "No Cherokee dare steal the Ulunsuti."

"Oh!" exclaimed John, struck with a new idea. He bent his head in study and pulled his lower lip. Could it be that he and Miss Wentworth had been followed by a spy from town?

The thing was not incredible. Suppose two men had tagged them in a car and one of them had been left in the lane, the other driving back to a prearranged place of meeting.

If that were so, then Matlock was at the bottom of it. He had learned of John's doings in Turkey-Fly-Up. When the prospector came to Kittuwa and called on Colonel Fielding, Matlock doubtless heard of it. Naturally he would set a watch. Then John drove away, with Fielding's niece in his car. She had been a visitor at Burbank's, near where Cabarrus prospected. Matlock would say to himself, "Something dead up the branch!" Then he would follow, to see what the couple was up to. He would leave one of his minions to spy upon their business with Degataga.

That eavesdropper must have been astonished at the outcome. And how his cupidity must have been inflamed by the revelation of the great flashing gem!

Yes: there was no longer a mystery about the affair. But the devil of it was that Cabarrus had not merely got himself into trouble— he had involved his innocent friends. Matlock would think them all in a plot together.

As John stood brooding over this awkward turn of affairs, Myra said something in Cherokee to the Indian boy. Taywa went aside, leaving John and the squaw alone. Myra looked up at Cabarrus with altered countenance, her eyes brimming with tears.

"I'm sorry, Myra," said he, "that this trouble has come upon you."

"Me, I'm so glad to see Little Jack once more!"

"God bless you, Myra! Maybe I can help you before long—get you away from here and make life easier for you. But first you must help me, if you can."

"I do anything for you, Jack."

"Well, you remember that after my grandfather's funeral there was no one left at the cabin but you and me. A lawyer was appointed to look after the old man's personal effects. They were sold to help meet his debts. But he had some papers in a small black metal box. Do you know what became of them?"

"Yes," answered Myra. "Before the sale Bill Matlock come to house and want see papers. I say, 'Don't know where at.' He say, 'You lie.' I say, 'Go hell, ask for papers.' He tear around, look, upset things, want trunk key. I say, 'No got key.' He say he bust um open. I get hatchet; say bust um his head. He cuss me out and go 'way. Me, I find key, open trunk, take box and hide um."

"Where did you hide the box?"

"Up holler, under big down-tree. Dig hole under tree. Put box in hole, all tie up in old man's slicker. Cover nice with flat rock; then leaves allover,"

"In Turkey-Fly-Up?"

"Yes. Little way up trail beyond fence. Big chestnut tree lay there."

"On the left side of the trail, about a hundred yards beyond the clearing?"

"Yes."

"I remember that fallen chestnut. Did you ever dig up the box again?"

"No. 'Fraid lawyer give um to Matlock. Keep hid for you. Then you run away. I come to Lufty, by my people."

"Then the box is still there in the woods?"

"Guess so. Nobody find um, I think."

"By Jove! Myra, you're a brick! I'll find that box. When I've got it, you shall have a comfortable home for the rest of your life."

"Me, I like to work for you, same as for old man."

"All right. Here's some wages in advance."

John handed her a yellow-back bill. Myra said nothing, but patted him on the arm.

"Call Taywa now," said John. "I must be getting back. You will hear from me again, before long."

The Indian lad came quickly at the call. They mounted their horses and rode away.

NINETEEN

When Cabarrus returned to Kittuwa he told Colonel Fielding and Marian what had happened on the Lufty. Then he went to a grocery, ordered supplies sent to Degataga's family, and got a new stock of provisions for himself.

As he was getting into his car the grocer said to him in an undertone: "I don't mean to meddle, but I've heard that Bill Matlock swore out a warrant for you yesterday and that he rode up Deep Creek this morning."

Cabarrus thanked him and drove off. No one stopped him as he went through the length of Kittuwa, but many curious eyes followed the young man in the sedan. His encounter with Matlock in the post-office was already the talk of the town.

At Terhune's he filled his pack-sack and set forth for Nick's Nest. He went around the Lumbo settlement, through the woods, and no one saw him after he left Terhune's.

It was late in the evening when he arrived at the Alcove. He was dead tired from carrying his pack over the long mountain trail; but he now had rations for two weeks safely stored in camp.

Next morning, about seven o'clock, he eagerly set out to look for the little black box that Myra had hidden, fourteen years ago, under a chestnut log in Turkey-Fly-Up.

John figured that since Matlock had come up the creek it was likely he was having the place watched. So John went by a roundabout route through the forest and came out on a ridge overlooking his first camp ground. Here he stayed for a while, quietly watching and listening. Nothing stirred in the woods below him. He was impatient to get at the old log.

He descended to the overgrown trail and went slowly, noiselessly down the hollow. Presently he came to the upper edge of the old field that had reverted to jungle. Thence he back-tracked a hundred yards, then bored his way at a right angle, through thick undergrowth, toward where he remembered the old tree to have lain.

After considerable search he discovered the remains of what had been the trunk of a big chestnut tree. It was half embedded in the ground. The mould on its under side had long since met and blended with the loose soil of the forest floor. Ferns and mosses and seedlings grew all over and around the rotting trunk.

John went to poking with his staff into the soft earth underneath the log. He was excited now. Would he find the precious box still there? If so, would it be intact, or would the thin metal have rusted away and let moisture in to ruin the papers?

In a fever of anxiety he prodded deep along the old log, striking a hard something now and then that turned out to be only a small stone, and growing more and more disappointed as he moved on toward the lower end of the log.

Then it occurred to him that the butt of the tree, when he was a boy, had been held high off the ground by the spread of the roots, which now had rotted and let the trunk down flat throughout its length. Naturally Myra would have buried the box under the upper part of the log, where it met the ground at that time. So he went to digging there.

Finally his staff struck a large and solidly embedded rock. Fast and furiously, now, he dug with his two hands, scattering the dirt backward like a dog after a burrowing animal. He worked around the rock. It was flat, as Myra had described. He tugged it out. Underneath it was something that was neither earth nor rock: it was a mixture of rotted cloth and dirt.

There was a firm oblong object sunken in the debris. He dragged it out into the open. It was the little bond box, once shiny with black enamel but now scaled with rust.

The box still fitted tight at the joints and its lid was locked fast. John whipped out his stout hunting-knife and pried the lid open. There were papers within, neatly folded, yellow and somewhat mildewed, but still intact. On bended knees he examined them.

The first document he opened was a duplicate of the deed by which his grandfather had conveyed the property to Matlock. The next was the old man's will, properly signed and witnessed. At sight of the signatures, tears welled in the young man's eyes. Reverently he folded the precious papers, thrust them into the bosom of his shirt, picked up his staff and arose to his feet.

At that moment a twig snapped behind him.

John wheeled around and found himself confronted by a burly man in woods dress: yellow duck breeches, high laced boots, a wool shirt open at the neck, an army hat. The fellow stood with fists doubled on his hips, his right hand touching the square butt of .45 Colt revolver that protruded from a Mexican holster. At first glance, Matlock was scarcely recognizable. Then his eyes shifted: the evil left eye, black with malice, turned and was fixed on Cabarrus with an intentness that seemed to bore him through.

"What in hell are you doing here *now?*" Demanded the bully. "What are you stealing this time?"

Coolly John answered him: "I have found some of my own property. Come out to the trail and we will have an understanding."

"*Your* property!" sneered Matlock. "Step out ahead of me. Don't make a false move, or, by God, you'll never make another!"

John walked out to the trail, never glancing back. When he came to an open space he turned and stood leaning on his staff.

Matlock stopped, three paces away, his hand now grasping the pistol handle.

"Take a good look at me," said John. "Haven't we met before?"

The big fellow scanned him from head to foot. Presently he asked, "How long ago?"

"Fourteen years," answered John, with a grim smile.

Slowly Matlock's mind groped. His memory of dates was none of the best. He had to figure that fourteen from twenty-five left eleven. What had happened in 1911?... Then, in a flash, came recognition.

"Jack Dale!" he cried, and his features became convulsed.

John said nothing, but simply stood awaiting Matlock's reaction.

There was a fateful pause. Then the explosion.—

"You damned skulker! What are you doing here? Sneaking about like a thief in the night! Going under a false name!"

John straightened up, no longer leaning on his staff, but poised, with the right foot forward. He lowered the stout hardwood stick, slanting it to the left and away from him, point to the ground.

"Listen, Matlock," said he.— "When my old grandfather was in distress, you came to him, uninvited, in the guise of a neighbor and a friend. You wormed your way into his confidence. He was trustful, having never dealt with sharpers. You loaned him money at an illegal and ruinous rate of interest. So you robbed him of his home—this cabin and its wooded acres—the last bit of property he possessed."

"Nobody else would lend him money," interjected Matlock. "He was mighty glad to get it, on any terms."

"So would a starving man be glad to get bread on any terms. You took deliberate advantage of his necessity. You were a blood-sucker. You drained his very life and he fell dead at your feet. After the funeral, you came to his wrecked home and even tried to steal the old man's papers, so that, in any event, you could snap your fingers at the law."

"Bah!" sneered Matlock. "Twenty percent on a great risk is no worse than four percent on a sure thing. All business is run on that principle. And you can't take long-term notes from people who have no income and may die on you any day. When they renew, of course the interest piles up. Usury laws are made *by* fools *for* fools. They're never effective, and shouldn't be. In evading them I was only fighting the devil with fire. Self-preservation is the first law of nature."

John calmly continued: "I'm not here to argue—I'm telling you where you get off. The poor, faithful Indian servant, left alone in the house, thwarted that last infamy of yours. She drove you off with a hatchet, then took the papers and hid them in the woods. I found them here today."

Matlock gave a quick, startled movement, as if a wildcat had sprung up in his path. His face paled for a moment, then turned to a violent red. A vein swelled on his forehead. His fingers twitched on the pistol butt.

Sternly John declared to him: "By the terms of the deed, as you well know, all mineral rights are reserved. By the will, which I now have in possession, I am my grandfather's sole heir. Henceforth I shall come and go as I please, build my own road on this property, dig and develop mines here as I see fit. If you interfere, Matlock, you do so at your peril."

In a twinkling Matlock realized that his estimate of this young man had been too low. Instead of having a mere prowling trespasser to deal with, he was now confronted by an antagonist armed with full legal powers and grimly determined to enforce them. Things had come to a showdown, and John Cabarrus held the winning cards.

"Fool!" cried the enraged usurer. "You'll never turn a spadeful of dirt on my land!"

Out came the revolver from its holster. Its blued metal flashed in the sunlight. Matlock thrust out his arm for deliberate aim.

Instantly John struck upward with his staff. It was a stroke from an unexpected direction. The stick caught Matlock on the under side of the wrist. It was an unbearably painful blow. The cocked .45 went off with a loud bang, its muzzle thrown upward so that the bullet flew to the sky.

John's stick was now in the air like an upthrust saber. He struck downward with the precision of a master of fence. The staff shivered on Matlock's head. He went down in an ungainly sprawl.

"You spawn of hell!" cried John. "You'd shoot me down in cold blood, would you?"

He seized the pistol and thrust it into his own belt.

Matlock lay bleeding from a scalp wound. His eyes roved with groping consciousness, striving to see a way out of his predicament. They worked in divergent axes, the white eyeball of one showing when the pupil of the other stared at John. They horribly suggested something inhuman. John remembered a bull alligator that he had seen shift its eyes independently of each other.

The young man stood over his stricken enemy, now wondering what to do with him. He hated to go away and leave him without knowing whether the fellow would be able to help himself.

But Matlock was not fully stunned. His strabismus, though it disfigured him, had one compensating advantage: it gave him abnormally wide field of vision. And now one or other of his eyes caught sight of something stealthily moving out from the bushes and coming toward John from behind. It was 'Poleon Lumbo, who, with his cousin Aleck, had been hired by Matlock, only yesterday, to patrol the property and keep a lookout for John Cabarrus. The discredited Youlus was not in on this deal.

Cabarrus, feeling rather than hearing something behind him, turned and found the muzzle of a Winchester rifle leveled within six inches of his face.

"Stick 'em up!" ordered 'Poleon. "Hands up, or I'll blow your head off!"

No trick or strategy could thwart such advantage. John's hands went up.

Lumbo snatched Matlock's pistol from John's belt and the hunting-knife from its scabbard.

Matlock struggled to his feet. Levelling his finger at Cabarrus, he roared: "Now, my pretty skulker, we'll hold a court-martial!"

Turning to 'Poleon he declared, with an air of questioning: "You saw this ruffian attack me?"

"Yes," answered the willing Lumbo.

"I wasn't doing anything to him?"

"Nary thing."

"You saw him point a pistol at me?"

"Shorely did."

"You saw me knock the gun out of his hand, and it went off?"

"That's right," declared 'Poleon, spitting for emphasis.

"Then he hit me with a club?"

"He did *so*."

"And you came to my rescue?"

"I did that."

"All right. Now hold your gun on him while I get what he stole from me."

Matlock unbuttoned John's shirt and took out the papers. He had wiped blood off his forehead with his fingers and it left red imprints on the manuscripts. Waving the documents at 'Poleon, he asked: "Did you see him rob me of these papers after he'd knocked me down with his club?"

"Yes, sir: I did."

Cabarrus blazed out: "You devilish liars!"

"Shut up!" cried Matlock. "I like that belt of yours: it's just the trick to keep your hands where they belong."

It was a web belt with a friction buckle that could be set at any point and would not slip. Matlock made John cross his hands behind him. He drew the belt tightly around his wrists, secured it with the buckle, cut off the superfluous length and threw it away. A gorilla could not have broken such a bond.

"Now march!" ordered Matlock.

The three proceeded down the trail to the old cabin. They entered it. The poor old place had been cleaned up a bit and some camping gear showed that it was now being occupied.

Matlock sat down on a rude pole bunk that had been set up in a corner. He made John squat on the floor with his back against the opposite wall.

"'Poleon," said he, "get on my horse, now, and speed into town like a bat out of hell. Don't say a word to anybody on the way, but bring the sheriff out here as quick as he can make it. If you don't find him, fetch a deputy. I've already got a warrant for this fellow; but there are bigger charges against him now—robbery and attempted murder. I'll stay here and guard the prisoner. Your cousin will be back in an hour or so. He can spell me at it."

"Shucks!" objected 'Poleon. "Me and you kin march this feller in to town, our own selves."

"Yes. We have a right to; for we caught him in the act of committing a felony. Any citizen has power of arrest, in such case. But it would excite the people too much. They might take him away from us and lynch him, if there was no officer in charge. We must see he gets a fair trial," declared Matlock unctuously.

'Poleon sniffed at such scruple, but he obeyed.

When 'Poleon had gone, Matlock leered at Cabarrus.

"So, so, so," he drawled. "You're one smart Aleck, aren't you? Let's take a look at these old papers you set such store by."

He drew them from his bosom and began to read, slowly, with close attention to the wording.

TWENTY

The tightly drawn belt, and its buckle in particular, was hurting John's wrists severely. He squirmed with the pain. In doing so, he felt a nail projecting from the old floor, where the end of a plank had rotted away.

He managed to press the buckle against the nail. By sense of touch he got a corner of the nail head under the belt, between the two ends of the buckle. Carefully he pushed until one edge of the belt was worked up and away from the buckle.

His enemy read on. The pistol lay close beside him on the bunk, where it could be snatched up in a fraction of a second.

John at last got the whole nail head under the webbing. Gradually he drew the end of the belt out from under the front end of the buckle. Then, pressing up the front against the nail, he released the tension at the rear. The belt slipped free.

Still holding his arms behind him, he chafed his wrists to restore circulation.

Matlock looked up. He stuck out his lower lip and half closed the eye with which he regarded his prisoner. For some time he sat thus silently studying the situation. Then he spoke, slowly, solemnly, as if pronouncing sentence.—

"You're the sole heir, eh? That simplifies matters. If you think I'm soft enough to take you back to town and go through all the rigmarole of a lawsuit, why, my fine young buck, you have another thing coming."

Cabarrus drew his feet closer to his body.

Matlock continued: "I sent 'Poleon away to get rid of him. I can now dispense with witnesses. When the sheriff gets here he will find that the desperado Dale, *alias* Cabarrus, has escaped. Somehow he contrived to slip that belt from his wrists. He batted me on the head again. He ran off, making for Tennessee. And this time he will be gone for good—yes, sir, forever."

"What's the idea?" asked Cabarrus.

"You're superfluous here," answered Matlock. "The place for such a meddler is six feet down in that swamp at the mouth of Dog-eater Hollow, with a pile of rocks on top of you, and the water and green scum over all."

Cabarrus caught his breath.

"You mean to murder me, before anyone comes?" he asked. "Sink my body in the swamp and tell the sheriff I escaped from you?"

Slowly Matlock answered, emphasizing each phrase with a tap of his finger in the palm of his hand: "I mean to mine all the radium around here, myself. You, as I said, are superfluous. In fact, you're a damned nuisance. Besides, I never forget or forgive an injury. You disfigured me for life—now I'll make you pay for it."

For a moment Cabarrus actually forgot that the hands behind his back were free. The horror of the swamp drove all other thoughts out of his head.

One reads in his morning paper that a gangster, Ruffo Sbarletto, has killed one Moe Schlossstein with a stab in the back. Does that murder come home to the reader? No: he passes on to the market news, or the sports, and the crime is immediately forgotten.

The murder was done by some creature of the slums whom the reader never saw, never heard of. The victim, likewise, is naught but an outlandish name. The killing might have occurred on Mars or Jupiter, for all the personal interest it excites. One does not live next door to murderers. One's friends do not die from the gunman's bullets or the assassin's bombs.

So Cabarrus had heard of such things. He had read about murderers and had seen their pictures. That was as near as he had ever come to the grim fact of their existence in his own world.

But he could not escape the reality now. There sat Matlock in flesh and blood, coolly weighing the evidence against himself, shrewdly preparing to destroy all traces of it, even to the dead body of his victim. There he sat, sane beyond doubt or cavil, yet actually gloating over the perfection of his crime!

The loaded pistol lay at his right hand. The swamp was less than two hundred yards away. Matlock could carry a corpse that far without any help. As for detection—there was not one chance in a hundred that anyone would see him as he went through the thicket, bearing his grisly burden.

The swamp—The green scum—

Cabarrus leaped.

His coordination was perfect; for he had known in advance just what he had to do. But Matlock, in the shock of surprise at seeing the prisoner's hands free, lost an irrecoverable half-second of time.

John's right hand seized Matlock's throat with the grip of a tiger's jaws. His left hand fastened on the hairy wrist beside the pistol. His knee drove like a ram against the big man's stomach. Backward they went upon the makeshift bed. Its poles snapped under the impact. The men went down in a heap, tangled in the bedclothes, but with John on top.

The revolver slid down within grasp of John's hand. He seized it by the handle and dealt blow after blow with its heavy six-inch barrel. No twinge of mercy restrained him now.

He arose, panting. In a dazed way he looked at the weapon he had wrested from its owner for a second time in this same hour. Its barrel and front sight were covered with blood and hairs. He made a grimace of disgust and dropped the gun on the floor. He wiped his fingers on a blanket and took the stolen papers from Matlock's shirt front.

"Well, Matlock." said he, when he had recovered breath, "you were partly right. The 'desperado' Cabarrus has escaped from you. He did slip his bonds; he did beat your head again. But you made two mistakes: he will not be sunk in the swamp; he is not going to run away."

John spoke aloud, as though his fallen enemy might hear him; but there was no stir nor sound from the figure on the broken bed.

It was time for Cabarrus to get away from there. Aleck Lumbo might show up at any time. So John went out, leaving everything in the cabin as it was.

He crossed the ford below the house and went on down the road a little way. Back in the thicket, not far from the roadside, he sat down on an old log. Here, from behind the screen of bushes, he could watch both the cabin and the road.

John looked at his watch and was surprised to find that it marked only nine o'clock. He noticed that his hand shook. It had been firm as iron while the crisis was on; but now reaction had set in and he was weak, trembling like a scared pup.

Would Matlock die?

He did not know. He had seized the pistol by its handle and had struck without shifting his grip, so as not to shoot himself if the thing went off. That is an awkward way to use a pistol as a billy, but steel is steel, and a desperate man strikes hard.

John tried to calculate how long it would take 'Poleon Lumbo to ride to Kittuwa and return with the officer. But he was so dazed that he groped in the simple calculation. Finally he made out that it would be about two hours. Two mortal hours to wait: Could he sit still that long? Why not go on down the road and meet the sheriff?

But he might encounter Aleck Lumbo on the way. Aleck would be armed, of course. He would hold John up, according to Matlock's orders. Seeing him so disheveled and smeared with blood, Aleck would suspect the truth and would search him for weapons. He would find the papers and would probably confiscate them. It would be folly for John to run such a risk. He must sit still and wait.

What day was this? Friday, the twelfth of June. It was on Tuesday, the second, that he made his first camp in Turkey-Fly-Up. And that was when he first met Marian Wentworth. Ah! much had happened in the last ten days.

He had come here expecting to find the old home place in the hands of some small proprietor or in care of a tenant. From such a one he had counted on the friendly greeting and hospitality that is second nature to the average mountaineer. By no stretch of the imagination could he have foreseen what actually did occur.

But, anyway, he had triumphed over Matlock—so far. He had found the will and it was in his possession. And now he must make good in Nick's Nest. It was still a gamble, to be sure; but he had faith in Nick's Nest.

There would still be the Lumbos to deal with. Even with Matlock outplayed, the Lumbos could give him trouble. What a vile set! Drifters, from nobody knew where, lodged on the outermost edge of the settlement, scorned by their honest neighbors, warring in their stealthy and stubborn way against the civilization that kept ever pushing them farther and farther back. In all the country round about, Matlock could have found few if any others to do his dirty work.

Two hours to wait!

His mind roved, skipping inconsequently, recalling trifles as well as serious things. Was Bupply still on guard with his bow and arrow?

What had become of the Ulunsuti? Yet all the time, in the back of his head, there was something neither trifling nor tragic, but very pleasant and soothing withal, that was content without seeking expression.

So he fell into a muse that drifted into day-dreams, and time passed unnoticed, and his watchfulness relaxed.

. . . .

The thicket vanished. It was all lawns and gardens now, leading by flower-bordered paths to a vine-clad chateau on the upland, where once a poor log hut had stood.

Far up on the opposite mountain-side a hundred miners delved and the smoke of a smelter arose. Drills whirred, over there, and ore cars moved along the tramways.

But here, amid the trees and shrubs and flowers, the Little People danced and beat their tiny drums.

Out from the chateau came a fair and bewitching girl. She listened, with hand cupped to her ear. Then down the path she came, glancing from side to side, parting the bushes, seeking something.

The Little People laughed and dodged behind the trees. They peeped out at her and were not seen. But the girl heard their merry laughter and her own throat thrilled with a glad song.

. . . .

What was that?

Pounding footfalls of a galloping horse.

Cabarrus came to himself, shocked into instant attention, and he rose bolt upright to meet the rude interrupter of his daydream.

It would be the sheriff, coming in hot haste, armed with a warrant. And 'Poleon Lumbo as eye-witness of an attempt to rob and kill.

John stepped out into the roadway.

Yes, it was a horse, coming full tilt and in a lather; but that small figure humped forward on the saddle, lashing the horse, was no sheriff or mountaineer.

She was in street clothes and bareheaded, just as she had been when news slipped out through loiterers at the courthouse that John Cabarrus was held prisoner at the Matlock place on Deep Creek, charged with robbery and attempted murder. Without a word to anyone, Marian had run to a stable, saddled a horse herself, and dashed off to overtake the sheriff.

She caught sight of John as he raised a hand to wave her down. With all her strength she checked her horse. Throwing the reins over its head, she leaped to the ground and stumbled forward, white-faced, all spent and breathless, quivering and wild-eyed.

John caught her in his arms.

"Oh, John, you're hurt!" she gasped, seeing the blood smears on his shirt.

"No, no: I'm all right, dear; but you?"

The girl was sobbing. She pressed her face against his chest. He strained her to him and kissed her hair.

"They shan't put you in jail!" she cried. "They shan't—they shan't!"

Then all John's restraint gave way. He raised her chin with his finger tips and passionately kissed her full on the lips.

"Marian—Marian!"

"How did you get away?"

"Worked my hands free."

"Where's Matlock?"

"In the cabin. He's harmless now."

"Did you kill him?"

"N-no; I think not."

"The sheriff's coming."

"How soon?"

"I passed them at Bridge Creek. He called me back; but I didn't listen."

"You raced up here alone—for what?"

"To help you."

They were in a rapturous embrace when a harsh voice interrupted them with an emphatic, "Well, I'll be damned!"

John wheeled to confront a tall, angular, stoop-shouldered man who had emerged from the thicket on the upper side of the road.

"All right," snapped John. "Go on and be damned. We won't stop you."

Aleck Lumbo dropped the butt of his rifle to the ground and stared.

"Did you hear me?" said John savagely. "Go up to the cabin and look after your boss. He's needing attention. We're not."

"What's happened?" asked Lumbo.

"The sheriff will soon be here to straighten out my affair with Matlock," John informed him. "If you know what's good for you, you'll not interfere."

"Mebbe," said Aleck Lumbo, spitting on the ground. Then without another word he passed them and went toward the cabin, looking backward from time to time.— "Them fools is still a-huggin'," he muttered.

TWENTY-ONE

The sound of horses splashing through a rocky ford. The rhythmic thud of hoofbeats coming at a sharp trot. Up from the creek and out in the old road appeared the sheriff, a deputy and a ragged woodsman, riding in single file.

Surprised at sight of John and Marian standing in the roadway, hand in hand, the three men reined in their horses and halted before the couple. The sheriff lifted his hat to Marian and smiled with quizzical invitation for her to speak.

She blushed, but she said nothing; neither did she let go John's hand.

"You beat me to him," observed the sheriff. Then of John he asked, "Where's Matlock?"

"Yonder, in the cabin," answered John. "He's hurt; but there's a man with him, now—Aleck Lumbo, I assume."

The sheriff frowned.— "I've heard this man's story," said he, jerking a thumb toward 'Poleon Lumbo, "and it sounds pretty bad. It's my duty to warn you that anything you say may be used against you."

"I have nothing to dodge or conceal," declared John. "And I warn you that the tale this hireling told you is what Matlock made up for him to tell."

"That's a damn lie!" blazed 'Poleon.

"Shut up!" ordered the sheriff.

"The whole thing, in a nutshell, is simply this," said John: "When my grandfather, Professor Dale, deeded this property to Matlock, he reserved the mineral rights. By his will he made me his sole heir. When he died, Matlock came here and tried to steal the will. It was in a little steel box, with other documents. Matlock was thwarted by our Indian housekeeper, Myra, who took the box and hid it under a log, up yonder in the woods. I found it there, this morning, with the papers intact."

"Oh!" exclaimed Marian. She squeezed John's hand.

"Matlock came up unawares," continued John, "and accused me of trespass and stealing. Then he recognized me as the little Jack Dale of long ago. He flew into a rage and leveled a pistol at my head. I knocked it out of his hand with my stick and I struck him down. But this fellow, 'Poleon Lumbo, came on me from behind, stuck me up with a Winchester, and disarmed me."

"Disarmed you of what?" asked the sheriff.

"Of Matlock's own pistol, which I had taken from him."

"Well."

"Then Matlock robbed me of the papers. He took my belt and bound my wrists with it, behind my back. The two of them drove me to the cabin. Matlock cooked up a lie that Lumho agreed to swear to. Then he sent the fellow for you. Matlock mounted guard over me and went to reading the papers."

"How did you get loose?"

"I worked the belt off my wrists, but kept my hands behind me. Then Matlock bragged that he was going to put me out of the way forever. He said he had sent Lumbo away so there would be no witness. He declared that he was going to kill me, right then and there, sink my body in the swamp of Dog-eater Hollow, and tell you, when you arrived, that I had escaped and fled to Tennessee."

"What did you do?"

"I sprang on him, beat him senseless with his own pistol, left him there in the cabin, and came down here to wait for you."

'Poleon Lumbo's face turned ashen. He fidgeted in the saddle.

The sheriff stroked the stubble on his chin.— "These two stories," said he, looking from John to 'Poleon, "are as much alike as a chunk of coal and a snowball. We'll go up to the cabin."

They tethered their horses and the little party of solemn-faced people climbed the bank and went around to the back door of the cabin, its only practicable entrance.

Aleck Lumbo, stern and dour, met them with a gesture that took in all the cabin room.

"I've left ever'thing jist pint-blank as I found it," said he, "savin' I drug *him* out on the floor whar he could breathe. I washed his face and tried to git him to swaller a dram; but he couldn't." Aleck was pointing to the unconscious Matlock, who lay on a pallet made from the bedding of the broken bunk.

"Are you awake, Matlock?" asked the sheriff, putting his hand on the man's brow.

There was no answer. Matlock's face was pale, save for the ugly contusions where he had been beaten with the pistol. He was in a cold sweat. His breathing was shallow; his pulse quick and weak. His divergent eyes were set in an unfocussed stare and the dilated pupils gave no sign of consciousness.

"This man is in a bad fix," said the sheriff. "And we're in a bad fix about getting him out of here. Dan," he addressed his deputy, "go hotfoot to Jim Terhune's. He's got a wagon. Tell him to put a good bed of straw in it and drive it up here, right away. Then ride on to the nighest telephone and call a doctor. You, Aleck, go up to Tom Burbank's and fetch him and his wife down here. She's a good hand to help with this man till the doctor comes."

"Let me go," suggested Marian. "I can get there in five minutes, on my horse, and Mrs. Burbank can ride back, behind the saddle."

"All right: go to it," agreed the sheriff.

"Cain't I do somethin'?" proffered 'Poleon.

"Yes," said the sheriff curtly: "you can stay right here till I leave. You're a material witness, and you're going back to town with me. Don't you step outside that door till I say so."

The sheriff looked round the room. He picked up the big revolver that still lay where John had dropped it.

"Whose gun is this?" he asked 'Poleon.

"Hit's the one this hyur feller pulled on Matlock," answered 'Poleon nervously.

"Where's Matlock's, then?"

"He didn't have nary gun that I observed."

"The hell he didn't! Look at that empty holster on his belt."

"I— I hadn't noted it."

The sheriff wrapped the pistol carefully in his handkerchief and put it in one of the big pockets of his hunting coat. He stepped over to the far side of the room and picked up a piece of web belt with a buckle on it.

"Whose is this?" he asked.

"Mine," answered John. "It's what they bound me with. I worked the buckle against that nail there, and slipped the belt through it."

"Where's the rest of the belt?"

"Up in the hollow, where Matlock cut it off and cast it away."

"Hum. We'll look for it, presently. Where are those papers you say you found in the woods?"

"Here." John drew them from his shirt bosom and handed them over. The sheriff was silently reading the will when 'Poleon bent over his shoulder and whispered: "Them's the very i-den-tical papers he tuk from Matlock."

"Can you read?" asked the sheriff aloud.

"No."

"Then how do you know they're the same?"

"'Caze they're marked by Matlock's bloody fingers. Lookee thar," said 'Poleon, pointing to the stains. "He'd wiped blood offen his forred afore he tuk 'em back from this feller."

"You'd swear these are the same papers you saw Cabarrus take from Matlock, and that Matlock afterwards recovered them?"

"Yes, sir: I'd swar to 'em on a stack o' Bibles a foot high."

"Better make it six inches," said the sheriff. He finished reading the papers and then put them away in his big wallet.

Aleck Lumbo winked at his cousin and they sidled to a far end of the room. Aleck whispered, "You dumb fool! You've put your own foot in it. Watch your chance and high-ballout o' hyur. By tomorrow you'd better be in Tennessee."

In fifteen minutes Marian returned, with Sylvia riding behind her. Tom soon followed, carrying little Margaret, as there was no one at the cabin with whom to leave the child.

"Build a fire and heat some water and some smooth rocks," directed Sylvia. She put a cold wet cloth on Matlock's head and went to rubbing his limbs toward the body, keeping him well wrapped up the while. When the rocks were heated she wrapped them in blanketing and put them against the stricken man's feet and body, like hot-water bottles. She held ammonia to his nose.

Matlock's eyes fluttered and he breathed deeply; but when the sheriff spoke to him he only groaned.

"Cabarrus," said the sheriff, "come with me and show where the rest of that belt is. The others, all of you, will stay here."

The two went up the hollow. They soon came to a trampled place where men had recently been in action. The piece of belt dangled from a nearby bush. The officer pocketed it, studied the tracks on the ground, and then said to John: "Show me where you found the box."

John led him aside through the thicket and pointed to the old log. The heap of freshly turned earth told its own story. The box itself lay there, with its lid pried open. The sheriff took it with him and they returned to the cabin.

"Where's 'Poleon Lumbo?" demanded the sheriff, as soon as he had cast his eyes over the room. Everyone turned and looked about. There was no 'Poleon Lumbo.

"Skipped, I reckon," said Tom Burbank, significantly.

The sheriff made a gesture of disgust.

Time dragged as they waited for the wagon. Matlock still appeared to be in a stupor, but he breathed normally. Sylvia, who had been watching him closely, whispered to her husband: "He's only addled. I do believe he could talk if he wanted to; but he wants time to think up somethin'."

At three o' clock Terhune came with the wagon. Four men raised Matlock on a blanket and transferred him to a deep cushion of straw in the wagon-bed.

"I hate to risk jolting him over that rough road," said the sheriff, "but it's the best we can do. The doctor will meet us somewhere on the way."

The Burbanks returned home and the others set out for Kittuwa.

John asked the sheriff, "What are you going to do with me?"

"I've a warrant for your arrest on a charge of trespass," answered the officer; "but there's nobody to appear against you till Matlock gets on his feet. As for this other matter, the physical evidence bears out your story; 'Poleon Lumbo has run away; Matlock is yet to be heard from. It's for the magistrate to determine whether he'll hold you for court. If he does, I suppose you can give bond?"

"I think so," said John.

"Of course he can," averred Marian, who had overheard them.

"When Matlock comes to his senses, he may decide not to press any charges. We all know that Lumbo was lying, or he would have stood his ground."

The sheriff smiled knowingly at John, "I reckon," said he, "that you won't lack friends in court." Then the unmannerly fellow tilted back his head and laughed.

TWENTY-TWO

Soon after Cabarrus and Taywa had left her, Myra Swimming-Deer put her son in charge of affairs at home and set forth on a long journey afoot. The first stage was fifteen miles to Degataga's place on the Soco. That was nothing, to a woman of fifty years who had climbed mountains and hoed corn and carried burdens all her life.

She went barefoot, but with shoes and stockings tied up, with some other light equipment, in the shawl that was her carryall. She would save shoe-leather until she came near the settlements where white folks lived.

It was late in the evening when Myra arrived at her half-brother's house. The wounded man was propped up in bed, fairly easy now, supping some corn gruel. Beside him sat a sturdy full-blood, He-who-runs-up-the-mountain-and-back, whom the whites called simply Runner.

And this was the news that Myra learned.—

It had been near midnight that Degataga's wife found her man lying senseless where he had been struck down. She and Kamama carried him into the house and then the girl ran for help.

Runner lived near and he was soon on the scene. Wasting no time in talk, but getting a lantern, he scanned the wet yard and its approaches. The storm had washed out all old tracks and softened the ground so that new ones were sharply outlined. It was no trick at all to "read the sign." Runner identified every footprint, according to the man, woman or dog that made it.

Among them he found tracks of an interloper. This fellow had worn run-down brogans studded with round-headed nails. He walked flat-footed, with the flexed knees and high-stepping gait of a rustic who was used to travelling over rough ground. He carried a thick walking-stick. Its prints were deep in the wet clay where he had hurried off down the slippery lane. No doubt it was with this club that he had killed the little dog and had felled Degataga from behind.

Down where Degataga's lane joined the public road, and off a little way in the woods, a mule had been tethered. The robber's tracks came from this place and returned to it.

The mule had rubbed some of its hairs off on the rough bark of the oak sapling to which it was hitched. They were black hairs. The animal had small feet and a short stride. Its right hind foot was malformed so that its fetlock left a print in the mud. Therefore it was a small black mule that was "rabbit-footed."

The mule's tracks were superposed on the wheel treads of John's car, both coming and going. So the thief must have followed Cabarrus to Degataga's lane and he did not go away until after John had left.

All this was simple as A-B-C.

Out on the public road the tracks were so plain, even by moonlight, that Runner could follow at a dog-trot. The full moon was but an hour high. So Runner left his lantern, ran to the end of the Soco road, crossed the bridge, and sped on past Birdtown to highway No. 10. Here he found that the mule had turned to the right, toward Kittuwa.

On the hard surface of the highway no tracks showed; but that did not slow up the human bloodhound. He trotted on, with easy but mile-devouring gait, and halted only when he came, here and there, to a by-road. At each of these a single glance showed that the mule had not left the highway.

But where N. C. 10 crosses the Tuckaseegee River, at the concrete bridge, the mule did turn aside. It took a shortcut to Deep Creek, along the old detour. Then it went up the creek toward the Smoky Mountains.

Runner had never been in that part of the country. Indians very seldom visited Deep Creek. Here, then, he slowed down. For five miles he plodded northward, still following the tracks of the "rabbit-footed" mule.

At a ford he came to a two-story house that had never been finished. The upstairs doorways and window-spaces were wide open to the weather and made him think of eye-sockets and nose-holes in a row of skulls.

Ten minutes' walk beyond this place, a rude stable stood close beside a ford. Here the man with the run-down brogans had dismounted and had led his mule into the stable.

There was no chance to examine farther, for savage dogs came baying from a near-by shack. The scout hastily retreated. He returned by the same route he had come by, and he finished his thirty-five-mile round trip as the sun came up over the eastern mountain range.

Good work, did they say? Pooh! a boy could have done it. This white clodhopper was a fool: he did not know how to steal!

Of course, Runner himself professed no skill in that art, being a church-member, but his own grandfather—now there was a man who could have pulled this job without leaving a trace, like a crow flying through the air! Yes: the white thief was doubly a fool, for he had stolen something that would destroy him. Then the Ulunsuti would bring itself back. They needn't worry.

The old squaw nodded. Kamama looked scared. But Myra was not impressed by his reassurance. She said that Indian magic was all well enough for Indians, but it did not work on whites. The investigation was only begun. She recalled that place on Deep Creek where the mule was stabled—she had passed it many times in the old days when she lived at Turkey-Fly-Up— but she had heard it had changed hands. The identity of the thief was yet to be learned.

They speculated on what the fellow had been seeking. What had brought him so far out of his way? Not the Ulunsuti; for he could have known nothing of it. In fact, nobody knew in advance that it would be brought to the house—that had come about by Kamama having made Degataga angry.

Finally Degataga suggested that an enemy of John Cabarrus must have been dogging him to see what he was up to. This fellow, spying on the premises and seeing a great flashing gem revealed, had been overcome by greed and he had turned robber. A shrewd surmise. It fitted the known facts.

But now, having got the Ulunsuti, what would he do with it? What could he do with it?

A professional thief from the cities could, no doubt, dispose of such a thing. But a backwoodsman of the Smokies— what would he know about the market for gems?

He would not dare try to sell the thing in Kittuwa or any other little town near-by; for everybody would hear of it at once. Asheville? Possibly. But more likely he would cross the Smokies to Knoxville, where perhaps he had acquaintances. The rag-tag of the Smokies often shifted base from one state to the other.

Myra thought that prompt action must be taken, if they would ever see the Ulunsuti again. But Degataga figured differently. The robber, said he, would expect the Indians to raise hue and cry, as white men would do, and make an appeal to the authorities through the Indian superintendent. He might fear that he had been seen, that night, on the Soco road, and even tracked to his lair.

What then? Why, naturally, he would cook up a story to account for his presence in the Soco country. Likewise, anticipating a search-warrant, he would hide the Ulunsuti in the woods where no officer could find it; also, if he had a spoonful of sense, he would stay at home, attending to his usual business, until the fuss was over. Then he could seek a purchaser in some far-off town.

The immediate problem was to find and positively identify the guilty man.

Finally Myra asked Degataga to leave the matter in her hands until he was able to go out and attend to it himself. She had hit upon a plan. Let her try it out.

And Degataga agreed.

So, early the next morning, Myra left them. She took a taxi that made regular trips from the upper Lufty. It brought her to Kittuwa just as the bank was opening.

The cashier of that bank got a jolt when this Indian squaw came in, laid down a yellow-backed bill, and called for change in goldpieces. He tried to quiz her a bit, out of curiosity; but "five dollah gold, fo' time" seemed all the English she could muster, and four fingers extended made the meaning clear. Questioning only brought out an unintelligible singsong in Cherokee. So he shrugged his shoulders and passed out the four goldpieces. When an Indian does not care to talk English, he won't, and that's the end of it.

Myra secreted the gold on her person and she departed. An hour later, as she went trudging steadily up the Deep Creek road, a horseman passed her at a gallop, going toward Kittuwa. It was 'Poleon Lumbo, riding a big black horse.

For fourteen years Myra had not been on Deep Creek; so she did not know any of the Lumbos, who were comparatively late comers in that neck of the woods. But she did recognize the horse and she knew that costly saddle, on which the ragamuffin was so conspicuously out of place. Last October, at the Indian fair, she had seen Bill Matlock pompously cavaliering with that very turnout.

At such reminder of the man whom she had never ceased hating, in all the years since she had faced him with uplifted hatchet, Myra broke out in an Indian imprecation. It was a terrific and comprehensive curse that took in Matlock's body, his soul, and everything he owned or controlled.

Thus having relieved her mind, Myra marched stolidly on, looking neither to right nor left, ignoring the curious stares of the few farm folk she passed on the way. It was nearing noontime when she paused at a brooklet that came merrily tumbling down out of steep woods on the left. Here a faint trail led up the hillside. Myra looked carefully about her for old landmarks to ensure her location. Then, satisfied, she turned aside and went trudging up the path.

Ten minutes of climbing through silent and deserted woods brought her to a small clearing that had been made by chopping out the smaller trees, burning the brush, and girdling the big hemlocks so that they died on their stumps. Four or five acres of steep and rocky ground had thus been opened to the sun. The plot was enclosed by a rickety worm fence of poles and rails. There was no gate. Myra let down a top rail, clambered over the others, and followed the path through a patch of spindling and weedy corn.

In a brier-choked gully on the far side of the field stood a few low trees so completely covered with wild grapevines and other creepers that they formed a bower, masking whatever might be underneath. There was no sign of a house; but a thin blue reek rose through the foliage, as from a chimney or a camp-fire, thus betraying some sort of human activity within the covert.

As she approached the place a dog gave warning and came rushing at her. She stopped and tried to coax it, but the suspicious beast bristled and showed its teeth. A shrill voice called it off, but no one appeared at the opening in the nook.

Myra stepped forward and saw through the tangle of vines an exceedingly shabby hut, scarce twelve feet square and ten feet to the roof-peak, that might well have served as a pen for animals.

The walls were of round logs small enough for one man to handle by himself. Where the clay chinking had fallen out from between the logs there were holes through which a cat could jump. The roof of the hovel was made of "shakes" or clapboards riven from trees that had stood near at hand. There was no chimney, but only a breast-high wall of field-rocks set, as a fireplace, in a gap left in the end wall. The floor was simply the native earth, tramped by years of occupancy to a hard and uneven surface.

The low door was but a shutter, made of split boards like those of the roof, and it opened outward on wooden hinges. There was no window, nor need of one; for light and ventilation came in through spaces between the logs, and down the fireplace, and through the doorway, which was always open, winter or summer, from dawn to dusk.

There was not a sawed plank—much less, a planed one—in the house, nor in its furniture. Everything but a few pounds of nails had come from the surrounding woods. The only tools used in its construction had been an axe, a crosscut saw, a hatchet, a froe and a jack-knife.

Myra stood still at a few paces from the doorway, and waited. There was no need of announcing herself by hallooing—the dog had attended to that. She knew that someone was peering at her through a crack in the wall, and that she would be admitted, or not, according to that person's judgment. If she were welcome, someone would presently come to the door and say so. If she were not, a gun-muzzle thrust out between the wall-logs would be sufficient hint to retire.

At last someone stirred within the hut. Then came an incredibly ugly hag and squared herself in the doorway. She stood with both hands on a crooked laurel stick that was carved with strange images or symbols. Her red-lidded eyes squinted at Myra, half-shut with the intentness of one who was dim-sighted or whose eyes were unused to the outdoor glare.

She was a filthy creature. The lines of her face were accentuated by grime, as though purposely painted in for a stage make-up. Her sparse white hair, apparently never combed, hung in wisps about her face, like old torn cobwebs. The dirty gown that seemed to be her only garment was ragged and unpatched. Its sleeves were quite gone, revealing gaunt but sinewy arms that were pied with black or blue splotches due to malnutrition. Her splay feet were bare. She stood silent as an apparition, hideous and revolting.

But Myra was not alarmed by the foul prodigy she had stirred out of this hidden lair. The Indian woman smiled and cocked her head as though challenging recognition.

The old witch in the doorway bent forward, thrusting out her chin and wrinkling her brows all the more, but her expression was still suspicious, even malevolent.

Then the squaw spoke: "Old Hex, how you do?" said she. "I'm Myra. You know me?"

TWENTY-THREE

She who was known to the countryside by the stigmatic nickname of "Old Hex" was one of those forsaken creatures who, in payment of their own misanthropy, are doomed to live apart, shunned and mistrusted by honest folk, baited by the ignorantly cruel, feared as something uncanny or diabolic by children and by adults with childish minds.

Old settlers in the Smokies still gossiped betimes over her wild girlhood. It was said that she came from a bad stock, "not our kind of people," but a ruck of shiftless, drunken and thievish drifters. Beaten and starved at home, she took to vagabondage and became depraved beyond the possibility of reform. The authorities gave up trying to tame or salvage this defiant piece of perversity. They took the easy way of driving her on and on, from county to county, shifting the burden from one to another, each in turn glad to be rid of her for a breathing spell.

Years of this wandering and harassed life bred in the outcast a contempt of all mankind and a malignant spite against law and gospel. Nothing but a gag could silence her wicked tongue. In fits of violence she would dance about with clenched fists and howl like a maniac, cursing even a minister in his pulpit or a court in session.

She became notorious, far and near, as a vixen, a spitfire, a fury. Preachers gravely declared that she was possessed with a devil. Common folk agreed, and called her a hell-cat.

But as age came sapping the virago's energies, she gradually subsided into a cold and sullen aloofness. She betook herself to a remote and sequestered hut, where her illegitimate son, Sang Johnny—himself harmless and diligent after his fashion—eked out a living for the two by gathering wild herbs in the forest.

In solitude, chewing the cud of sour and bitter recollections, brooding in a realm of weird fancy, a prey of hallucinations, bedeviled herself by strange perversions of a damnatory creed, this fearsome hag gained the reputation of a witch.

Illiterate and credulous folk among the backwoodsmen began to whisper it about that there were "quar doin's" in the neighborhood. Butter would fail to come in the churn. Cows suddenly and inexplicably went dry. Dogs had fits. Cats went crazy. The old mare's mane was matted into "stirrups," showing that a witch had ridden her in the night.

Mary Ellen Pringle, who took special pride in the clean down and goose feathers of her bed, found that she couldn't sleep o' nights. Suspecting something gone wrong with the mattress, she opened it and found, to her horror, a matted ball of all sorts of dirty feathers—chicken, duck, turkey, owl and crow feathers—a "witch-ball" in her virgin bed! "And, hope I may die if there was ary sign of a hole in that thar tick, whar the like o' that could a-got in!"

One day Old Hex came down from her far-off hill and intruded her presence on Sairy Ponder for an hour's gossip. They were sitting on the porch when down the road from the clay-mine came a six-mule team hauling kaolin. Old Hex stood up and she said to Sairy, "Now look!"

She took a lower corner of her apron in each hand, raised the apron vertically like a sail, and commanded, "Stop!"

The team came at once to a halt and balked. The driver flogged and swore; but not a mule would budge.

Then the crone raised her apron again, reversing the corners, and she said "Now go, damn ye!" Instantly the six mules sprang forward, straining at their traces, and the wagon creaked on out of sight.

"There's no gittin' around sich as that, when you're knowin' to it bein' true," said a gossip. "And you-uns mighty well recollect that when Joshua Judd was drownded in the swift water, and a hunderd men failed to find the corp', Old Hex kem and told 'em she had seed him in a vivid, hung by tree roots deep in a sartin pool downstream. They follered her direction, and—sure enough, thar hit was lodged, in the very i-den-tical way she'd described!"

So went story after story of Old Hex's uncanny prowess. And in time she came to glory in the mean advantage this reputation gave her. She would cackle in triumph when people cowered or when they cursed her from very fear.

It was said that she was not merely possessed by *a* devil, but that she had deliberately sold herself to *the* Devil. Someone who claimed to know how it was done explained that on nine successive days she had gone to a mountain-top at dawn and there she had cursed God. On the ninth, Satan himself appeared to her. The Fiend placed one hand on her head and the other on her feet, taking her oath that all between his hands should thenceforth be his and devoted to his service. In turn he gave her power of second sight; power to read the thoughts of others; to put a spell on man or beast; to transform herself into an animal; to ride a stick through the air at night; to produce sickness, insanity or even death.

Myra had heard these tales. But canny Myra smiled to herself. Whatever superstitions of her own race might be harbored in her dusky breast, she was a thorough rationalist about these tomfooleries of the whites. To her, Old Hex was an impostor, shrewdly playing her neighbors for fools, making a bit of money out of it, now and then, when credulous or malicious people came to her for secret aid.

Now Myra herself needed help, and she was ready to pay good money for it. But the aid she sought from Old Hex was of a sort that called for no faith in the witch's supernatural powers, though she trickishly would profess such confidence.

As the old woman still glared at her with suspicious or hostile eyes, Myra went to clucking surprise and disappointment at the failure to recognize her. Then she broke out in laughter.—

"You not know me any more?" she asked. "Myra fetch you Indian medicine, long time 'go."

Then a light came into the crone's eyes.— "Aye, aye," she exclaimed; "now I make you out. Hell fire! come in and set."

To this polite invitation Myra responded by following Old Hex into her slubbered hut. She sat down on a bench made from a split log.

It was a weird interior, quite in keeping with its beldame mistress. A clapboard table, the log bench and two similarly fashioned stools, a pole bed in the corner, strewn with filthy old quilts: such was the hut's furnishing. A few tattered clothes and many strings of dried herbs were suspended from wooden pegs driven into the walls. A cast-iron spider and a Dutch oven stood, uncleaned, at one side of the fireplace; a sooty coffeepot at the other.

In one corner of the room a ladder gave access to a low cockloft overhead that might be Sang Johnny's roost at night. To the loft beams were racked a hoe, a mattock and a long crosscut saw. On wooden forks over the doorway a cheap shotgun rested. The premises exhaled a sugary and sickly odor that disgusted the Indian woman, but she bore it stolidly.

"Whyn't you brung me medicine, no more?" complained Old Hex.

"Me, I been long time gone—far," answered Myra. "Now I come back; fetch you some."

She untied her shawl and spread some of its contents on the rickety table.

"This, it is *ahawi aktata*, for your sore eyes," she explained. "This, *unnagayee*, for the black spots on your body. This, it is mixtry of three kinds roots: makes man crazy for gal, like buck runnin'—you sell heap powders, this stuff!"

"Aye, aye! How much you want for them leetle yarbs? I'm very poor!"

"I give 'em you, present."

Old Hex clutched the medicaments and the love potions, with no word of thanks, and stored them away. Then the two women went to exchanging news and gossip about their old acquaintances on Deep Creek and the newcomers who had settled there. Myra learned about the Terhunes, the Lumbos and the Burbanks. Finally she inquired who lived now at the third ford above Terhune's.

"Youlus Lumbo—damn his yaller hide! I bite my thumb at the dirty cur!" exclaimed the witch.

"You no like um?"

Old Hex burst out in a profane tirade against Youlus, his family, his mule, and everything that was his.

"He got rabbit-foot mule?" asked Myra.

"Yes, a limpy, little black devil!"

"This Youlus, he big thief," asserted Myra.

"Allers has been; but how did you know?"

"Steal magic stone from my brudder, Degataga," declared the squaw. She gave a brief account of the affair, keeping much of it to herself and particularly saying nothing about Runner's scouting trip.

"How do you know Youlus did it?" asked the witch.

This was the opening Myra had been leading up to. She arose and drew from the bosom of her dress an ancient flint arrowhead to which a waxed string was tied.

"Look," said she.

She held up the string so that the arrowhead depended from it like a plumb-bob. The arrow spun round and round, then settled and pointed straight to the doorway. Myra stepped out of the hut, Old Hex trailing behind. At a bend of the path the arrow swerved and pointed to the new direction. They went on over the field. At each turn of the path, the arrow turned correspondingly.

"How do you do that?" asked the witch.

"Not me," lied Myra smoothly; "arrow, he do it. Indian magic. All time arrow point right way. I go from Degataga, his house: arrow show where. Come big road: arrow point to Kittuwa. Come Kittuwa: arrow show one street. Me, I go wrong way: arrow git mad, spin round and round. Go right way: arrow still. Come Deep Creek: arrow point up here. Come Lumbo, his stable: arrow point straight down to ground. Me, I find anything lost, that way."

"Let me try it!" cried the old dame.

"No good," declared Myra. "Medicine man, he conjure first; then give me arrow. I talk all time to arrow. Must talk Cherokee—English no good. Indian magic."

Old Hex was awed. In common with ignorant whites everywhere, she believed that the Indians possessed medicines and charms of extraordinary potency; that they had strange gifts of divination and a gypsy-like faculty of discerning events in distant places. They could beat her at her own game.

"If I could do that, I' make it pay me rael money," she declared.

"You make it money now," said Myra. From somewhere about her person, as by slight of hand, she produced a shining yellow coin and held it before the rapt old woman. "You see this!" she exclaimed.

"Gold!" cried the witch. "Gold!"

"Yes, it is gold," murmured Myra. Then in a low voice, as though fearful of eavesdroppers, she confided her secret to Old Hex.—

"Indian magic find who got stone. Lumbo got it. But me, I go to Lumbo, say, 'You give me stone,' he hit me on head. White magic must get stone. You make white magic. Tell Lumbo terrible charm, that stone: better give up—strike him blind, that stone; make him heap sick, he die. Lumbo 'fraid o' white magic; 'fraid o' Old Hex. He give um up. You git gold."

The hag's eyes glittered with understanding. Her fingers clawed the air.

"Tomorrow I'll git it," she declared. "Tonight, when the owls hoot, I'll conjure and set all the devils of hell to work on Youlus. He'll writhe in torment till he gives up that Indian stone."

TWENTY-FOUR

Matlock was taken to a hospital. An X-ray examination showed that his skull was not fractured; yet there was a lesion of some sort that kept him in a torpid or dazed condition for many hours. When he recovered complete consciousness he was interested in nothing but his aches and pains. He had severe recurrent headaches. In the intervals of ease he lay in a state of lassitude as if not caring whether he ever got out of bed. This was in such marked contrast with his normal habit of restless energy and impatience of restraint that the doctors shook their heads and forecast a slow recovery.

Questioning irritated him. When foolishly inquisitive visitors tried to quiz him, he only growled and stared them down; or, if they persisted, he swore volubly and told them to mind their own business. When the sheriff asked him what he proposed to do with Cabarrus, he said, "That can wait," and he then turned his face to the wall and complained of headache.

Confidentially the sheriff gave his own view of the case to Colonel Fielding.— "Matlock realizes that he has overplayed his hand. He knows when he's beaten: so, gambler-like, he takes his medicine in silence, not fighting it or whining. If he has any plans for the future, he's wise enough to keep his mouth shut."

In the absence of any charge against Cabarrus, no action was taken against him. His papers were returned and he stored them safely in bank. Free, now, to go his own way, he resumed his prospecting in Nick's Nest.

Everything in the Alcove was as he had left it, save that wood rats and white-footed mice had chewed up some of his cotton things for nest material and a family of flying squirrels had made themselves at home in his pack-sack. Tracks in the dust showed where skunks and raccoons had prowled and tried to raid his larder; but they were foiled by the precaution he had taken of hanging his bacon and food bags by wires from a high rack.

John's natural resilience of temperament brought him back in rebound from the fears of yesterday to the hopes of today. He got busy at once, following the fault-plane, taking specimens every here and there, testing with his blowpipe kit. Down in Nick's Run and along its feeders he labored with his pan. Frequently he found traces of interesting minerals; but nowhere did he locate a vein that would be profitable to work.

As the days went by and he still found nothing of commercial value, the strain of disappointment began to tell. He grew stern and haggard; lost zest and appetite; felt himself slipping.

One day he suddenly realized that he was talking to himself, not quite aloud, but in a muttering, grumbling way. "Good God!" thought he, "am I becoming senile? Is solitude turning me into a doddering fool?"

The sky was gray and lowery. The glen had fallen prematurely into shadow. A cold wind came down the trough of the mountain and a dreary drizzle of rain set in. The woods took on a somber aspect. The birds were silenced. Foxes slunk to their dens amid the rocks and timorous rabbits shivered miserably in their coverts.

The breeze died down, but the wretched mizzle continued and the hollows of the hills were filled with a stagnant fog. The woods were too wet for John to keep on at work and the air too cold for him to sit still, even in the shelter of the Alcove.

He collected some dead laurel for kindling and started a fire. This was the fuel he had been using all along to do his cooking; for laurel is of such sprangling growth that the dead tops mostly stand free from the ground and so they season snap-dry, instead of getting sodden and rotten. Besides, the dry laurel or rhododendron ignites readily, gives out an intense heat, lasts well, and raises no smoke.

Heretofore, Cabarrus had been very sparing of fuel, making no fires except to cook by; for a regular camp-fire would have betrayed his whereabouts. But now he piled logs of down-wood on the fire and warmed the whole Alcove by their reflected heat. The pyre gave off volumes of smoke, but that did not matter now, for the reek blended with the mist and was indistinguishable.

With nothing to do but sit and brood, John's mind was led into melancholy speculations, influenced, no doubt, by his wild and awesome surroundings. He glanced upward at the dragon carved on the Alcove wall.

Was it a mark to fix location, as a woodsman would blaze a tree? Not likely. Savages need no waymarks other than those that Nature supplies. It might be a totem, the emblem of an individual who had here performed some feat of daring that he thus recorded on the rock. Or possibly it was a talisman to keep off evil spirits while the solitary hunter slept in these haunted woods.

Cabarrus realized that the vivid imagination of primitive man peopled the earth and the elements with spirits, some of them malevolent, which could only be warded off by use of amulets and sacred rites. To him they were no mere poetic images, such as John himself fancied sometimes in his lighter moods, but dreadful realities in which the savage believed with his whole heart and soul. Ah! no wonder men were cruel and bestial in those days when life was a bedlam of superstitious fears.

John shrugged his shoulders and strove to turn his thoughts into pleasanter channels. But it was no use. Who could be jolly on such a day as this? It is all well enough to be alone in the wild forest when the weather is fair and bracing, and a body has something strenuous or interesting to do; but this abominable chilly fog and the dripping wetness of the woods oppressed him with a feeling of futility and an eagerness to get away.

After all the toil and danger, what did this venture of his amount to? He had won the first round of his fight, to be sure: he had established his right to take any mineral treasure he might find on Matlock's land, or in the rocks under the land, as far as China. But if he should fail—fail to unearth anything of value, after all this fuss over a title, he would be a laughing-stock, a fool for his pains!

Aye, worse: he would have spent his savings to no avail. He would be left as poor as Job's turkey— hard pushed to make a living for himself alone.

And John Cabarrus, in this last week or so, had learned, beyond self-delusion, that he no longer wanted to live alone.

Good Lord! was he growing morbid, timorous? Snap out of it! He sprang to his feet. There *was* treasure in Nick's Nest. Hadn't his grandfather known where it lay? Well, it was there yet, waiting for the man who knew how to utilize it. He, himself, was that man. He would find it. He would make good!

Chunks of it, big chunks, the old naturalist had brought out of here. Beryl—massive crude beryl, from which beryllium is derived. There must be a bed of the precious stuff still hidden, unmined, inviolate, somewhere in the nooks or pits of Nick's Nest.

The pits! By all the Thunders and Thunder Boys! Why the devil had he been pottering over the surface? Down below—down in the darkness under the earth—down where the mountain had been split apart—that was the place to look!

John seized the new staff that he had cut for his climbing. He set things to rights, closed his little tent, and strode off along the secret trail that led out from the Alcove along the jungly side of the ridge. Off through the dribbling fog to Kittuwa! Tools he must have, and dynamite.

He had no more than reached the top of the ridge at the Pullback trail when the mist rose streaming from the glens and valleys. Then the sun burst out and covered all the mountains with its glory. The cheer of its warm rays and the pulse of his own activity put him in good heart, so that he whistled as he hurried forward.

When he came down off the ridge at the Lumbo settlement he observed a strange flustered ado about the shacks. At the Youlus place a farm wagon was loading with household furniture, a pitifully meager outfit. A red-haired woman and some tow-headed children were bustling about, carrying things out of the house and stowing them awkwardly in the wagon. He caught a glimpse of Youlus, who, recognizing him, dodged out of sight, moving in a queer jerky way and with his face twitching. Youlus looked sick and haggard.

Down at 'Poleon Lumbo's hut another wagon was similarly employed and another family of ragged folk was hurrying to pack up. 'Poleon himself was not there. The woman and her brood had a frightened air.

John wondered what had broken loose, but he marched on without speaking to anyone. At Terhune's he found Kit and Bupply. To Kit he remarked: "The Lumbos seem to be moving."

"Yeah," grunted Kit. "Good riddance to bad rubbish!"

"What got them in the notion, all at once?"

"Youlus has done gone crazy."

"How do you mean, crazy?"

"He thinks he's bewitched."

John burst out laughing.— "What do you think about it?" he asked the boy.

"Well," judicially, "d'you ever see Old Hex?"

"No. Who or what is Old Hex?"

"Sang Johnny's mother—the yarb hunter's. They live 'way yander on the fur side o' the creek, high on a hill, among the woods, in a pen I wouldn't keep hogs in. She's as ugly as ha'nt-bait, and if the Devil's tuk a fancy to her, he ain't got no taste, is all I can say."

"What's she got to do with the Lumbos moving?"

"I don't know the ins and outs of it; but there's been some quar doin's around hyur."

Bupply looked up at John with a frightened stare.— "I've swallered a live minner to keep from gittin' 'witched," he confessed.

"Swallowed a live minnow! Bewitched! You!"

Kit slapped Bupply till the child bawled.— "You dumb fool, to believe the like o' that!" he cried. "They's enough idgits in this settle-*ment*, without the Terhunes losin' their minds."

John soothed Bupply with a new dime. Then of Kit he asked: "Do many folks around here believe in witchcraft?"

"Naw!" answered Kit, scornfully. "Thar's jist a few, hyur and thar, that cain't read or write, and got no sense, nohow. All the Lumbos are that sort. My pap done seed 'em, one time—the hull kit and caboodle o' growed-up Lumbos—a-squattin' around a tub o' clar water on the floor. Each and everyone, by turn, dipped a gourd in the water, helt it high over the tub, and spilt the water back agin. The one for which the biggest bubbles riz from the water was the one had done been bewitched.

"That happened to be 'Poleon. Nex' day was Sunday, and they all went to Church and prayed the masterfullest praars—all o' them, that is, but 'Poleon: he wasn't fitten, 'cayse he was bewitched. So 'Poleon stayed at home and moulded him a silver bullet to kill the witch with. The fust visitor would be either the witch or the Devil hisself.

"Pap didn't go nigh that place for a week, fearin' to git shot. Said he druther keep silver in his pocket than his innards. But I went thar—they don't take boys into 'count—and I told 'Poleon I seed a raven big as a turkey flyin' hell-bent for Thunderhead and a-squawkin', *I got to go—I got to go-o-o!* Ravens kin talk, you know."

"Well, what then?" asked Cabarrus.

"W'y, 'Poleon got easy in his mind. Said the witch had emigrunted."

"So you're a witch-doctor, eh?"

"Yeah: I cured him with a damn lie."

Cabarrus chuckled.— "Which of them is bewitched this time?" he asked.

"Hit's Youlus. They *is* somethin' quar about that. Nigh about a week ago, as I was fishin', who should I see but a Indian squaw comin' barefoot along the road. Fust Indian I seed on Deep Creek in my time. Natcherly I drapped my pole and spied on her. She turned yan side and climb the hill to Sang Johnny's.

"Well, sir, nex' day—believe it or not—hyur kem Old Hex waddlin' by our-unses place. I tuk my foot in hand and follered, to see what the old devil was up to. She went right to Youlus Lumbo's stable. He was inside, feedin' his mule, and had his back turned. She coughed, and he turned, and—thar stood Old Hex!

"Youlus turned pale as a corp' and for a time he was, in a manner o' speakin', stone dead. Old Hex went to havin' speech with him. I was too fur off to rec'nize what she said; but hit must a-been somethin' orful; for Youlus went to tremblin' and a-beggin', and, by John Thomas, a-cryin' like a kid gittin' a lickin'. Hit was hateful to see!"

"Then what?" asked Cabarrus, who was stirred by Kit's mention of the squaw.

"Old Hex she raised her squawk and yelled, 'You git it—you git it *right now!*'"

"And what did Youlus do?"

"He shummicked off inter the woods, up the hill, and was gone some time. Old Hex moved back down the road to whar they's a dead tree the lightin' killed; and thar she stuck. Bimeby, hyur kem Youlus, toterin' along like a old man with the palsy. He retched out his hand to Old Hex and give her somethin' wropped in a yaller rag—mebbe 'twas leather. Then he knelt down and said somethin', as though he was prayin', and got up and went away. And, by grannies, then what you think happened?"

"What did happen?"

"That Indian squaw riz right up out o' the bushes, from behint the dead tree, and Old Hex give her the passel. The squaw give Hex somethin'—I dunno what—and away she highballed, might' nigh runnin', down the road towards Kittuwa."

"That was a week ago, you say?"

"Nigh about. Well, ever sence then, Youlus has been crazy. He got the jerks and the weak trembles, so's he cain't hardly walk nor put a cup o' water to his face 'thout spillin' hit. His face has the jerks, too, and one eye is nigh shet.

"Ma went thar to see could she do anything fer 'em, and Youlus told her: 'I've a sentiment like bugs crawl in, over my skin; but when I look, they ain't none thar. I've a bumbly noise in my head, like bees buzzin' or wheels goin' round. My heart gits spells o' flutterin' and I choke up till I'm nigh sifflicated. Whut you reckon ails me?' And his wife told him: 'You know good and well what ails you. Old Hex lied to you. She did *not* take the spell off.' So, as I say: that pizen old woman did do somethin' to him—I dunno what."

"And now they're moving away," said Cabarrus thoughtfully.

"Yeah. 'Poleon left fust, all by his lone self. Then all the Lumbo fam'lies got narvish. I snuck up thar a time or two, and they was all cussin' and cryin' around, havin' a big through. Aleck is aimin' to move, too—soon as he can sell his yearlin's. Hit's jist as well; for Pap says ever'body on the creek was sick and tired o' them trash and there was talk o' runnin' them out, anyhow."

"Well, I'm glad to hear this," said Cabarrus. "With them gone, this will be a decent community. Everybody else around here, that I've met, is honest and kindly and a good citizen. I don't know better folks anywhere than your mountaineers, taking them as a whole. But there's always and everywhere a riffraff that gives trouble and gets talked about so much that they can give a whole settlement a bad name."

"I reckon we're shet o' Matlock, too," said Kit approvingly.

"I think so," said John.

"We-uns used to wonder what you was up to. You kivvered your tracks so durn well."

"Oh! So you noticed that?"

"I'll *say* we did. I tried my own self to foller you, but lost your tracks at Lick-log Gap. Then Pap obsarved that Youlus Lumbo was out, day after day a-huntin' you, and comin' back all wore out and mad. That's when Youlus fust begun gittin' the jerks. He tuk to thinkin' mebbe you was a ha'nt."

"How do you know?"

"Pap follered Youlus."

"Oh, and did anybody follow Pap?"

"Uh-huh," grunted Kit, nodding.

"Who?"

"Me."

TWENTY-FIVE

When Cabarrus drove up to Colonel Fielding's home, Marian met him on the porch.

"Oh, John," she cried, "they've found the Ulunsuti! One of the Lumbos had stolen it. Myra went up Deep Creek and somehow she got it back. She stopped here, on her way home, and showed it to me."

"I know how she got it," said John; and he told her what Kit had reported. "I suppose Matlock was at the bottom of all this," he added.

"No," said Marian, "I've learned that Matlock had a falling-out with this Lumbo before the robbery occurred. Youlus must have been trailing you over the country and he followed us to Degataga's home."

"How is the old chief now?"

"He's up and about, so the sheriff says, and little the worse for wear. What luck have you been having, John?"

"So far, I've found nothing worth while; but I know the stuff is there. I'll plug along till I do find it."

"Do you believe in hunches?"

"No."

"*I* do, and I know you'll succeed. Myra is sure of it, too. She says the Little People like you."

"Oh! So she's been telling you fairy tales."

"Well, you believe in fairies—don't you?"

"I believe in one with all my heart."

"You goose! Come in and tell Aunt Kate what you've been up to. She's all in a flutter over your doings and wants to hear about them from your own lips."

Of course John went in. He was shy and made a poor start; but Aunt Kate was adept at drawing him out. In five minutes he was talking about himself and the wild Smokies as freely as if he had known her all his life.

"The hidden glen that you call Nick's Nest must be an awful place to stay in, all alone," said she.

"I wouldn't mind, but for one thing," explained John. "It is so deep and narrow and heavily wooded that the sun doesn't shine directly into it till nine in the morning; then it leaves so early in the afternoon that the nights are very long."

"What on earth do you do, to pass the time, from dark till bedtime? Surely you don't go owling around in the woods."

"No: if a man tried that in Nick's Nest, he'd break some bones. I potter around in camp, plan the next day's work, and listen to the voices of the night. For amusement I make up—well, bedtime stories, rhymes, nonsense."

"A poet! And we've been taking you for a scientist, with nothing but rocks and metals on your mind."

"I am a scientist," said John; "but rocks and metals grow burdensome at times. One must play, you know; and Nick's Nest is no golf course."

"Why don't you read or write? Have you no lantern or candles?"

"I haven't dared show a light. It would have guided the spies to me."

"Horror! You had to sit there, silent, through those long black hours, for fear of being shot from the bushes!"

"Not just that; but I couldn't afford to let Matlock and his gang know where I was so long as I hadn't recovered the will."

"Ugh! I've heard things about that hideous Matlock that made my blood run cold."

"He is out of the way, now; and the Lumbos, too. I'll be left in peace. It will be fine to come and go in the open, once more, and do everything aboveboard. That hiding out was the hardest of all to bear—covering my tracks like a fugitive."

"How did you get in and out of Nick's Nest without leaving traces? I'm told those backwoodsmen can trail like Indians."

John laughed.— "I had to have a pathway, of course; but it was a labyrinth in the tall undergrowth. It was in segments, like a disjointed snake, with blind ends leading nowhere. The segments overlapped, but were some distance apart, with dense brush growing everywhere between them. In passing from one to the other, I never went twice over the same ground. The ends of the segments were bent away in confusing directions. The entrance to the Alcove was very narrow and I masked it with dead laurel with the tops bristling outward, I'd pull a laurel bush aside, to enter, and then replace it."

Marian had come in. She asked: "When may I see your cliff-dwelling, John?"

"Whenever you wish."

"I'm going back to the Burbanks tomorrow."

"Day after tomorrow, then, I'll come over and guide you to the Alcove. I must set my house in order," he laughed.— "Make a camp broom and sweep the cave floor."

"You shall do no such thing. Fancy a cave-man with a broom! Just stay in character."

"Well, look for me at nine, day after tomorrow. The dew will be off the bushes by that hour."

"But if it's raining?"

"I'll come for a visit, anyway. On rainy days I'm lonesome."

"Oh, just on rainy days?"

She read the answer in his eyes.

John took his leave and went to a hardware store for tools and dynamite. The sheriff, seeing him, came across the street.

"Matlock is selling out and leaving the country for good," said the officer.

"Is he up and attending to business in person?" asked John.

"No: his affairs are in the hands of lawyer Grimes. Matlock is worse hurt than I thought: the doctors say he'll never be himself again. They're sending him to Florida with a nurse."

John stood with hands in pockets, for a time, studying.

"Well," said he, "if that's the case, there'll be no more trouble between him and me. I've won all I was after. The incident is closed."

"That's right," said the sheriff gravely. "He's a broken man."

Cabarrus stowed his supplies in his car and then went to see lawyer Grimes.

"Is Matlock's property on Deep Creek for sale?" he inquired.

"Yes, sir."

"What does he want for it?"

"There's a rock-bottom price of three thousand dollars; one-third down, balance in one and two years. I think it's a bargain."

"How about a ninety-day option?"

"Speaking for yourself?"

"Yes."

"You can have it. Five percent down."

John took out his purse.— "Draw it up," said he.

Soon he had the option deposited with his other papers in the bank.

An hour before sunset he was back in Nick's Nest, with his hammer, drill and dynamite. In his pocket was left barely enough money to carry him back to New York.

"Now I've staked my last cent on it," said he to himself. "Hurrah for Nick's Nest!"

Then came the longest night he ever spent in the Alcove. By this time in June the moon rose late; so there were several hours of utter blackness following his lonely supper. He built a roaring camp-fire, not caring, now, whom or what it might attract. The firelight dispelled the immediate gloom and dried the interior of his little tent, which heretofore had been coldly wet to the touch, at night, from the excessive humidity of the forest atmosphere.

In the first week of his seclusion here, John had not been much affected by physical discomforts. It was lonesome, of course, without even a dog to keep him company; but he had been so stimulated by the thrill of exploration and buoyed up by the hope of immediate rich discoveries that he had kept in good cheer.

But another week of hard work unrequited had narrowed the chance of success. It brought him up against a possibility, if not a probability, of failure.

Ugh! that infernal recurrent doubt that haunted the back of his mind! In broad day he could put it away, while going actively about his business; but in wakeful hours at night it ate into him like a corrosive poison.

So, this night, he had but a fitful rest. More than once he came upright in bed with a chill at his heart, as though some bloodless, clammy thing were clutching at his vitals.

But at peep of day he was gently roused by the chirping and cheeping of small birds welcoming the dawn. Their gaiety was contagious. He hurried down to Nick's Run and bathed in a cold, fern-bowered pool. Then a vigorous scramble up the roundabout way to his cliff-house put him in a glow. He got breakfast over the big, smoke-less bed of coals that was left of his all-night fire. He ate with zest and felt like a new man.

To the devil with doubts! He was strong enough now to tear the mountain apart and make it give up its secrets. He took up his prospecting pick and his electric torch. Over the rampart of broken rocks he clambered toward the farther fault-plane.

Over there was a great fissure that went down to an unknown depth: an abyss blacker than midnight. He had observed it the day he crossed over to Burbank's side of the ridge and found Marian; but he had never examined it with particular attention.

Now he went directly there and dropped a pebble into the rift. The round stone dropped vertically about six feet, then rolled off downward at a slant, and again it dropped straight down, striking bottom with a thud.

The opening at the top of the crack was too narrow for a man to descend; but Cabarrus found, by poking with a long stick, that it rapidly widened below. The cleft was thin-edged at the ground surface. The rock was cleavable stuff that broke rather easily under the hammer. He chipped off enough on each side, with the hammer-head of his little pick, to widen the entrance so he could slip down sidewise without danger of sticking fast.

The beam of his light showed that there was good footing below and that there were no snakes. John lowered himself. He stood, then, at the upper end of an incline, the top of his head just level with the entrance he had made at the surface. Stooping, he found room to move in a crouching position.

He flashed the light down the slope and then worked his way cautiously to the edge of the drop-off. Here his torch revealed a wider and deeper fissure, twelve feet to the bottom, with walls converging where he squatted but widening below in what appeared to be a chamber of considerable size, with a flat floor.

John scrambled back out of the hole. He said to himself: "So far, I've only been scratching the surface of the mountain. Down below, I can find what this formation is made of. I'm going to do it!"

He hurried back to the Alcove, whistling as he went. There he got his hunter's axe and chopped down a stout young tree that bristled with branches almost to the ground. He lopped off the limbs, leaving stubs of them sticking out, and so made an "Indian ladder," which he carried back to the rift. Lowering this and sliding it along the incline, he let it down to the floor of the chamber. The upper end he jammed firmly into a crevice, so it could not slip or turn.

Then down his pole ladder he went, carrying only his electric torch and the short-handled pick. Alone, he disappeared into the black pit, where no man ever had ventured before him.

At the bottom of the chasm John stood erect and found himself in a rectangular space like an arched vault, about ten feet wide and twice as long. A dim light filtered down from cracks overhead, like fading twilight. It seemed to be warning him to be gone, lest long night entrap him here.

He shuddered at the tomb-like silence and the chill of the darkness under the earth. He cleared his throat. The sound gave him a nervous start, as if he had profaned a sanctuary of the dead. There was a creepy sensation on his skin: invisible fingers seemed to reach out from the shadows and touch him with cold, unfleshly tips.

Phantoms—bugaboos! A fine explorer, he, to shiver here like a scared urchin in a cellar at night, venturing after apples!

John threw the beam of his flashlight along the wall at his right. It revealed a pegmatite dike of coarsely crystallized quartz, feldspar and mica, with other minerals embedded in the matrix. There was a great bed of this rock running through the basic granite of the mountain.

The opposite wall of the chamber was plain granite, sparkling with tiny facets of mica. Some convulsion of nature in byegone time had cloven this formation apart, splitting it cleanly along the face of the dike.

As John approached the farther end of the chamber he saw something strangely different from either pegmatite or granite. A great columnar crystal protruded vertically from the right-hand wall, reaching from floor to ceiling like a buttress. It was over three feet thick, greenish white, with a pearly luster.

With bated breath he regarded it for a moment, then stepped forward to give it close inspection. He broke off a piece and studied it with enforced skepticism, curbing his eagerness lest he suffer a maddening disappointment. But there was no mistaking this. Here was his opaque beryl in massive form—source of that remarkable metal, beryllium, on which his hopes were centered.

It was identical with the stuff his grandfather had discovered in Nick's Nest. He had not found it here in the depths, of course, but on the surface—an outcrop now hidden by the underbrush.

Poor old man! To him the chunk of beryl had been nothing but a cabinet specimen for collectors to linger over.

Where the column protruded from the cave wall the passage narrowed to a mere ledge, about three feet wide, with a gaping black gulf on the left that went down into God knew what. John ignored the abyss and strode forward, eager to see if the beryl continued as a vein on the far side. There was another and larger chamber beyond.

As he rounded the buttress and threw his light ahead into that inner room he beheld an astounding spectacle.

A blazing coruscation! Sparkles of dazzling brilliancy burst from pockets in the pegmatite with a glory that made John doubt his senses. They came from exposed crystals, of all sizes and colors, that were set like jewels in the rock. The parting of the dike from its neighbor granite had uncovered them as though lids had been lifted from so many caskets.

"Great God!" cried Cabarrus: "Has the crude beryl deposit of my dreams turned out to be a gem mine?"

Dazed, with heart bounding, he stepped quickly forward toward the scintillating lures. He was no longer mindful of his footing, no longer conscious of the black chasm lurking on his left.

Then terribly, without an instant's warning, he was swept out of his entrancing prospect into the very grip of death.

His foot slipped. He fell in a flash. His right side struck with cruel, numbing violence against the edge of the abyss.

He whirled with cat-like quickness, face downward, striving to save himself with palms and finger-tips desperately clinging to the smooth, moist rock.

But there was no roughness to catch and hold; no friction to check him. The sloping rock was slick as if it had been oiled.

He shot over the edge and down into the awful blackness of the pit.

He struck and stopped. The impact jarred every bone in his body and the brain in his brain-pan.

Utter darkness!

Were his eyes out?

The flashlight had dropped from his hand. Somewhere it lay shattered and forever useless. The pick, too, was gone.

For a time John lay on his side, gasping, unable to move a finger. His heart was in the clutch of horror. O, that solid blackness! It pressed him on all sides like water against a deep-sea diver. The very rock around him seemed to contract, slowly, inexorably, with a creeping compression that nothing could withstand.

He was sinking into a stupor. Pitifully he struggled to command his senses. A spark of will-power came aglow. He moved one hand—it hurt. He moved the arm—it hurt worse. Pain helped him to think. Deliberately he increased it by rising to his elbow. Ah, that arm was not broken!

He sat up. His feet stuck out over a void. He felt of himself. No bones seemed to be broken: he was only bruised and stunned. Blood trickled down his face from a scalp wound.

He braced himself with back against the stone wall of the rift. Courage! Pretty soon he would be fit. But, O, what darkness!

He had matches. They were in a waterproof box that he always carried and kept filled. Thank God for matches! He got out the little box from his breeches pocket. The tiny flare of the match did not penetrate far into the dark, but it did reveal his immediate surroundings. He had been caught by a ledge of protruding rock, so narrow that a man could barely stand up on it. He would try that when his legs quit trembling.

The rift was not quite vertical. It sloped inward from the point from which he had fallen. The ledge on which he sat was on the farther side, across the chasm. The granite at his back was far too hard for him to carve handholds in it with his knife. There was no chance to escape that way. The opposite wall was too far across the gulf to reach, and it sloped inward, toward the pit, instead of away from him.

He managed to get to his feet. Holding a match high overhead, he saw the place from which he had fallen. It was four feet above his utmost tiptoed reach. A treacherous smooth groove, only two feet wide, slanted downward through the middle of the passageway to the inner chamber where the crystals blazed. He could easily have stepped across it to good footing, if only he had cast a glance down to the rock floor.

O fool—fool!

The match burned out. He sank down again upon the ledge and strove with all his might to think up some way of escape from the horror of the strangling darkness.

He struck another match and dropped it into the pit below; but it immediately went out. He felt of his handkerchief: it was dry enough to burn. With a third match he ignited it and dropped it as a flare into the dismal chasm. Alas! There was no exit below. The blazing rag showed forty feet of gradually narrowing crack in which a falling body would wedge fast forever.

He was entombed. With sickening certainty he realized that no possible struggle or device of his could ever free him from this awful trap. Through everlasting night he would linger, suffering the torments of hunger and thirst, the greater torture of the crushing darkness, gradually losing his mind, until in agony he would writhe over the ledge and plunge to merciful death in the black pit below.

He sank upon his face and groaned, "O God—my God!"

TWENTY-SIX

Marian was ready for the woods. Sylvia had cooked a chicken and put up a nice lunch for the young couple.

"I betcha that'll taste good to a man that's been livin' on bacon and canned stuff," she said.

Tom had stayed at home this morning. He was uneasy in his mind. What was this pair of "furriners" up to? Why was Cabarrus still staying on in Dog-eater Hollow, of all abominable places on earth? Tom himself had never ventured there but once, and that was plenty. Its evil reputation for "ha'nts" had never daunted him—Tom was a born rationalist and feared neither spooks nor devils—but the gulch was so confounded rough that nobody of sense would think of camping there, unless he had to.

Still, of course, Cabarrus was not what you'd call a fool. Tom had sized him up, noting how he carried himself under strain. Yes, the fellow was a man, all right, and he went about his business in a practical way. It was right for him to have holed up in Dog-eater Hollow till he found the will—Tom himself could not have hit on a shrewder way to circumvent Matlock and the spying Lumbos—but that was over. What was Cabarrus doing there now?

And this college girl? As pretty a picture of enticing womanhood as man ever saw. Fit to bring up a family of bouncing kids, as God intended. But just fribbling around in the woods, picking up weeds for keepsakes. Weeds! Good God A'mighty!

If they were in love with each other, these two, as Tom more than suspected, why in thunder didn't they stay in the settlements, eat ice cream, see the movies, dance, go joy-riding, sing together in church, and raise Cain generally, like young folks ought to? Huh! This prowling around in the woods was one devil of a way to go a-courting!

Nine o'clock.

Marian was in the doorway, looking for John. Her cheeks were flushed, her eyes sparkling with eagerness to greet him.

Sylvia came and put her arm around the girl, humming a woeful ballad in a minor key, as was her custom when her spirits were high—just as Tom would roar out a melancholy revival hymn about sinners in torment, when he himself was full of moonshine and feeling bully.

Nine-thirty.

What was delaying John? He had said so distinctly "nine o'clock," and had promised to come, rain or shine. It wasn't like him to be late in keeping an engagement.

Marian went back into the "company room" where she could be alone with her disappointment. Sylvia was getting fidgety. She went out into the yard, time and again, to look and listen. Even little Margaret had sensed something wrong.

Ten o'clock.

Tom paced back and forth in the yard. Margaret toddled after him, to and fro, to and fro, with curly head bent and plump little hands behind her back.

"What's the matter, Marjy?" asked Tom.

"Daddy, you let me be," replied the child. "I'm narvish."

Sylvia ran and caught Margaret to her bosom, kissing her.

Marian, checking a sob, came out to Tom and asked him how to get into Nick's Nest.

"There ain't no way," said he, "but jist to smash through the brush. I'm goin' over thar, myself, right now."

"I'm going with you," declared Marian.

"You! W'y you'd never make it. That's a perfec' pant'er-den of a place. You stay here with Sylvy till I git back. If ary thing's wrong with your young man, I'll help him and bring him out."

"I'm going with you!" The girl's eyes flashed as she repeated her decision in a higher key.

Tom regarded her with stern eyes, but the corners of his mouth twitched and his lower lip stuck out.

"I don't ginerally, usually let no woman boss me," he declared. "But if nothin' else'll do you but to git all scratched with briers and your clothes torn off, w'y, all right, all right."

Tom went into the house. On the wall was a Philippine bolo, shorter than a machete and with broader, heavier blade. A timber cruiser who had used it in slashing his way through Smoky Mountain thickets had left it with Tom as a present. Burbank now took it down and strapped it to him.

"There's never been no trail cut into Dog-eater," he explained to Marian. "I reckon now's the time to make one."

He pointed to the high ridge south of them.— "You see yon knob with the three pines on it, and a deep gap to the left?"

"Yes," said Marian.

"We'll set our course for that gap. Come on."

Sylvia asked: "What if Mr. Cabarrus shows up while you're gone?"

"Blow the horn," answered Tom. "I'll be listenin' for it."

The hound came looking up into Tom's face, wagging its tail furiously and trembling with eagerness to go along.

"All right, Don," said Tom. "We may need you, old boy."

They crossed the branch and went on into the same woods where Cabarrus had made his courtly bow to "Maid Marian" and announced himself as a henchman of Robin Hood.

Then up the steep side of the ridge they toiled, Tom slashing in advance, wielding the bolo with tireless arm, cutting out only the chief impediments, wasting no time on niceties, zigzagging this way and that for secure footing, "breasting the mountain," as Tom called it. Yes, breasting sixty-degree slopes and rubbing shoulders with the cliffs.

In half an hour they came out of the laurel and into the gap. Tom stopped to slow down his breathing and to reconnoiter.

"I ain't never been right hyur, before," said he, "and a feller cain't see what's ahead of us, down below. But I know, in reason, Cabarrus must have found a bit of a flat som'ers up hyur on the side o' the ridge; 'caze there jist ain't none down in the gulch. But is it to right or left? We'll have to project around till we find out."

"Call him," suggested Marian,

Who-ee-ee-ee: Tom let out a shrill hunter's call that rang over the hills with bugle clearness. They listened with strained ears. Don understood it and stood tensely acock, listening, scenting.

There was no answer. The forest was silent as the grave.

Tom drew the heavy revolver from under his armpit and fired two shots in quick succession, paused, and fired another.

No answer.

"Durn it!" exclaimed Tom. "A deef man ought to hear that, if he's anywhar in the holler, or on the Pullback trail comin' to my house. D'you reckon he changed his mind and went to Kittuwa or som'ers?"

"No, no: he wouldn't do that. O Tom, he's been hurt! I know he's hurt! Hurry! My God, we must find him!"

Tom seized the girl's shoulder as she started forward.

"Fust thing," said he calmly, "We got to find his camp. If he ain't thar, there'll be traces o' some sort. We'll track him from his hide-out, whar he must a-spent the night. This dog o' mine ain't no bloodhound, but he's got a heap o' sense."

Marian patted the dog's head. He looked up at her with wistful eagerness to do his part, whatever it might be that they were after.

They went on down from the gap, over rough rocks, slashing through laurel and briery vines, until presently Tom emerged in a plain trail, recently trimmed out but little used.

"Hyur we are," said Tom cheerily. "It's his'n."

Quickly they moved off to the left, following the sinuous path as it wound in and out among the spurs and furrows of the mountain. They came to a bend, and then abruptly to a blind end of the trail.

"Huh! He quit hyur," observed Tom. "I see: he started a trail to the top o' the ridge, but only got this fur. Turn around. His camp's yon way," and Tom pointed backward toward their starting point.

They returned. A hundred and fifty yards to the west they were checked by another blind end. Tom peered about, but the dense undergrowth, higher than their heads, was matted all around them.

"Well, I'll be damned!" exploded Tom. "He done this a-purpose."

"Yes," said Marian. "I remember he told Aunt Kate how he masked his trail. It's continued off to one side. Go aside, to right or left, and you'll strike it again."

Tom wielded his bolo, cutting through to a lower level, and, sure enough, here was the trail again. Presently they came to the edge of a cliff and to a barrier of great tumbled rocks that seemed to forbid farther advance. There was a lot of dead laurel bristling toward their faces like a *chevaux-de-frise.*

"That looks natural; but 'tain't," said Tom, pointing to the laurel. He pulled some of it away and discovered rude stone steps leading down into.—

"The Alcove!" cried Marian. "And there's his little tent! O John—John!" she called.

The girl rushed ahead of Tom, and so did the dog.

"Cain't keep ary one o' them at heel," grumbled Tom. "They got no manners a-tall."

Marian cast one swift glance all about the place and then ran to the little tent. She cast off the bobbinet front and peered within, expecting to find John sick abed.

He was not there. The blanket was neatly folded over the short air-mattress, the pillow at the head of the bed, a pair of moccasins at the foot. On a flat rock to one side were a small toilet case, a first-aid kit, binoculars and blowpipe kit.

"Oh, where can he be?" she moaned.

Tom appeared not to notice her anxiety.— "That bit of a tent, now, is the trick!" he approved. "Cabarrus don't need it in this place as a shelter from the el-e-ments, 'caze they's a good stone roof overhead; but it keeps out the snakes and polecats and wood rats and daddy-longlegs that are so darned neighborly at night."

He cast an appraising eye over the camp in general.

"Ain't many men so tidy in camp," he observed. "No litter on the floor; no old tin cans or rubbish. Cookin' vessels all washed and hung up. Clothes on a line to sun and air. Lookee how keerful he is about stowin' his grub."

Tom pointed to a rack of poles from which hung, suspended by wires, a slab of bacon, half a smoked ham, small paraffined bags of flour, cereal, sugar and dried fruit. On puncheon shelves, neatly arranged, were cans of corned beef, boned chicken, milk, coffee, tea and salt, along with some lemons and a carton of eggs.

"Right old-maidish," he remarked.

"How can you?" cried Marian. "For God's sake, Tom, get busy and hunt for John!" She burst into tears.

"Now, gal," said Tom sternly: "don't you take a conniption. I ain't makin' fun—I'm huntin' sign. We got to use our eyes and do some common sense thinkin', afore we rush off. For instance, look at this fireplace: he's burnt a lot o' wood, lately; but not this mornin' to git breakfast by. No, nor last night, nuther," he declared, after poking all through the ashes and finding no live coal nor even a spark.

Tom picked up the little camp axe that leaned against a short log used as a chopping-block. He felt its edge.

"Keeps his tommyhawk in good order," he commented. "I never seed one o' this brand. Bet it's extra good steel. Got a long, straight sarviceable handle. Huh—the edge is gummy: he's been choppin' green pine. Now I wonder what he did *that* for. 'Tain't fitten for nothin' around camp: you cain't burn it, and the rosum seeps right out o' every cut and gits your hands and ever'thing all sticky. Whar did he cut it, and what fer?"

Tom left the Alcove and went to where a clump of young pines grew. Immediately he found a freshly cut stump and a lot of clipped boughs lying about. He studied the ground and found plenty of boot tracks.

"That gits me," he confessed. "Green pine pole."

He came back, rubbing the bristles on his chin. Meantime the hound had been running all over the place, delighted with scents of foxes and raccoons and all sorts of things exhaled from the dens among the broken rocks.

"Don!" cried Tom sharply. The dog came leaping to him.

"If you stir up a polecat, damn you, I'll wear you out with a hick-'ry. We got use for that nose o' your'n: so keep it clean. Come hyur with me."

Tom got John's moccasins out of the tent and held them under the dog's nose. He took the underwear from the line and did the same. He led the hound back and forth, holding his nose to the cave floor, giving him an occasional whiff of the clothing, and so on until the dog seemed to understand. Don began circling about. Presently he trailed over to the spring. Then he lifted his head, scenting, and sprang up over rough rocks and out on the talus barrier.

Tom and Marian followed as fast as they could over the confusion of uptilted rocks. The surface was treacherous with moss that slipped off from under their boots.

"Gimme your hand, gal," said Tom, "We don't want no broken legs today."

"Oh, Tom, do you think the dog really knows what he's doing?"

"We'll soon see is he a real trailer or only thinks he is."

They struggled on. The hound disappeared ahead of them. Presently he barked—once—twice—thrice.

Marian's face had been pale enough, but now it went stark white with fear of finding Cabarrus dead. Tom grimly clamped his lips and forged silently ahead.

Now they saw Don. He had halted before a long fissure in the rock. His bony head was lifted in another peal of discovery.

They came to freshly broken rock at the surface of the rift, with chips of it scattered about. Tom got down on hands and knees and shouted into the black chasm; but he got no answer.

"Hyur's whar he brought his pine pole," observed Tom, pointing to scratches and scrapings along the surface.

"He must a-shoved it on down below."

"He's down there, himself!" cried Marian. "Oh, if only we had a lantern!"

"Stay with the dog," said Tom. "I'll soon git a light."

He returned to the Alcove, took up the hunter's axe, scouted around, found an old pine log that lay rotting on the hill-side, knocked off two or three of its resinous stubs, hacked their butts so they would easily ignite, and brought them to the rift.

Tom lit one of his torches and thrust it down into the pit as far as his arm would go.

"This is a tight squeeze for a feller o' my bulk," said he, "but I can make it. You set still while I see what's down thar."

He slipped down through the narrow crack, crawled along the incline, and called back to Marian: "Hyur's his pole ladder!"

The stubs on the pole hardly looked strong enough to support his weight; but Tom took a good grip with his left hand on the pole itself and down he went, bearing the torch in his other hand.

When he stood on the floor of the outer chamber he called to Cabarrus; but still there was no answer.

He stepped warily forward, holding the smoking torch aloft, and in a moment he saw where a chunk had been broken off from a column of greenish rock.

"Yeah," he said aloud to himself: "He done that. Took him a specimen."

"Where?" asked a trembling voice at his back.

Tom nearly jumped out of his skin.

"God A'mighty!" he exclaimed. "You give me a jolt. What the devil you doin' down hyur? I done told you to stay with the dog."

"I'm here, where I belong," said Marian. "Go on. Hurry!"

"Don't you git into a swivvet, young lady," replied Tom. "Did you fetch another torch?"

"Yes: here it is."

Tom lit it from his own flare and handed it back to her.

"Now mind your step," he ordered, gruffly. "You ain't got no hobnails, miss. Hang on to me."

The big fellow edged past the column of beryl. As he held his torch low to pick his way, he saw a treacherous smooth channel in the rock floor directly in front of him. The thick black smoke from the fat pine knot obscured all view of the chamber beyond.

Tom stopped so abruptly, at sight of the dangerous footing, that Marian bumped into him. He said: "Wait a bit; they's a bad place ahead."

Just then a faint cry came up out of the black chasm on their left. It had a weird, unearthly sound, not of a human voice but of something uncanny—the wail of a spirit of the underworld.

Marian's overstrained nerves responded with a scream.

The cry from below was repeated; this time in a louder, more human tone.

Tom bellowed an answer.—

"Hello-o-o! down thar. That you, Cabarrus?"

"Yes," came a weak voice from the pit. "Oh, be careful! Don't slip!"

"John—John—are you badly hurt?" called the girl.

"I'll—be—all—right."

She struggled to pass Tom, that she might peer into the gulf where her lover lay.

"Set down!" thundered Tom, "Don't you wiggle a finger. I'll git him up."

Tom took out a fish-line from his pocket. He tied it to his torch and lowered the blazing pine knot into the pit. Lying flat, with face over the brink, he looked below. In the ruddy flare he saw a ghost of a man lying on a narrow ledge some twelve feet down. Cabarrus was striving to sit up. Then he reached out and secured the torch.

"Steady, thar!" Tom called to him. "Rest easy till I fetch the pole."

Tom brought the Indian ladder. He lowered it, butt foremost, to the ledge on which Cabarrus lay, and wedged its upper end in a crack of the rock.

Marian held her own torch over him as Tom slowly descended. Carefully he tested the pine stubs with his feet before trusting much of his weight on them. Gripping the pole with both hands, he went on down, across the sickening chasm, to firm footing on the ledge.

Tom put his arm around John and whispered: "Have you bruk ary bones?"

"No," answered John weakly. "I can climb when my legs stop trembling. My nerves have been shot to pieces."

"No wonder! God A'mighty! How long have you been down in this hellish place?"

"I don't know. It seems a week—a year. The darkness has been awful. I'd given up. How did you ever find me?"

"W'y, betwixt me and your gal and the dog, we tracked you. Rest easy, a bit, while I rub your legs. Wish I had a dram for you."

"I need water worse."

Marian called: "Tom, is he able to move?"

"Yep—purty soon, gal. Jist be patient."

Tom chafed the exhausted man's limbs and worked up the circulation. By and by, Cabarrus got to his feet.— "I think I can make it, now," said he.

Tom steadied him from below, as far as he could reach, but he dared not lean far forward nor add his own weight to the slender pole. Up above, Marian, with one arm around a spur of rock, reached down toward Cabarrus with the other.

There was a short but dizzy interval over which the exhausted man had to climb unassisted. He summoned every nerve to a supreme effort. His rescuers watched, with hearts in their throats, as he climbed painfully, desperately, inch by inch. Then Marian seized his shirt at the shoulder and pulled upward with all her strength. Out on the passageway he gained, at last, and sank into the girl's arms.

Tom climbed up beside them.— "I reckon you're bodaciously damn nigh dead," he said to Cabarrus.

Nobody heard him but himself. The young couple was oblivious, now, even to the cavern gloom and the smoke of the torches.

Tom busied himself in drawing up the Indian ladder. He found John's prospecting pick where it had fallen aside when the unlucky man slipped and fell.

Marian was murmuring things to John, and he was gasping answers, that Tom deemed it unmannerly for him to listen to. So the big woodsman moved off to one side and waited, with what patience he could command, for them to get through.

In such case, a third party, who is naturally a man of action, soon gets to fidgeting.

"I wish that gal would do her whinnelin' outside whar they's daylight," he complained to himself. "This cussed black hole don't seem like church nor home to me."

Presently he called: "Hey, you folks! Let's git out whar the sun shines and we'll find water and grub for that starvin' man."

He carried the pole ladder to the entrance. They followed and climbed up out of the rift.

The hound sprang joyfully upon one after the other and almost knocked them down with his felicitations.

TWENTY-SEVEN

"O, the blessed sunlight!"
John's parched lips gasped the salutation with all the reverence of a prayer. He had been immured in the dense blackness of the pit for twenty-seven hours. Thirst and hunger and wounds he had endured; but they were nothing to the mental agony, the terror of long-lingering death in the dark.

Tom hurried to the spring for water and to John's tent for the first-aid packet. When he came back with them Marian gave the famished man sups of water at intervals and she sterilized his wounds and bandaged them.

"My dear, my dear," she gently chided him, "what ever made you go into that awful place alone?"

"I was hunting beryl. It's there, Marian—I found it—but just then I slipped."

"All the beryl in the world isn't worth such a risk."

"But the slip was my own fault. The place is safe enough if one minds his step."

He did not tell her what the magic was, on the cavern wall, that had charmed away his vigilance and had caused the accident. Maybe it would turn out to be only false glitter, after all, from worthless crystals of quartz or other common minerals. But the beryl—ah, that was there!

Tom made another trip to the Alcove and brought up their lunch. Quickly he built a small fire and made coffee. They warmed up the chicken Sylvia had prepared and had a hot, stimulating meal. John basked in the life-giving rays of the sun. By and by he stood up and limped about, testing his legs.

"I'm a new man, now," he declared bravely. "Give me your arm, Tom, and we'll toddle back to camp."

When they came in sight of it, John let out a faint cheer.—

"Good old Alcove!" he cried. "All the comforts of home!"

Marian looked up at the vaulted ceiling.— "It's like the apse of a stone church," she observed. "It's not a cave: it's a sanctuary."

John answered: "Many a man in the roaring city might wish for a sanctum as quiet as this."

That sort of thing was over Tom's head, and so, as he was not used to staying dumb in company, he interrupted with the directness of a practical mind.

"What's this beryl you've been looking for?" he asked.

"A mineral that I propose to mine."

"I ain't never heered of the stuff. Beryl—ugh—it sounds too much like 'burial' for me!"

"Oh, Tom," protested Marian, "that's an abominable pun! Forget it. John isn't ready to go mining."

"I'll be ready tomorrow," declared John. "The kinks will be out of my legs, after a good night's rest. I'm figuring how to grade a road into this hollow. I can corduroy it across the swamp and connect with the Kittuwa road near our old cabin."

"Got a legal right to do that?" asked Tom.

"Yes, by virtue of the mineral reservation. And, as a matter of fact, if the beryl deposit turns out as good as I hope, I'll buy this whole tract, so as to have absolute control. I've already secured an option on it."

"From Matlock?" asked Tom, surprised.

"Yes, through his attorney. Matlock himself is out of the picture. They say he'll never be strong again."

"I wish you'd busted every brain out o' his head, while you were about it," declared Tom bluntly.

"Oh, no: it's better so," said Marian. "He'll never come back to Kittuwa, even if he should get well. Everybody hates him so. Besides, he'll never want to look again at the place where he was so thoroughly beaten and disgraced."

"Tom," said Cabarrus, "when I go to mining, I'll need a foreman: somebody who knows the country and the people and would be loyal both to them and to me. How about taking the job yourself?"

Tom studied. Presently he answered: "Well, I'm right handy to your hole-in-the-ground. If they's anything in it, let me know. I've sort o' promised Sylvy I'd be a foreman some day. She gits spells o' hintin' that I'm a triflin' feller."

"Suppose you come over here tomorrow. We'll go down in the rift and see what's there."

"I wish ruther we had a way o' kerryin' you over to my place for a rest. The rift, as you call it, will stay hyur till you're fitten to work. Tell you what—when I've tuk this young lady back to the house, I'll hike over hyur agin and spend the night with you, if you don't mind."

"All right. Bring a lantern, if you have one."

"I've a lantern and a flashlight, too. I'll fetch 'em both."

"And, by the way," interjected Marian, "this young lady that you mentioned has a flashlight of her own. She will be here at nine o'clock tomorrow, dew or no dew. The trail Tom cut is so plain that one can't miss it—anyway, Don will come with me. So you'll have to put up with my company."

"Now lookee!" mocked Tom. "You see what's come from givin' the women the vote. By grab, they boss everything!"

"Oh," retorted Marian: "and so the world's going to the devil, eh?"

"Shucks, no: it's done gone."

Cabarrus smiled.— "I rather think I need a—a camp cook. Consider yourself engaged."

"Thank you, kind sir. But understand this: I won't cook you a meal—no, not a bite—till I've been down in the rift and have seen you build a safe bridge across that slippery place."

Tom and the dog went up the stone steps and out on the trail.

Marian was following; but Cabarrus caught her and put his arm around her.

"I—I'm rather tongue-tied, somehow," said he; "but you know, dear, what's on my mind. When we first met in the wild woods, it was like two children in a garden, each finding a new playmate in the other. It didn't take long for the shyness to pass off. We didn't say anything about our feelings—didn't need to. We just went along naturally together, understood each other, without many words. Then troubles came; but we stuck together. We were tested, and we bore the strain. We've been through risks and hazards together. Oh, Marian, let's go forward, now, into the great adventure. Let's go on through life, hand in hand and heart to heart."

She answered: "True love needs no declaration, John—save this—"

With soft, warm arms around his neck, lips pressed to his in passionate abandon, she sealed their troth.

Then up she sprang with the lithe grace of a young doe, ran up the steps and out to where Big Tom was waiting.

Cabarrus, left once again alone, soon lost himself in happy daydreams. Here in Nick's Nest there would be man's work to do; but over yonder, at the old home place, a new home should arise, and there would be man's recompense. The vision of the chateau came to him again, the questing maid, the gambols of the Little People and the beat of fairy drums.

So, an hour or two later, Tom Burbank found him, still basking in God's blessed sunlight, still deep in happy reverie.

They spent the night together and were up at peep of day. Cabarrus was still stiff and sore, but he knew that exercise would soon limber him up. They had breakfast before a jolly camp-fire; then tidied up the camp, got in a supply of firewood, cut some white oak poles and fashioned a real ladder, for which Tom had brought the nails from home. Then they cut down a slender ash tree, split puncheons from it with wooden wedges, and carried them up to the rift for making the bridge that Marian had insisted on.

A little before nine o'clock, Don came bounding into camp, barking and wig-wagging his message of "Ready, sirs—ready for anything that's up!"

In a moment, Marian appeared and gave them a jaunty salute.

"Good morrow, merry gentlemen, and how are you, this fine, brave day?"

"Fit as fiddles," answered John, "and all in tune."

They clambered over the rocks and on to the fissure in the mountainside. The two men managed to slide their new ladder down into place and they carried the puncheons on to where they were needed. In ten minutes they had bridged the dangerous slant where John had met misadventure, and they passed over it, Cabarrus in the lead, Tom bringing up the rear.

Then John threw the beam of his flashlight along the scintillating wall of the dike.

"Oh, oh, oh!" cried the astonished and delighted girl. "It's unbelievable! It's magic! The mountain itself has wrought magic here! What are those crystals, John?"

"I don't know yet. This is as far as I got. Let's see what the mountain has done for us!"

They stepped slowly forward.

Along the face of the dike, much of the glitter came from muscovite and black mica, good for nothing but to catch the eye and disappoint a treasure hunter. But here and there, amid the coarse rock, were pockets that had been riven open by the parting of the dike from its neighbor granite. These pockets or druses, some of them two or three feet in diameter, were lined with brilliant crystals of various shapes and colors: white albite and brown smoky quartz, glassy rock crystal, and a surprising variety of sparkling, deeply colored stones that were unmistakably true gems.

There were dark red garnets, green beryls and aquamarines, rare blue beryls and still more precious ones of golden yellow. John identified an extraordinarily brilliant crystal of the rare gem called hiddenite, a lithia emerald.

In one of the druses were slender red crystals of rutile, queerly interlocked at angles, like miniature frameworks or scaffoldings. In another, protruding two inches from the quartz, was a prism of marvellous beauty, green throughout most of its length, but crowned with red shading into violet. It was tourmaline, of gem quality.

Marian was in an ecstasy, not only at the wonder of the discovery itself, but because John had made it—her John—whose gallant endurance of discouragements and dangers was now, at last, so gloriously rewarded.

And John himself, elated, thrilled by the sudden coming of good fortune, could not restrain some show of triumph.—

"There's enough wealth here in gems alone, exposed and ready for picking like ripe fruit, to buy Matlock's holding and finance my mining operation. Beyond that, there's no telling what other pockets may be revealed when we go to mining farther in. This formation is honeycombed with them. It's, as we say, drusy."

Marian sighed like a contented child.— "Myra was right," said she: "the Little People like you, John."

They passed on, beyond this chamber, by a narrow passage that led upward into fathomless darkness. Thus they came presently into a wider space.

As John picked the way over uneven footing, a startled exclamation broke from him and he stooped to pick something up. It was a rounded stone, thick as his wrist and about eight inches long, that looked like an artifact: something shaped by man.

It was indeed a stone hammer, fashioned to be held in the hand without a handle. Near it lay two flint chisels, both of them broken at the edges.

"Look!" said he. "I'm not the first man, after all, to enter here, though first through the crack back yonder. There's another entrance somewhere, or has been, probably up at the end of this passageway."

"Why, John: then this is a prehistoric mine, worked, heaven knows when, by men of the Stone Age."

"Queer," observed John, "that they left all those sparkling gems in place."

He looked about him. Five feet above the floor where the stone hammer lay, he saw a druse that had been rifled. Evidently some large crystal had been pecked away. Beside this empty pocket an ancient carving faced them. It was the figure of a dragon, with only a broad line for its head, from which fangs protruded.

"The original," mused John. "Those on the Alcove wall and the wrapper of the Ulunsuti are replicas of this."

Marian pointed to the empty pocket in the wall.— "There," said she, under her breath— "there's where the Ulunsuti came from!"

"But why did those men of the Stone Age take nothing else?"

John's ready fancy carried him back to a time primeval. His knowledge of Indian psychology helped him to frame a theory.

"It seems," said he, "that I can see some savage hunter following a wild animal here to its den. Instead of a mere burrow or cranny in the rock, he finds a deep fissure in the mountainside. Thinking of nothing but the chase, he lights a pine knot and ventures in. He comes into this vault where brilliant colored stones flash back reflections from his torch.

"What awesome magic, this! Unwittingly he has intruded into a sanctuary of the gods of the under-world!

"In fear and trembling he hurries out of the charmed cavern, lest he himself should suddenly be turned to stone.

"Religiously he consults the shaman, the priest and doctor of the tribe. And that one, after conjuring and offering propitiatory prayers, takes the hunter as guide and ventures into this holy place.

"He removes only one flashing crystal, to use in his religious rites and to prove his own supernatural powers before his tribe. Then he leaves, seals up the entrance, and forever after keeps this location secret. The origin of the Ulunsuti then passes into myth."

Dropping the primitive tools, John scanned the wall again. Near the Ulunsuti's pocket he saw a bulge or boss of quartz. Idly, with no conscious motive, he tapped it with the hammer-head of his pick.

The protuberance gave forth a hollow sound. He struck sharply, with a quick withdrawing stroke. The outer shell of a druse cracked off, revealing the interior, which instantly flashed back at him a miracle of chromatic lights. The pocket was lined with limpid rock-crystals, all of them growing inward toward the open center of the pocket—all of them transfixed by long, slender needles of dark red rutile.

Gently he removed the largest and finest crystal and handed it to Marian.

"A sign! A token!" he exclaimed. "Love's arrows—*fleches d'amour!* It's yours, Marian. You have an Ulunsuti all your own."

"Oh, John—John! What woman ever received from her lover such a gift as this?"

"What woman ever was the guiding star of such adventure? What are gems of cold stone in the presence of a love like yours?"

John turned his back upon the jewel-studded wall. He drew the girl tightly to his breast. Then reverently he raised his hand in salute to the invisible genii of the grotto.—

"Little People," he said, "this is what I want. I want—to take—this!"

The End

About the author of the introduction

Writer and naturalist George Ellison has written frequently about Horace Kephart. Since 1976, he and his wife, the artist Elizabeth Ellison, have resided in a cove adjacent to the Great Smoky Mountains National Park several miles west of Bryson City, North Carolina. One of their recent collaborations is *Blue Ridge Nature Journal: Reflections on the Appalachian Mountains in Essays and Art*.

About the author of the foreword

Libby Kephart Hargrave, great-granddaughter of Horace and Laura Kephart, is well known for her accomplishments in professional music and theatre as well as a private vocal, piano and acting coach. Her award-winning song, "Living on the Comfort" (USNS COMFORT), written during operation Desert Storm, received written recognition from President George H.W. Bush for its positive uplifting message.